PEAK
PLAGUE
MYSTERY

Typeset by Typo•glyphix, Burton-on-Trent DE14 3HE
Cover design and photography by Cactus Images, Derby DE24 8BF

The moral right of the author has been asserted.

This novel is the work of fiction and, except in the case of
historical fact, any resemblance to actual persons living or
dead, events or localities are purely coincidental.

Matador
9 Priory Business Park,
Wistow Road, Kibworth Beauchamp,
Leicestershire. LE8 0RX
Tel: 0116 279 2299
Email: books@troubador.co.uk
Web: www.troubador.co.uk/matador
Twitter: @matadorbooks

ISBN 978 1838594 596

British Library Cataloguing in Publication Data.
A catalogue record for this book is available from the British Library.

Printed and bound in the UK by TJ International, Padstow, Cornwall

Matador is an imprint of Troubador Publishing Ltd

PROLOGUE

Dr Bence Kovac slowly pushed open the door. The warmth of the room washed over him as he entered. A small, twelve-year-old girl lay sprawled on an iron-framed bed in a corner of the room. She was asleep and that pleased him. Her black, shoulder-length hair looked unkempt and a deep memory stirred. The image of his beautiful loving wife fused in his mind. She had now long gone, and he was pierced by a pain as though someone had punched him. He tried desperately to clear his head. He was after all doing this for his Lidya, but not just for her. This was for all humanity and he alone would save thousands of lives. He firmly believed his work would one day be known worldwide.

Bence stood at the side of the bed and intently watched the rhythm of the child's breathing. It was not laboured; the girl looked peaceful. He glanced down at the record chart in his hand: *Patient 1607*. He couldn't remember her name, perhaps Jane or Jill. It didn't matter. She was recovering and recovering well. The bacterial disease had initially concerned him, but he had remained confident his cure contained the necessary virus to eat this bug. It had, after all, worked well in his lab. He looked up and out of the window at the cloudy sky and reflected on the money this new mix would earn him, and more importantly, how he could invest it in his real quest. He had made a vow and it was one that he would not break.

The girl stirred, naturally taking in a deeper breath before a long exhale. Bence turned and slipped out the door.

ONE

REBECCA'S TALE

SATURDAY 24 APRIL 2010

Rebecca Johnson walked out of High Peak School, down the access road and turned left up the hill towards St Peter's Church. She practically skipped as she went, breathing in the scent of spring daffodils and the witch hazel that floated on the morning breeze. A low, dry-stone wall separated the footpath from a dense wood that now blocked any sight of her school. She wore a striking, pale blue coat with a neat collar and large matching buttons: a genuine sixties garment that had once belonged to her aunt.

At the peak of the hill stood a little parish church, its grounds bathed in sunlight, that prompted a moment's review. She watched an elderly lady she sometimes spoke to disappear inside. After a brief pause, she descended the other side into High Peak village. Just three outlets gave homage to a community centre: a butcher combined baker, a newsagent, and in between, a post office.

'Good morning, Aunt Lilly,' Rebecca said, as she entered the shop.

'Ah, Rebecca. You got my note then?' replied the elderly lady, appearing from a back room. With sagging cheeks and aged lines below the eyes, Lilly's face conveyed a constant expression of sadness.

'Yes of course. I like sorting the books,' Rebecca lied.

'You've a good heart, my girl,' said Lilly, opening an integral door to a security screen and pushing a box through with her foot. 'I can't bend like I used to. I'll probably give these up when you leave.'

'Oh, don't say that. The villagers come here to sort through them,' replied Rebecca.

'Yes, but they don't buy anything.'

Rebecca looked at the shelf. 'But more than half have gone.'

'Well, not by your classmates, I do know that,' said Lilly, her eyebrows lifting.

'Admit it. You wouldn't want them in here anyway.'

'Weird school that one,' said Lilly, under her breath.

'Not really,' said Rebecca defensively.

'Only one year of students... it's not natural.'

'It has other years.'

'They're miles away, other side of Derby, and only a handful of children to a class.'

'Well, that's what I like most.'

'I can't see how it balances the books with so few pupils.'

Rebecca exhaled, wondering whether there was much point in once again going over how the Academy supported itself.

'I've told you, the Academy rents out the health centre and then there's the activity centre. Loads of people use these facilities.'

'No one around here does. Anyway, how's Annie? Has she written lately?' asked Lilly, closing the door and returning to the counter.

'She's fine. Sends her love. She asked me to let you know that Burt Braithwaite died last week.'

'Really? The mechanic from Chesterfield? He was a charmer he was. Did alright for himself in the end. Had a big car sales place.' Lilly looked out, focusing somewhere beyond Rebecca. 'I remember Annie and I meeting him at Palais de Dance one night in Chesterfield.' Lilly turned back slightly, looking more directly at Rebecca. 'I thought he died years ago.'

'Well, apparently not. The funeral's next week.'

'My Alfie didn't like him. Thought he had eyes for me, but we knew it was Annie he fancied all right. What did he die of?' asked Lilly.

'Pneumonia I think,' replied Rebecca.

'Don't know what the world's coming to.'

The sound of the doorbell pinged, breaking the conversation, as a tall wiry gentleman of advancing years entered the shop. Rebecca recognised him instantly.

'Hello, Dr Kovac. I've been expecting you,' said Lilly.

'I believe there's a parcel, special delivery,' he replied.

Rebecca watched him from the corner as he marginaly leaned forward, placing his hands on the counter.

'Yes, came early this morning,' said Lilly and disappeared into a back room, which then left an unnatural silence. Rebecca busied herself working through the box of books, sticking price labels on the covers and placing them on the shelf in alphabetical order. She chanced a further inquisitive sideways glance at the man. He was looking directly at her so she immediately returned to the job at hand.

'Here we go, Doctor.' Lilly clicked a release bolt and slid a section of screen upwards, allowing passage of the parcel.

Rebecca watched him again as he took the package, feeling he intimated a special regard for whatever lay within. He turned with intent to leave.

'I'm afraid I'll need a signature for that,' said Lilly.

'Oh yes. Yes, of course,' he replied hurriedly, signing a slip and departing with no further communication.

'He gives me the creeps,' said Rebecca.

'Don't be daft. Shouldn't judge a book by its cover, Rebecca.'

'It's nothing to do with the way he looks.'

'Old Mrs Ascot swears by him. Gave her some special treatment for an infection on her leg after her op last year,' Lilly explained. 'Brilliant, she says. Cleared it within a week. She'd been on and off antibiotics for months.'

Rebecca pondered the information, but remained silent.

'And you want to be careful what you say up at that school. Dr Kovac's sibling is a well-respected teacher there,' announced Lilly.

In a small, three-bed detached house on the outskirts of the remote High Peak village, deep within Derbyshire's national park, a tall man with profoundly pointed features and eyebrows that defied logic sat heavily ensconced in his favourite chair. He reviewed a note, a note sent with a parcel:

> *Enclosed 2010/11 potential epidemic bacterial strain, centre originated Carcassonne. Package to be returned no later than July.*

'They're being demanding,' Bence said to himself, straightening his back. He tore at the brown paper, staring at the thick metal box and then reflecting on the bacteria within. For those in society who were old or with existing disorders, such as asthma and emphysema, this cell could be deadly.

Bence scribbled on the note *VO21*. Within his vast collection, he had a virus that showed a fondness for this newly sent bug, which was more than fortunate because locating such a molecule was the most difficult part of his therapy. His mind focused on being back in the laboratory with purpose; to study, investigate, deduce and conclude, and he felt a surge of warmth.

FRIDAY 17 MARCH 1989

Vladimir Orbelin sat quietly. Not one part of his body was allowed exposure; droplets formed on the inside of his mask. He looked down with immense sadness at his sleeping wife. It was some small comfort. Maybe she had no awareness, no knowledge of the imminent inevitability. She had known, yes, just some few days previously, but that was different. Then there had been a slim hope, but better than nothing. 'No one should suffer like this,' he said to himself as he slipped a small cylindrical tube of plastic containing a tiny element of sharp steel back into the folds of his sealed suit.

Lidya stirred, her eyes struggling to open. She stared into his eyes through the clear shield. She looked frail. Her hair, that he remembered being full-bodied, lay wispy and unkempt. The skin around her eyes had sunk and shone white with a tinge of purple. No words were spoken, yet he knew what they were saying. Goodbye, my darling. Lidya involuntarily inhaled and on release of that last gasp her spirit lifted and she was gone. A pain, greater than any he had ever known, shot through him. He wanted to rip off all the garments separating them and embrace her, hold her close, feel her skin.

The image of his son filled his mind: his one and only descendent. All that stopped him at that moment from taking his own life was the vision of his boy, for whom he was now solely responsible. Looking at his wife he made a vow. He wouldn't stop until he held in his power the ability to snuff out this variation of bacterium known by millions as the 'Black Death'. His gloved hand held her delicate fingers tightly.

'Vladimir,' said Nikolaz, a similarly clothed physician.

'Five more minutes,' replied Vladimir. He knew exactly what they would do. They would use bleach on his Lidya, killing any potential loitering bacteria. The thought repulsed him.

'I apologise, but I've been instructed to advise you that Mikhail wants to see you in his office,' said Nikolaz.

'Surely he can wait,' replied Vladimir.

'They're nervous, my friend. You've found a deadly bacterium,' said Nikolaz, placing his hand on Vladimir's shoulder.

'They have my report,' rebutted Vladimir.

'If there is anything else I can do, you know where I am,' Nikolaz replied, his tone ending the conversation.

Vladimir looked at the colleague who had also been his friend. They had laughed about life and intimately discussed work. Now he realised things had changed. He gently released Lidya's hand and walked out, brushing past Nikolaz with no apology. The hard grey floors and white clinical walls of the secured treatment centre offered no warmth as his ID pass buzzed the metal doors along his journey. He would tell Mikhail what he thought of his lack of compassion. He paused barely a moment outside the research centre's head office before entering without knocking.

Mikhail Nozadze, an elderly man, sat upright, initially startled at the intrusion. Sliding some papers together on his ornate wooden desk, he leant forward intertwining plump fingers. He tried to show a kinder face to Vladimir but it didn't fool the receiver.

'I'm so sorry for your loss, Vladimir. I want to be the first to offer my condolences.'

Vladimir's tall slender frame and milky blue eyes elicited no communication.

'Please have a seat,' said Mikhail.

Vladimir swept the chair back from the table and sat waiting with crossed legs.

'Would you like a drink? Coffee? Or perhaps something a little stronger?' asked Mikhail.

'No thank you,' Vladimir snapped and he watched Mikhail look to the side, avoiding his gaze.

'It is with regret that we must have a chat, Vladimir, but sadly I need to close out some issues in respect of the mutated strain of the plague *Yersinia pestis*: your YPX1.'

'You have my report,' replied Vladimir.

'Yes, but understandably it's not your normal full account, which saddens me on this occasion to reflect on such lack of... content. I suggest you take some time off and review the document,' said Mikhail.

'The report outlines all the details about the mutated strain. Which parts do you not feel fulfil the brief?' asked Vladimir.

'I'm sure you know already.'

'Humour me.'

'You're one of our best bacteriologists, but it is apparent that you're deliberately holding back information. Your account neglects to accurately describe the location. We are aware you have been south east of Diyarbakir in Turkey, but we need specifics.'

'I contained the outbreak locally. We were fortunate that the casualties remained at two.' Vladimir paused, realising that this was now incorrect and willing himself to keep control, he continued. 'Three ... and as long as we monitor from a distance, there is nothing to suggest a major incident.'

'Don't play games, Vladimir, for your sake.'

'My team and I took hundreds of samples of decaying matter from the area, which I'm certain will contain the killer virus that will devour the parasite. I need time to work with the substances.'

'You have avoided my question, Vladimir, and thus my problem.'

'The precise location is sacred. We don't want the area

swamped with scientists looking for the same virus we're seeking. They could inadvertently spread the disease. It remains vital the area is safe from that. I'll find the cure, Mikhail.'

'Vladimir, I worry you don't appreciate the severity of your actions should the West get hold of this deadly disease and find a solution. It would be catastrophic and you will be held personally responsible. Failure is not an option.'

Vladimir looked hard at the old man. 'I'm a doctor, not a military man.'

Mikhail replied, 'Vladimir you're a clever man, but sometimes incredibly naïve.'

THURSDAY 29 APRIL 2010

Rebecca entered the dining hall too late. It had been a long day and she had missed the main evening meal. The shutters of the serving hatch were down. Her stomach ached with emptiness as she walked along the corridor to the main kitchen. The door was open just a fraction, which allowed the narrowest view of any occupant within. Rebecca slowed, hesitated and observed, but didn't enter or make her presence known. Isolated images of a tweed jacket and grey hair flitted across the gap; she leaned forward and glimpsed snippets of movement, covered hands manipulating food.

She retreated rapidly through the dining hall and up the stairs, all thoughts focused on getting to the girls' dormitory. At the top of the second landing she ran directly into Brian Lambert, the PE teacher.

'S-sorry, sir,' Rebecca said between gasps.

'Rebecca, you need to be more careful. Run around outside, not on the staircases.' He paused. 'Is everything alright?'

'Yes, sir, sorry.'

Moments later she watched through her window as the familiar intruder, complete with satchel, left the adjacent school building just as she had often noticed, just as she had known he would tonight. But tonight things felt different.

Later that same evening, Rebecca re-entered the dining hall. The stained wooden floor and half-oak panelled walls had lost their warmth due to the bright light from the more modern LED bulbs suspended from traditionally styled lamps. The hall was now packed with students and teachers grouped around the various tables. The hum from voices telling teenage tales interspersed with spasmodic laughter gave her a weird sense of exclusion. She spotted Martin Holloway, a tall boy with blonde hair and a round face – a person with whom she always felt comfortable. He sat in a corner surrounded by classmates, enjoying the supper items of cakes and biscuits. Rebecca noted he was consuming the food she had earlier witnessed being touched by the intruder. She closed her eyes, willing the knot in her stomach to pass and almost sprinted from the dining hall, not stopping until she was outside and breathing the cooler air.

'What now?' she mused. Should she warn Martin? Doubt niggled at her. Perhaps she was mistaken. Perhaps there was some innocent explanation. She should go to a teacher, but how could she broach such a concern? The teachers would say she was making things up, trying to get attention, and they'd want to know who she'd seen. Rebecca thought about her mother. She hadn't lived with her for years, so why she should be reflecting on her now she didn't know. Then the vision of Aunt Annie came to her. Thinking of her always brought a sense of peace that took the edge off the night. Annie was old, her grandfather's sister; she couldn't worry her.

'Hello.'

'Oh Martin! You startled me.'

'Sorry, are you okay? You looked... well, a little shocked.'

'I, um, yes I'm fine.' Rebecca closed her hands together, her thumb rubbing against the palm of her other hand as she felt its dampness. 'I'm struggling with that computer programming that Mr Joins set, and well, you're good at that. I was hoping you could help me.'

'You know I will. What's really the matter?' replied Martin.

'Oh, well, it's just all those people around you. I um, I didn't want them to get the wrong idea.'

'Rebecca, I know you better than that. You don't worry about what other people think!'

Rebecca shifted. 'Perhaps you don't know me. Perhaps you only think you do.' Rebecca's eyes looked deeply into his and she saw disappointment.

Martin moved a strand of hair that had fallen across her eye, his fingers drifting around the back of her ear as he continued.

'No problem. it's late now but we can look at it together tomorrow after lessons.'

'Right, tomorrow then,' whispered Rebecca, and she left for the sanctuary of her dormitory.

The next evening after classes had ended, Rebecca stood at the entrance to the computer room. She watched patterns on the wall cascading with the sun flowing through the end corridor window and dancing on the dull, straw-coloured paint, but she remained alone. Odd, she thought, as Martin had never been late or missed a meeting with her before. Had she misread the signals? She waited ten minutes before heading off.

Pushing open the door that led to the tutor class corridor, she heard the muffled sound of music playing inside the ground floor common room. On entering, the clarity and volume of the music changed. She winced. A group sat in a corner at an isolated table doing homework. She wondered how they could possibly construct a sensible piece of work amidst the din. On the left she saw Catherine Banks. Catherine was wearing a bright pink and pastel green all-in-one suit, copious accessorised costume jewellery, and her long flowing dark hair also boasted colourful additions.

'Hi Catherine. Have you seen Martin?' asked Rebecca.

'He's been out of lessons this afternoon, not feeling well, so he left around lunchtime to see Dr Kovac. I've not seen him since,' replied Catherine.

Rebecca looked away, clutching her folder tightly.

'I'm sure he'll be fine. He'll probably be back tomorrow,' said Catherine, as she gently touched Rebecca's arm.

'Right, well thanks,' Rebecca replied and left the room.

Moments later Rebecca knocked on the staffroom door.

'Yes, come in.'

Brian Lambert sat at his desk. Not the stereotypical teacher, he was rather unkempt, with determined eyes and dressed as he often was in outdoor gear.

'Hello, Rebecca,' he said, turning around in his swivel chair to face her and leaning back slightly.

Rebecca fought against allowing her stress to show.

'Oh... Mr Lambert, I... I was wondering if you could tell me whether Martin is okay, Martin Holloway. Apparently he left school today feeling poorly,' Rebecca said, her hand now unconsciously rubbing the seam of her skirt.

'Yes, yes. He's fine, just some bug he's picked up. I'm sure he'll be back before you know it.'

'Do you know where he is? Can I go and visit? I could take him some grapes.' Rebecca's words spilled out.

'I'm afraid not, Rebecca. He's in the sick bay next door; just a precaution you understand. We have to be careful in our tight-knit little community. These bugs can spread fast and we don't want the entire school off now, do we?'

Rebecca looked at him, a little more confidence creeping in. She tilted her head slightly with a pleading look.

'Martin is in safe hands. Let's just say we have to be seen to be proactive in these situations. As I said, he'll be back soon so don't worry about him. Now, if that's all, I need to complete my reports.'

THURSDAY 3 JUNE 2010

Again Rebecca stood motionless, a stealth-like figure amidst the furnishings. A mingled smell of foot odour and polish filled the air from the discarded footwear beneath the stairs. She thought about Martin. He had looked thin and pasty. She remembered him glancing in her direction, smiling at her as his classmates fussed around him on his return. Relief had flowed through her, the voice in her head saying, 'thank God he's okay'. Her inquisitive nature would need to be quelled.

She moved around, peering down the corridor leading past the kitchen. She took another look and after so many weeks was finally rewarded. A familiar figure drifted in, straight from the main entrance across to the kitchen door, a swift move that could easily have been missed in the blink of an eye. A buzz of heat flowed through her and she found it difficult to think.

Some short moments later, her heart still pounding, she found the strength to move out with a plan. Just as she started to leave, a noise from the main entrance halted her advance. She watched Brian Lambert stride towards the kitchen door that had been left slightly ajar. He pushed it open and entered. Rebecca gingerly moved closer so she could hear but remain concealed.

'And?' said Brian.

'And you will have to trust me,' replied the intruder.

'That's not fair,' replied Brian.

'I need to save lives and this has nothing to do with you.'

'It has everything to do with me. I need an explanation,' said Brian.

'Not here, not now.'

'When?'

'Maybe... tomorrow.'

'Not good enough,' said Brian, his voice edgy but determined.

'Definitely tomorrow.'

'If you don't, it's over. Is that clear?' Brian came out, closing the door behind him and leaving through the main entrance.

A sense of stillness ensued and the quiet bade her remain hidden. A few minutes passed before the tall thin figure returned to the foyer. He entered a code on the electric panel and left via the sick bay door.

The next evening Rebecca found Martin in one of the study rooms off the classroom corridor.

'Hi Martin. How are you now?'

'Still a little weak, if I'm honest,' he said, placing his hands in his pockets and Rebecca thought he was trying to look casual.

'That's not surprising, but you're okay?' she enquired, concern simmering under the surface.

'Enough about me,' said Martin, 'what are you up to?'

'Well, I've thought about doing a project as part of our maths statistics work; make it more interesting and practical.'

'Really,' said Martin in a raised tone. 'And how do you propose to do that?'

'I'm going to look at schools in the area, including this one, and plot school absences, compare the number of school days missed. See if there are any trends,' she said.

Martin's eyebrows lifted.

'That's great. What gave you that idea?'

'Well, you, of course,' she said. 'Has anyone in your class taken ill?'

'No one in my class, but my friend Guy Weaver may have the same bug.' Martin's eyes glazed. 'I've never felt so poorly. It makes you feel weak, all bunged up and sweating, yet you're cold all at the same time.'

Rebecca looked at him before asking, 'When did Guy go off sick?'

'Just today, I think... why?'

'I can add that to my stats project. And you were off for four days?' she asked, looking at him for confirmation.

'No, six. The annoying part was that male nurse. I find him a little weird. He constantly asked whether I was feeling better. Talk about getting on your nerves.'

Martin's attention drifted again as though an image was displayed behind her.

'Then he wanted samples. So embarrassing.'

'Samples?' enquired Rebecca.

'Yeah, well,' he started to go red, 'you know,' he lowered his voice. 'Urine and,' he paused, 'the other.'

'Right,' said Rebecca, and reading Martin's discomfort she changed the subject, but she remained with him for a short while before making an excuse to leave. It was getting close to the hour before supper and that meant her surveillance time would begin again.

SATURDAY 10 JULY 2010

Rebecca ventured into the village to send a letter to her aunt. She looked across the three shop fronts and approached the tiny central post office, but before reaching the door, she spotted Mr Lambert leaving the newsagent's. He was holding hands with a woman. They were looking at each other and giggling over a private joke.

'Hello, Rebecca. This is Miss Harper. Stacey, Rebecca,' he introduced.

'Mr Lambert,' Rebecca replied, as her heart thumped.

'Rebecca,' he said, lowering his voice as though parting with a secret. 'Stacey will be working at our school.'

Rebecca looked at Miss Harper's pale skin and bright red hair, both emphasised by the sun. She forced a smile, but Miss Harper remained fixed on Brian.

'Brian, stop. Don't be so mysterious. I only agreed to help out part time at the school. You promised me your father...' She stopped mid-sentence. Miss Harper turned to look at Rebecca and continued, 'Well, Rebecca, see you at school.'

In the darkness of a clinical laboratory, the smallest of midges buzzed around a pure space. A totally inconceivable parasite within a vat of nothingness, apart from one corner where, within a locked box, there lay potential sustenance. Determination filled the smallest of minds imaginable as a mystic yet barely detectable odour emanated from a tiny cell. Just how the insect procured access would remain unknown, along with its exit strategy. But it did. It had been successful. *Yersinia pestis* X1 moved microscopically around its new space. Cells a thousand times smaller than the human eye could distinguish lay hidden within a parasite's gut. Its host was oblivious to its new cargo, giving it time to spread, grow and survive. Within minutes the tiny mind of the flying insect clicked to feed mode.

Roger, the school's Golden Glavcot rabbit, wriggled its nose as it sucked in the evening air and his ears gave an involuntary flap. The dark fur barely moved as a tiny insect penetrated the surface of its newly found food source, sinking its feeder to quench its natural desire. But the smaller parasite within had other ideas. Its skill was to block the passage of digestion. The insect was replete, yet remained hungry. Devouring further fresh fluid, it then released its full capacity in an act of vomiting. Deadly bacteria flowed over the newly opened wound. It was free at last while the remaining particles were engrained within the gut of the insect, to be carried to the next innocent host.

As Rebecca walked around the school grounds later that evening, there was a lingering warmth and an orange glow silhouetted the trees on the school boundary. She reflected on the doctor. What was he doing? The weight of knowledge was overbearing.

As she approached the rear of the school she heard a banging sound, not to any rhythm but spasmodic. She saw the source as she moved around the edge of a low wall. Roger, the school rabbit, was jumping and kicking oddly, clearly distressed. Warily she stepped up to his hutch.

'What's the matter, Roger?' She looked back across the grounds as though expecting to see a fox then returned her gaze, bending lower to look more closely. The rabbit carried on flipping and bouncing around his enclosure, and then two things happened. Roger leaped forward, hitting the front of the cage, causing Rebecca to jump back, taking an involuntary breath as she did so.

She felt something hit the back of her throat. The sensation set off an instant fit of coughing. She leaned over hand on knee, willing herself to be calm, to breathe slowly and take in air. She retreated to the nearest toilet and drank copious amounts of water using nothing but her cupped hands.

SUNDAY 11 JULY 2010

The next morning she awoke to pain. Her chest burned. Her head felt confused and she ached. Her joints felt as if they had been replaced with sandpaper. Panic overwhelmed her as a coughing fit began. It was violent and raw, the soreness in her throat unbearable. Completely alone, she pulled a jumper on over her pyjama top, the seams and the tightness sensitive against her skin. She concentrated hard to lift her jeans to her waist as her tension increased and she collapsed in a heap on the floor. She tried to remember what Martin had described, although she was sure he hadn't mentioned difficulty in moving.

She staggered into the foyer of the health centre. A male nurse was flitting around as Rebecca stumbled forwards.

'There's no surgery today. Come back tomorrow and make an appointment with Doctor Kovac,' said Nurse Stephen.

'I can barely move,' wheezed Rebecca.

He looked at her as she clutched the back of a chair. 'Can you describe your symptoms?'

'I ache... so weak.'

'Why are you on your own?'

'It's Sunday,' she breathed. 'They must've gone on the walk.'

Rebecca coughed. Small red spots of blood speckled her hand.

The nurse froze, his eyes fixed on the girl's outstretched fingers. He grabbed a chair.

'Sit,' he said, and examined her. Seconds later he snatched the phone, fumbling as he pressed numbers. 'Hello, Bence, is that you? Listen, I have a girl in reception. She's –' he looked across to determine whether Rebecca was listening then lowered his voice. 'I believe she's extremely ill. I wouldn't call otherwise, Bence. She's coughing up blood.'

Rebecca watched him, straining to absorb words.

'Yes, well, she's complaining of aching, weakness and looks white, more grey, and I can see patches on her skin, below the neck, a dark red. No, blue to black in colour.' A pause then the nurse's eyes widened. 'Okay, okay, I hear you. Yes, I will. Yes, I said I will.'

The nurse clicked off the phone and walked to a cupboard. Rebecca imagined him retrieving medication, tablets or perhaps an injection. He took out a white box, extracted something from it and applied a mask to his long, thin face. Finally he added gloves, pulling and stretching each finger into its folds.

Rebecca felt numb. The pain was reaching proportions beyond endurance. Her mind swam with visions of Martin and her aunt, wishing she were with her now. She watched the nurse locking the front door and she thought he said the doctor was coming. Then, against her will, she passed out.

MONDAY 12 JULY 2010 – 01:30

A mist carrying an odour of bleach wafted from a small narrow space as intense flames engulfed it with ferocious devastation. Inside, an isolated figure – one that had long since left this world.

TWO

DALE SCHOOL

THURSDAY 9 JULY 2015

A shrill, ear-piercing sound rang through the corridors of Dale School as Jason Palmer, the youngest person in the school by two years, shook a traditional brass bell with an ornate wooden handle. He methodically ran around each dormitory, classroom and lounge area announcing mealtime. He was always the bell ringer on his class's duty week. There was only a momentary lapse prior to the thunderous sound of feet hammering on the stairs and travelling down various corridors.

The smell of hot food and the heat of the kitchen hit Adam Brant through the serving hatch as he used a folded tea towel to grab one of the stainless steel tubs. Along with Adele Martel, a French student, with long dark hair, brown eyes and naturally tanned skin, they delivered hot beef and vegetable stew to five circular tables. Looking across, Adam saw Jason return with the school bell, red-faced and panting.

'Jason, grab one of the gravy pots for our table, please.' Adam returned to the serving hatch. 'Chloe, you and the others should go and start your dinner. We can finish taking out the tubs. Then you'll be ready to start clearing away.'

'I'll be glad when this week's over,' replied Chloe.

'Only two more days and then we're off,' said Adele, smiling widely as she took a tub of boiled potatoes.

Adam and Adele joined the others some short moments later at their table. Adam was marginally the tallest in his class. He had an olive-toned complexion with freckles sprinkled around his nose. His long blonde hair offended some teachers. His stomach growled as he ladled food onto his plate.

'Only one day left on duty then our week's done for some time,' he said.

'Try ten weeks,' said Adele.

'Really?' replied Adam, as he stabbed a steaming potato from the tub and flicked it onto his plate.

'Think about it. We have refreshment week next week at High Peak School, then six weeks summer, then because of the duty group rotor being four, we'll have three weeks when we return,' she explained rationally.

Refreshment week was always a welcome end to the school year: a whole week jam-packed with exciting activities.

'They'll have us cooking this stuff before long,' said Jason, tugging at a particularly gristly section of beef with his fork and separating it from the remainder of his food.

'Don't be so melodramatic. Of course they won't,' said Adam.

'It's just those wet activities that put me off, making us do that barrel roll in the canoes, and the waters are fast flowing at times,' said Chloe.

'Random warning,' sang Adam.

'I was just thinking about refreshment week, Adam,' she said scornfully to her twin brother. Apart from the shape of their noses and chin line, the two looked nothing alike. Chloe had a fair complexion, like that of a painted porcelain doll. Her green eyes and full lips, coupled with hair that had tight natural curls, gave her a slightly Afro-Caribbean look. She nearly always wore a wide black hair band to tame the frizz.

Adam looked up. 'We decided as a group to go to High Peak during refreshment week. Remember our democratic discussions?'

'Yes, Adam, but I'm not one to spoil everybody's fun,' replied Chloe.

'Come, come, now children! Let's not squabble,' said Jonathan, who was slim, black and had the knack of communicating and understanding. He continued. 'Come on then, team. We need to clear away.' He stood and eyed the others who had sat down first.

'Don't forget to serve the staff table first with puddings. Mr Ingham looked a bit miffed when I placed the stew on one of the other tables and they had none,' said Adam in a subdued tone.

Once back at the table, Adam viewed the pudding's white swirls tinged with brown peaks. Lemon meringue pie was his favourite dessert.

'I'll be Mum,' Jonathan announced, and then proceeded to go around the table.

'Chloe?'

'Just a little, please.'

'Adele?'

'What is that?' she asked.

'Lemon curd set on pastry with an egg meringue on top,' replied Jonathan.

'I think I'll give it a miss, thanks.'

'Adam?'

'Yes, please.'

Jonathan piled a significant helping onto Adam's plate and then looked across at Jason.

'I'm full thanks,' said Jason, putting his hand in the air in a stop gesture.

'Jason, you've hardly had any dinner,' said Chloe, looking at him with some concern.

'Well, it's just me then,' Jonathan continued, ignoring Chloe's over-motherly tendency, and piling a portion onto his own plate.

Later, on entering lounge Level C, Adam saw Jonathan sprawled on one of the settees reading a book. Jonathan had short, wispy black hair, pronounced cheekbones and a majestic chin line.

'Is it good?'

Jonathan lowered the book slowly and looked at Adam. It seemed to take a moment for the question to register.

'Oh, err, yes. Quite sad though.' Jonathan stared at Adam. 'What's up?'

'It's Jason. I'm worried about him. He seems so,' Adam paused, carefully choosing the correct word, 'reserved.'

'Well, I guess it's just the trip. I'm not convinced about him being at this school, two years ahead of his peers. Big IQ's one thing, but it doesn't give you life experiences.'

'Deep, but I know what you mean. I'm sure Chloe senses something or she knows something, but if I approached her she would either start panicking or clam up. You know how close they are.'

'Yes, but it could be that he's just growing up. Why do I have a feeling I'm getting a challenge?'

Adam looked across and smiled.

'If anyone can get through to Jason, you can.'

'Well, I'm flattered, of course, but not totally convinced. Adam, it's not your job to sort out the world, you know.'

'Really, I thought it was! And it's not a challenge, just, well, if you get the chance. Right time right place, you know.'

'Only too well, and you're not listening... to me.'

'Thanks.'

'I haven't done anything yet.'

Adam raised his eyebrows then gave him a pleading grin.

That same evening Jonathan felt as if he'd looked everywhere for Jason. He eventually found him sitting on a wall near the school boundary. Sitting himself down next to him, Jonathan looked at the stream in front of them and remained quiet. Jason started fidgeting, picking up small stones and casting them across the water. He eventually broke the silence.

'It's starting to get dark.'

'Yes, I'm surprised to find you out here on your own,' said Jonathan.

'I like it here. Not many people come around this side of the school.'

Jonathan gazed at their silhouetted reflection.

'Well, just a few days and we'll be at High Peak.' As he mentioned High Peak, he thought he saw Jason stiffen. He decided to press on. 'The students there are younger. Maybe you'll find some new friends.'

'I may do, possibly. There's a class going from Park View and they're my age. But Jonathan, can I ask, do you believe in ghosts?'

Jonathan suddenly felt immensely pleased with himself, but knew he must remain composed.

'It's not true, you know.'

'What?' said Jason.

'That High Peak School is haunted.' Jonathan continued. 'It's just kids spreading silly stories.'

Jason looked up at him. 'You haven't answered my question.'

'The truth is, I don't know. But if there is such a thing, then I do know they can't hurt you. Is that what's bothering you?'

Jason looked ahead and nodded slowly.

'We all have fears, Jason. It's perfectly normal. There's absolutely nothing to be frightened of, and I can say that while we're there, you'll never be alone.'

'Thanks,' he said, exhaling as though all thoughts of ghosts were being blown away and his body was releasing concerns that no longer belonged to him.

'Come on, Jason. It's almost supper time and I think they have some lemon meringue pie left over.'

Adam watched Jonathan and Jason enter the dining hall as members of staff were serving supper from one of the kitchen hatches: hot drinks and leftover puddings were being offered and even some homemade biscuits. Ron Jameson sat in a corner of the dining room. He was a tall man of slim build and dark handsome appearance. His well-trimmed beard appeared fractionally more than stubble and was perfectly manicured. It had been ten years since Ron had embarked on his dream. The Academy now offered a host of facilities to locally based companies and ran courses covering many areas, including academic, motivational and legislative advice. The schools shared resources, including most of the teachers who travelled around delivering their subjects.

The students piled in for snacks and drinks, their speed and briskness changing instantly once they noticed the school's head teacher and academy founder was present watching their movements. Jonathan motioned to Jason to join the others in their class who were already seated whilst he retrieved the necessary beverages.

'I wonder why our Ronald has decided to join the lesser ranks,' Chloe said quietly.

'Shh, Chloe. He'll hear you.'

'I think we're a little too far away, Adele. He's probably considering whether to stop the supper, you know, to save money.'

At that point Adam noticed Jason walking towards them. He was smiling widely and appeared to bounce on each step.

'Well, supper has obviously brought out the best in you.'

'Yes, I'm pretty hungry actually. Jonathan is bringing the grub over, so if you want anything, you'd best be quick.'

Jonathan joined them, carrying a tray filled with four helpings of lemon meringue pie, a plate of homemade biscuits, some squares of fudge and a pot of tea.

Chloe's gaze went from Jonathan's face to the tray of goodies and back again.

'Are you hungry, dear?'

'Only for you, my precious,' replied Jonathan, eliciting giggles from around the table.

Ron Jameson left the dining area, acknowledging their table with a nod as he made his way back to his prestigious office, conveniently located opposite the main staffroom. The atmosphere in the dining room lifted.

'I'm really tired,' said Jason, with a relaxed yawn.

'Me too. I'll see you all tomorrow,' said Chloe. She got up and walked around the table, then waited for Jason before they both left.

Adam watched Adele as her gaze followed Chloe's every move. He felt life was odd and definitely not fair. He turned back to Jonathan. 'And...'

'He was scared of ghosts.'

'Pardon?' replied Adam.

'We're going to High Peak next week, and Jason had obviously heard the rumours about Rebecca and how she haunts the place. He was nervous. That's what's bothering him.'

'Rebecca Johnson? Jonathan, you're a genius!' said Adele.

Adam looked at her and wished he had directly obtained this information.

'She committed suicide, didn't she?' he asked.

'It's not so surprising in this system. Washing up half the night. Just look at my hands. They're like sandpaper,' said Jonathan.

'That's not funny,' Adam snapped.

'You can't save her, Adam. It's too late,' he replied. Adele looked confused.

'Jonathan thinks I have issues – that I want to save everyone.'

'Well...'

'Oh great! Just great!'

'You want everyone to be, well, how I can put it... normal.'

'Surely that's a good thing,' Adam replied.

'I feel you're missing the point.'

'Well, on that note I'll leave you two love birds,' said Jonathan, and he disappeared through the door to the dormitory stairwell.

FRIDAY 10 JULY 2015

Adam joined Jonathan after breakfast, avoiding Adele, and they went down to their classroom. Three steps led off the dining hall that gave entrance to a wide corridor containing several classrooms, lecture hall and two common rooms; theirs was the first classroom on the left.

The room had walls of barley white covered with their work, from artistic drawings to flow charts and photos of pupils at various events: skiing in France near Adele's home, Chloe holding a trophy for winning the interschool tennis tournament and multiple pictures of Graham Alan Bates' tutor group in twos and threes, mostly pulling silly faces. At the front of the class was a central white board with the capacity of a large monitor connected directly to the internet. Deep windows gave views of natural greenery, with a wood to the left and fields disappearing to the right as far as the eye could see.

Adam sat next to Jonathan, struggling to find enthusiasm. Mr Joins was a smooth devil with dark overlong hair and a well-shaven face. Adam was sure the girls swooned over this man, although he felt he was a little too thin and he noticed his legs were bowed. However, Adam had to admit he was also one of the best teachers. He'd set today's tasks on the white board, each one focused on statistics. The subject made absolutely no sense to Adam; he could do the required questions, understood the formulas, but that wasn't the point. Calculating the likelihood of picking a red ball from a bag that contained ten red, ten green, ten blue and ten yellow balls was easy enough to establish, but he believed you could do the task all day long and still never actually pull out a red ball. Adam sat back in his chair disgruntled and started fidgeting with his pen.

'Adam, is everything ok?' asked Mr Joins

'Yes, sir, just reflecting on the fact that odds or likelihoods, well, they don't really help. I can't see a benefit unless you're in the gambling business, and then the only people who really gain are the bookies. Everyone else will lose eventually.'

'Adam, you've just hit the nail on the head. You appreciate the likelihood of a horse winning does not necessarily mean it will, and understanding that is half the battle in life. But if you were to play the same race under the same conditions over and over again, I can assure you that a specific horse would win against the others pretty much as was expected by the odds that were originally predicted.'

'But that can neither be proven nor disproven, sir, so we would never know,' replied Adam.

'Actually we can prove it and have done many times by carrying out the experiment with the balls-in-a-bag question.' This statement got a humorous hum from the class to which he gave a smile of acknowledgement and continued.

'If we carry out the task of pulling the coloured balls from the bag and note the results, we would get a pattern that followed the odds which you are calculating as predicted.'

'Has there been any specific work related to stats that we could use practically in our lives, sir?'

'I recall a bright young lady doing a project on school absences – a superb piece of work, very detailed, and the results were somewhat surprising. She compared student absences within her own school against other schools in the area and even got some figures from a local health centre to review the likelihood of illnesses against the size of the community. All sorts of interesting patterns and probabilities were explored. This sort of information can be put to good use by relocation resources in order to deal with patients.'

Adam could certainly see the benefits in this scenario.

'Was that a student from this school, sir?'

'No... actually a girl from High Peak.'

'What was her name, sir?' asked Adam.

Mr Joins paused. 'Rebecca, and before you or anyone else asks, yes, Rebecca Johnson.' The name resonated within the room.

'Sir, what happened to Rebecca?' asked Adam.

Mr Joins looked at him for a moment as though deliberating then shook his head.

'Let's not go there. Just concentrate on your work.'

Adam watched Mr Joins as he went around the class helping other students. His movements appeared laboured and his shoulders now drooped as he went.

The English lesson after morning maths dragged apart from

the last forty minutes when Mrs Chambers, the tiniest, kindest, and Adam thought, certainly the oldest lady in the school, handed a book around to each student. They were to read a chapter, randomly selected, and then write what was good, bad and surprising about the chapter.

Adam picked up the book he had been dealt and read the title *Elizabeth Robey and the Peg Tower*. He looked over at Jonathan.

'Have you ever heard of this book?' he asked.

Jonathan shook his head. 'Looks riveting.'

Adam watched Jonathan struggle to contain his laughter.

'Right,' he replied through gritted teeth. He thumbed through the book and without warning randomly chose a page. Adam read, 'Chapter Eight'. Its title was *Backdraft*.

Elizabeth slowly came round. A powerful flicker of light dancing above her stripped the small film of moisture her eyes had left and she closed them, which felt like soft skin being pulled across sandpaper. Her senses were beginning to register more effectively as every second passed. A sweet charred wood mixed with manmade fibres burned into the soft tissue linings of her throat, and deeper within her lungs, as her chest rose then fell rapidly in an involuntary reaction to rid herself of the pollutant. She coughed and felt a rawness pierce her throat. She rolled over, bringing her knees up and lifting her central mass in an attempt to help expel the unwanted foul mucus. If only she hadn't opened that door, the fire would have been contained. Elizabeth moaned outwardly with the pain of melted fabric adhering to the skin of her breasts.

Adam looked up and across the classroom, breaking his intimate vision as though wondering if anyone else was aware of this woman's plight.

'Is everything all right, Adam?' asked Mrs Chambers.

'Yes. Absolutely. Just fine,' replied Adam, in a quick succession of statements. He felt Jonathan's gaze silently questioning him. He didn't want to explain.

After dinner Adam returned to the room that was practically a second home. Mr Miller was the largest man he had ever known. Visually he reminded him of the villain from *Toy Story* who took Woody for personal profit. Mr Miller, however, had a totally different manner and was one of the most approachable teachers. He adored his subject with a passion. One of his very notable characteristics was the strength of his cologne; it always made Adam think of deep woods on a summer's day.

'Today, class, this being the last one before the summer break, I want to introduce you to a remarkable subject. Jason, what do you think is the most amazing thing on Earth?'

'Well, I suppose the Eiffel Tower,' he said.

'Good answer,' said Mr Miller, and Jason suddenly became taller in his seat, beaming.

'Chloe, same question.'

'Mobile phones,' she said.

'Interesting.'

'Jonathan, what do you think is the most incredible thing on our planet?'

'We are, sir. All of the people in this very room.' The class broke into laughter.

'Yes, exactly! Spot on!' said Mr Miller, which instantly stilled the room. 'Our bodies are the most amazing things on this planet. The topic I wish to discuss is a remarkable process that occurs within all of you, all of the time. In nearly all cases you will not even know that it's happening. It's your immune system. This will form part of next year's exam, so you will need to review it over the break, along with revising the other topics we've covered.'

He handed out some sheets that contained diagrams and pictures of tiny dots. These had been labelled *invaders (bacteria and viruses)* and *fighters (killer cells)*.

'We are under attack every day by bacteria. Some of these we need, for example, the ones within your stomachs. These help you digest your food. Others are not so friendly. You need to imagine yourselves as a wonderfully warm, salty and moist sack, a very nice place for our little invaders to insinuate themselves and reproduce.'

Adam winced as the class murmured, disgusted at this particular image. Mr Miller smiled at the reaction and continued.

'Our fantastic immune system works like soldiers in a battlefield from the very moment we are born. So look then, class, at our first diagram. An invading bacterial cell breaks through our outer wall... oh, and consider your mouth, throat, stomach and back passage as your outside, not inside.'

There were looks of confusion.

'The inside bit is sealed: no air or food is allowed unless our organs have processed it, checked it and allowed safe passage to the chemical you.'

Adam raised his eyebrows: thinking of himself as a chemical was certainly a first.

'So, if a bacterial cell penetrates and starts attacking, multiplying and locally changing our chemical structure, then we have cells equally ready to fight back and kill the invaders. These tiny invaders are known as pathogens and our initial fighting cells are called neutrophils and microphages.'

Mr Miller clicked a button that turned part of the white board into a screen showing mobile microscopic cells. Adam watched intently as one dot surrounded the adjacent one then engulfed it.

'Right, so these neutrophils and microphages eat the invaders, but if they start to struggle, they can send for backup. Some invading cells have difficult shells to break. Now, here is the clever bit. A special cell comes along to the battle and rips one of the invaders apart, placing bits of it all around its outsides. It will leave the fight and go to the lymph node, a place where our bodies have an army production centre. Once there it will look around for the right killing equipment.'

Looks of surprise stared back at him.

'I can imagine it saying,' said Mr Miller, cupping his hands like a megaphone to his mouth, "Is there anyone here that can deal with this?" then showing what it has brought. When it finds the right support, a reaction occurs and the found cell starts reproducing itself. Some of these then produce millions of little weapons known as "proteins". These flood the blood, travelling back to the battlefront. These weapons can attach themselves to the invaders because they have been specifically matched. This has two effects. Firstly, by smothering the blighters, they struggle to reproduce. Secondly, they can contact the bigger killer cells that can now, through their attachment, deliver a toxic serum directly into the bad bacteria. When our personal tiny microscopic killing machines have won, we don't want them causing any further harm so we naturally pass them, but this whole process leaves a memory, so we can watch out if this particular bug ever comes back.'

'Pass them, sir?' Jason asked.

'We lose them amongst the waste we pass.'

Jason still looked confused.

'Toilet,' said Chloe.

'Oh.'

'Right, now fill in the blanks on the attached pamphlets. We have some simple videos online that you can access by following the links on the sheet, and I would like you to write a summary in your own words of our immune system. And Jason, for clarity, that does not mean copy and paste.'

Adam stretched his legs walking around the school grounds. His hands were buried deep in his pockets; he was looking out beyond the trees but seeing nothing.

'Want to talk about it?' said Jonathan.

'I'm not sure; nothing makes sense.'

'Are you talking about Adele?' Jonathan's tone was smooth and understanding.

'What? No... Rebecca.' Adam turned to look at his friend. 'That book I had today, it described a woman being burnt in a fire. Surely no one would choose to end their life that way.'

'You're back on this Rebecca thing again aren't you?' Jonathan replied then continued after a brief pause. 'There are times when there's no explanation, and Adam –'

Adam stopped walking and turned to face him, feeling hot.

'What?'

'Accept people don't conform or act the way you want them to.'

'I accept people are the way they are.'

As he said this he turned away again but not before he'd seen Jonathan raise his eyebrows. He inhaled, savouring the smell of moist wood that lingered in the gap between the school and the dense trees, and kicked at a stone sending it into the long grass.

'I know I can't help her, but I do want to know more, to

understand, to make sense of how miserable she must have been.'

'Maybe you have a desire to prevent anyone else from doing the same thing and that's good.'

A distant buzz rang out from the school.

'Come on Adam. Mr Ingham will be furious if we're late.'

They went back inside through the main dining hall and down the steps leading back to the class corridor. They entered just as the others were taking their seats.

Mr Ingham stood to the left of the white board, fiddling with his electric piano keyboard. He was a stocky fellow with a rotund belly and well-trimmed dark hair thinning on top. The students tried to guess his age at about the late fifties or early sixties, perhaps not far from retirement. No one actually felt comfortable enough to ask. A general assumption was that he'd originally come from Poland as he still held onto a slight accent. He exuded a look of kind grumpiness. However, he was always pleasant enough and could play the keyboard with skill and passion.

'Afternoon,' he announced.

'Afternoon, Mr Ingham,' came the response like a well-rehearsed choir.

'Now, today, and as a final lesson before the end of term, I thought we should set a challenge for the holiday period.' This initiated a low hum of disapproval. Mr Ingham ignored it and continued.

'I have three sets of music that I'll play, tunes which you may or may not know. What I want you to do in groups is to alter them. Either write words to the tunes, or change the tunes by way of speed or location of chorus. Make them your own. It's not an easy project. Don't forget you can use the magic of Music Maker apps to compose the work.' Mr Ingham then played the three pieces of music: Liszt's Hungarian Rhapsody No. 2, then Mozart's *Alla Turca* and, finally Beethoven's *Moonlight Sonata*, which got a cacophony of approval.

Adam sat in the end lounge of their dormitory. The TV was off and he fiddled with the paper on the immune system. The door opened and Jonathan walked through wearing a particularly smug expression.

'I have something for you,' he said.

'Right.'

'Don't brood, that's not you. Look at this newspaper extract.'

Adam took the paper and read:

Sunday 1 Aug 2010

SCHOOLGIRL'S DEATH REMAINS A MYSTERY

Verdict remains open after inquest into the death of Miss Rebecca Johnson of Chaddesden following a tragic occurence at High Peak School, Derbyshire.

Rebecca Johnson's remains were discovered at 02:00 on Monday 12 July following an intense but localised fire in a store room. Forensic evidence has confirmed that the fire was caused by a 'winkie' candle, allegedly belonging to Miss Johnson. It is not known whether Miss Johnson intended to take her own life.

'Chloe spoke to me after our conversation.' Jonathan threw his hands wide. 'She knew what was bothering you. I said nothing.'

Adam smiled.

Jonathan looked directly at him. 'We go to High Peak on Sunday 12 July 2015, the five-year anniversary of her death. How coincidental is that?'

'I'm not brooding, but I'm disturbed by this. It doesn't matter whether it's one year or five, we should definitely nose around to see what we can discover. Mr Joins was clearly affected by her death, that was obvious, and we know she'd done some work analysing illnesses at her school,' said Adam.

'And you now think that's a motive for murder? A little far-fetched!'

Adam shrugged. 'Who knows? But seriously, would you set yourself on fire?'

'No, no, I wouldn't. But surely that just means it was an accident then.'

'Why use a candle for light? Wouldn't you get a torch?'

'People don't always act logically, Adam. And there won't be any pupils left who were there at the time. And something tells me any teachers that work there won't be very open to you asking questions.'

Adam looked down, deep in thought. He knew Jonathan was right, but he also knew he had to satisfy his curiosity. Something within was compelling him; he needed to know more.

'Are you sure this is not just something to take your mind off... well, going home?' asked Jonathan.

Adam looked up, his breathing becoming more audible.

'What do you mean?' he asked, although he was sure he knew exactly what Jonathan was talking about.

'Now don't go all defensive, Adam. I worry about you, that's all. You always get... edgy when it's close to the end of term.'

Jonathan was touching his shoulder now and his face showed

a concern Adam wanted desperately to ignore. He wanted to quash what he thought might be pity as images of his stepfather stomping around the house and shouting at his mother flashed through his mind.

'Really, well, I'm sorry you feel I become edgy. Anything else?'

'No, nothing.'

Adam looked at him. He anticipated the statement that was on the tip of his tongue, desperate to be released.

'Come on, Jonathan. Let's have it.'

'It's not just you, you know. There's Chloe as well.'

'She doesn't clash with him like I do.'

'Just because someone doesn't react or retaliate doesn't mean they like the person that is being horrible or nasty to their brother.'

Odd, thought Adam, now Jonathan had put things that way, he couldn't remember actually ever discussing John Simms with Chloe. They had often talked about their real dad, and enjoyed imagining what he was like and where he lived, but somehow John never featured.

'That's ridiculous. He's never so much as said "boo" to Chloe. I'm sure he thinks the sun shines from you know where, as far as she's concerned.'

'Still, it doesn't mean you like someone though, does it?'

Adam was not sure whether Jonathan knew more than he was letting on, but he felt uncomfortable debating this particular topic.

THREE

VIOLATION OF
REBECCA'S REST

FRIDAY 10 JULY 2015

Within the dark wood-panelled walls of High Peak's common room, Louise and Lisa Holloway sat opposite one another like a mirror image. Their symmetry was captivating. Both had long, jet-black hair that fell well below their shoulders, brown eyes and facial features that suggested melancholy. Lisa had a distinctive talent – her artwork which was superb for any age, but at thirteen, most precocious. Many of her drawings were featured in the pages of the Jameson Academy prospectus. Darren Cooper sat with the twins. He was small for his age, with a face so covered in freckles that at first glance he looked tanned.

It was quiet, apart from a tiny scratching noise as Lisa etched the drawing of a girl who had once walked this building. The black-and-white shaded sketch, copied from a photo Lisa had taken earlier that day, was of a picture hanging in the school's entrance foyer. Its piercing eyes now looked out to its creator. Its nose and mouth were perfectly formed with just some shading and general shaping to complete a striking likeness.

Darren looked across towards the girls and quietly asked, 'Can you smell –' he paused analysing the odour that had broken his study, 'bleach?'

Boom! All three jumped, their hearts pounding, as music erupted and bounced around the room.

'Shit!' said Darren.

'What the...?' said Louise.

Lisa physically jerked and then glanced across at Darren, pointing at her phone. It had connected via Bluetooth to the room speaker with three small bars in the top left corner dancing to a beat.

'It's my phone,' she said, pressing the screen, and instantly silence fell again. 'Odd. I didn't touch it.'

'You must have done, and it's late and we've probably woken half the school. We're directly below Level B, which is Miss Harper's,' Louise retorted.

'Sorry, I didn't mean to. In fact, I'm sure I didn't go near it,' Lisa replied, 'and look what I've done to my work.'

Darren and Louise peered over her shoulder and felt a shudder run through them. Lisa had smudged her work, giving the distinct impression that the girl she had drawn was crying.

'Now that looks spooky,' said Darren.

He watched Lisa look down, her eyes widening and initial annoyance clearly dissipating. She obviously understood what he meant. The image of Rebecca Johnson now burned deeply into Darren's consciousness and a sense of fear dwelled numbly in his mind. The thought of leaving the present company and wandering alone to his dormitory was not a pleasant one.

SATURDAY 11 JULY 2015

Fraser Johnson jumped out of bed, not bothering to pull up the covers. He dressed and ran down the stairs of their semi-detached Derbyshire stone-built house.

'Mum, I'm going out. Meeting Clive and Darren at Whaley,' he shouted, wrestling with trainers and tugging at the backs without touching the laces.

'You've not had any breakfast, Fraser.'

'I'll get a hot chocolate or something in the village.'

'Teeth!'

The sound of Fraser tramping back up the stairs and spitting water around a basin followed his mother's request before the front door slammed shut.

Fraser joined his friends who were waiting outside the café on the edge of Whaley Bridge.

'Hi Fraser! Are you looking forward to next week?' asked Clive. Clive Ross was a tall, gangly lad who was thinner than looked natural, with blonde hair and pearlescent hazel eyes.

'You bet! Luckily the rest of my class voted for the High Peak refreshment week. Where did you go again?'

'Wales, camping – last week. It was wetter than you can imagine. Wish we hadn't bothered,' replied Clive.

'Come on. Let's get in before all the seats are gone,' said Darren.

The boys chained their bikes to a metal hoop positioned close to a canal boat access point. They entered through a slatted wooden door with a wrought iron handle. It gave access to an internal wooden staircase giving an odd sense of homeliness. Once at the top, the space opened into a light, airy room that looked out over the start of Upper Peak Forest Canal. The boys walked over and sat at a corner table covered with a white cloth with a yellow porcelain vase sprouting wrapped cutlery. They watched the narrow boats taking passengers on a moving breakfast trip along the canal.

A young lady brought them three cups of hot chocolate topped with cubes of marshmallow. Fraser watched Clive whose gaze didn't leave the girl. She wore a badge with the name *Nicola* printed on it. Fraser reflected how odd it was that somewhere on life's journey one learnt that you mustn't call someone by their actual name unless they gave you permission, and he didn't know the girl. She was older than him, yet surely still of school age, with hair that hung below her waist. Clive was clearly mesmerised. Fraser thought about *The Addams Family* film and the image of Cousin It flashed before his mind.

'Thanks,' said Darren, as Nicola placed his drink in front of him, bringing Clive out of his trance.

'Oh yes, thanks,' Clive added, a little too early, as she hadn't taken the mug from her tray at that point, causing the other two to giggle at him.

Fraser sipped the frothy drink, enjoying the milky, sugary texture. Surely life couldn't get much better than this, his mind full of images of fun at High Peak activity centre, no schoolwork and then a further full summer of nothing but lie-ins, cycling and watching TV. Plus he had a couple of weeks with Mum and Dad in Devon to look forward to. No, he figured, this is pretty much the best time of the year, even better than Christmas.

'Come on, Darren, get out the old OS map,' said Fraser.

The map was worn and covered in squiggly lines from the many multicoloured crayons of trips long gone. He perched it on the edge of the table.

'It has to be the bike track on the hill just down the canal towpath,' said Darren, looking pleadingly at his companions.

'Good for me,' added Fraser.

'Okay,' agreed Clive.

Once the drinks had gone, Fraser and Darren let Clive pay Nicola prior to leaving. They watched with amusement as, with some skill, he managed to pay the bill without taking his eyes off her. Once outside they could no longer contain their mirth and they laughed until their insides started to hurt. Clive lifted his arms defiantly.

'What? What's with you guys?'

The summer sun was strong, peering out between scattered clouds that blew spasmodically across the sky, switching the intense rays on and off. This was great for the three boys as they peddled hard over the stony path waving at some of the boats and their passengers.

They carried on down the path then turned off to the right and climbed through a wood that stretched upwards away from the canal. At one point all three were off their bikes and pushing their beloved machines hard with effort at every step. The hill started to level off and the foliage reduced, giving way to an expanse of ground that gave rise to a hidden track they had visited many times. The track had twists, turns, humps and hollows of smoothly curved ground. Its naturally raised banks on either end had lost all vegetation where the loose surface had been worn away.

The three boys raced each other, timed laps, and pulled wheelies with youthful energy. Then they sat by the track looking over the valley below. The canal meandered majestically around the landscape, disappearing in the distance.

'Are you going to tell Fraser about... you know.'

'Clive... idiot!' said Darren.

'Tell me what?' replied Fraser.

'S... nothin',' said Darren.

'Come on, you've got to tell me now.'

'You really are a prat, Clive Ross. You know that, don't you?' said Darren.

Clive looked away, as though suddenly distracted by the view; the abundance of trees looked like the top of a broccoli head. Huge shadows, cast by the sun's light shining around the moisture-filled clouds, washed over the greenery.

'I'm still waiting,' said Fraser.

'Well, last night, me and the Holloway girls had a bit of a fright.'

'And?' Fraser encouraged, shifting around to view Darren.

'It's probably nothin'.'

'You're starting to wind me up now.'

'Late last night Lisa's phone set off the common room speaker. Shook us, that's all.'

'I think I know what you're trying to say and it's stupid,' said Fraser.

Clive cleared his throat, willing Darren to continue.

'You want to get that seen to mate,' said Darren.

'Tell him about the smell,' said Clive.

'Right, I've heard enough,' replied Fraser.

'Fraser, don't be like that. It's him, he shouldn't have said anything,' said Darren.

'No, he shouldn't, but it's clear you've all been making up stories. Gossiping about, about my cousin.'

'We haven't, honest,' Darren pleaded.

'I'm going to head back now anyway. Mum told me not to be late.' It was a lie. He paused. The others looked at him and he continued. 'We're going to see Auntie Annie this afternoon.'

The journey back down the hill and through the wood was intense and pretty scary as the incline increased and control became more and more difficult. Fraser's was not a mountain bike and didn't absorb the shocks as well as the others, which gave him an increased degree of difficulty in keeping the back end on the ground. Clive and Darren were both quicker and now stood at the bottom of the hill on the edge of the path.

Fraser concentrated on avoiding the large tree trunks,

branches, rocks and hollows. Relief filled him as the incline started to level off and he could see the other two watching him from the towpath. He wanted to go in a different direction, one that took him away from Darren, and especially Clive.

It was at that point that it happened. Just that split second lapse of concentration, the act of momentarily looking across, and an inner release of the stress from the hill descent. His front wheel dipped unexpectedly and lodged firmly in a rut that ran at ninety degrees to his momentum. The bike stopped dead but eight and a half stone of flesh, blood and bone didn't.

Clive and Darren looked on helplessly, as though watching a slow motion movie, although it was all over in a matter of seconds. Fraser catapulted over his bicycle, his arms stretched out in an instinct of natural protection as he rapidly lost height. Fraser's splayed hands hit the ground, struggling against an invisible force that pushed on, causing his elbows to bend over his head, affording it some protection. He flipped over, pivoting on his shoulders. The rest of his body carried on until his backside hit the ground with a bounce, creating a double thud that sounded worse than it actually was. The bike, obeying the laws of physics, tumbled down after him. Fortunately the wedged front wheel had caused it to travel sideways so that it narrowly missed the spot where Fraser now lay motionless.

'Fraser! Are you all right?' asked Darren, his raised syllables emanating concern.

'Um, I think so...' came Fraser's subdued and cautious reply.

'Don't move, just take your time,' said Clive. Fraser thought Clive sounded like something he'd heard on TV, and was perhaps feeling guilty.

Fraser looked at his hands, grass-stained mainly, but a couple of grazes were starting to sting and throb, along with the centre

of his lower back. He got up slowly, moving each joint in ᴜ
his head analysing and his prehistoric conditioning running   .
evaluation-of-injury report. He was looking and sensing for any
sharp pain or lack of movement.

The boys were staring at him, stuck to the spot.

'I'm ok, honestly,' said Fraser, picking up his bike.

'Are you sure?' Darren asked again.

'Yes, just a little shaken. I'll be fine, honest.'

Fraser walked somewhat gingerly to the path and turned in
the opposite direction to the one he knew the others would take
home.

'See you Monday,' he said to them.

'Yes, see ya,' Darren replied.

Fraser glanced back at the boys. Only Darren looked anxious
torn between watching him leave and staring at the floor. It gave
him a wave of guilt, but he wanted to be alone.

Fraser went through a well-used gap in the hedge line that
separated the road from the canal path. He stuck to the roads, their
smoothness offering relief as opposed to the rugged hill that had
ended the morning. As he rode he thought about Rebecca. She had
lived with Aunt Annie and he remembered playing badminton
with her in his aunt's back garden, which was large and seemed
to go on forever. He recalled hitting the shuttlecock and getting
it lodged in a tree, and then laughing with Rebecca as they both
jumped, whacking their rackets into the foliage. She must have
been about thirteen when he was around nine. He had been fond
of her, as she always seemed to have time for him. Now, as she lay
cold and lost to his world, the High Peak students were making up
stories about her soul being trapped and roaming the corridors.
He hated them for that and his thoughts urged him to change
direction: a new purpose, a new mission, that wouldn't take long.

He cycled further around the dale to the top of the hill and entered the churchyard from a side gate. Once through, he left his bike leaning against the stone wall just inside the closed-off area. Parts of the dry-stone enclosure had long since been lost, either to the natural movement of the ground or the cruel elements that penetrated the high, remote spot. There were other theories from people in the community that outsiders had raided and removed some of the sacred stones, and these stories had been expressed with revulsion at such an act of violation in a religious and historical place.

From a grass verge at the side of a road bearing little traffic, Fraser had gathered some bright yellow daffodils mixed with bluebells. He clutched them as he made his way towards the grave. Trees and bushes filled much of the graveyard and images of roots penetrating coffins flooded Fraser's mind. He shook his head unconsciously, squeezing the stems of the flowers in his hand, causing their sap to ooze and seep across his broken skin.

He heard voices ahead. He moved sideways and hid behind the trunk of a large oak. Two men were standing either side of Rebecca's grave. They wore dark green overalls like workmen and thick brown boots similar to those he himself had for going on long walks with his parents. The men blended into the background. The only colour given off was a dirty yellow from their rubber gloves.

Between the men stood a metal grey tripod with a motor-type housing at its centre. Leading from the bottom of the motor and pointing downwards was a rotating tube, twisting as it spun slowly, appearing to travel downwards into the soft soil. Perhaps it was an optical illusion and maybe the tube was merely rotating.

Fraser felt a sudden urge to vomit; his hand and back throbbed even more at the sight of this violation. He wanted to run at them, kick them hard and shout 'leave her alone'. After all, what could she have possibly done to them? He didn't move. He stood there utterly paralysed, his head spinning. Surreptitiously he looked over from behind the tree. A small white van was parked alongside a track running adjacent to the church and graveyard and giving access to the fields beyond. One of the rear doors of the van was ajar, allowing a cable to pass over the wall and disappear into the housing at the very tip of the tripod.

The men were talking. They appeared unconcerned about being seen. Fraser could hear them but couldn't detect what they were saying. He dropped the flowers and stole back to where his bicycle lay, picking it up slowly and slipping away quietly, only half glancing back to see if anyone was following.

He cycled down the hill and away from the church. At the bottom his momentum started to slow, but his passion to get home didn't wane as he passed the entrance to High Peak School. His attention was diverted by a stationary vehicle ready to pull out and turn left up the hill to the church and perhaps beyond, in the direction from which he had just come. Its intentions were clear by the flashing orange light that pulsed on and off. His eyes met and fused with the driver momentarily. A lady with buoyant red hair watched him intently as he passed at a right angle to her path.

FOUR

HIGH PEAK

SUNDAY 12 JULY 2015

Gillian Johnson pulled into High Peak School and activity centre with a sense of trepidation; she had stayed here some seven years previously with work colleagues. That particular memory was bright and happy as she recalled seeing people she worked with every day doing things that were very much outside their comfort zone. There mingled another memory, one of immense sadness, as the image of her niece intruded.

Gillian didn't see her sister-in-law much either before or after Rebecca had died so tragically at this very place. Despite the awfulness of it all she felt she had no right to deny Fraser his own opportunities at the school. She was not about to change her ways and turn the boy into a recluse or make him miserable. Nonetheless, a strange sense of fear pulled at her as she said goodbye to her boy in the car park and watched him disappear inside the entrance to the building.

Fraser wandered around to the main office. His class would join him later. No point in travelling all the way to Park View this morning and then catching the minibus back here to where he lived. His backpack pulled on his shoulders from the weight of all the stuff his mother had insisted he take. His back still ached from the fall the previous day and he momentarily reviewed his

48

hands as he stood waiting. The office was similar to the one at his own school, with a light wooden desk, and a glazed screen protecting occupants from visitors. Fraser now wondered why such isolation was necessary. Then his insides tensed and a sick feeling rose in his throat. Through the window he saw the red-haired lady again. She was talking to the two men he had seen desecrating Rebecca's rest. They were chatting as bold as brass and then they handed her a metal case that looked strong and industrial.

'Hello!' A lady behind reception broke his gaze and brought him back inside.

At first Fraser just stared at her before finding his voice.

'Oh... er, I'm Fraser Johnson from Park View School. We're staying here for refreshment week.'

'Okay, yes, here we are. You're on Level D, dormitory six.'

'Thanks. Can I go up and take my stuff?'

'Yes of course dear. Do you know the way?'

'I'll find it.'

'Okay, have a good week.'

He turned just as Stacey Harper came walking along the corridor behind him. He couldn't help himself. He stared intently at the metal case she was carrying.

'Are you all right?' Stacey asked.

The lady behind the counter said, 'This is Fraser Johnson, Stacey. He's here for refreshment week'.

Fraser saw Stacey momentarily falter. She involuntarily glanced sideways at the picture that hung on the lobby wall; he feared she could see the likeness to him.

At that moment, Darren Cooper strolled up.

'Hi, Fraser! Which dorm are you in?'

Fraser turned to look at Darren then back at the stationary

Stacey. It broke their reverie and Stacey headed off without so much as a word.

'Are you okay?' Darren asked.

Adam sat against the internal wall of the minibus, pinned by the weight of Adele who was leaning comfortably against him. His arm rested over the chair behind her as they travelled towards High Peak Hostel. He wanted to wrap his arm around her and hold her tight, but he knew that would be going too far.

They were being driven by their personal tutor, Graham, a middle-aged and balding man who found it increasingly difficult to maintain a waistline.

'Graham, I actually believe you'll be sad that the summer break is almost upon us.'

'How did you know, Chloe?' he sarcastically replied.

'Because you love our little group.'

'Right.'

'Oh, you so do, sir,' Chloe replied.

'This may be a shock, but I do have a life beyond these school walls.'

'Really, oh please do tell,' she encouraged.

Adam watched Graham lean over to peer in the rear view mirror at Chloe with a wry smile and a small shake of his head. He saw Chloe stare straight back beaming. But Graham didn't expand: Adam interpreted from this that either his other life was private or he was indeed going to miss his tutor group.

The minibus meandered around the hillside, turning onto the main road and passing through High Peak village. Adam focused on this quaint, chocolate box location and could well imagine it had adorned many postcards depicting a tranquil lifestyle, an image that in the main didn't resonate with this particularly youthful group of new inhabitants. However, for a short and adventurous break, it did offer a volume of excitement.

They passed three shops on the right, two of which shared a mix of commodities. The butcher was also the baker and the newsagent had window displays of wool and craft-type products. Centrally, a tiny post office remained fairly insulated from any changes resulting from capitalistic expansion, with perhaps the exception of the odd book in its windowpane fading from the sunlight.

The road climbed as it left this communal sign of life amongst the rural expanse, until it reached a peak where an isolated parish church stood, its spire pointing to the heavens and visible for miles. The van travelled on and down towards High Peak School. On the left, standing deep within the hillside and surrounded by trees, Adam could see a building resembling an old hall. It was fixed at the end of an overgrown track. Its windows were boarded up around the bottom and it had the general appearance of neglect shown by the missing tiles on its roof, with many broken and twisted out of symmetry.

'What's that building, Graham?' Adam asked.

'I believe that was the old schoolhouse and perhaps a hall for the villagers. Now, of course, they make use of the school. I believe it still sits on part of the school's property, although Ron has tried to get permission to demolish it. The local parish council refused. I think it's a bit of a bugbear as the kids keep vandalising it.'

They continued on and shortly turned into the drive of High Peak School and Activity Centre. The more newly constructed driveway flowed around it, twisting through the woodland, which Adam thought was probably to avoid removing large trees or perhaps to add a more impressive feel for visitors than a straighter route.

'Here we are then, the old manor house, High Peak School,' Graham announced. Adam and Jonathan were the last to leave the minibus. They joined the group at the main entrance just as Brian Lambert introduced himself as the Head Teacher of High Peak and their tutor for the week at the activity centre. Mr Lambert certainly didn't look anything like a normal head teacher, particularly as he seemed quite young. Adam thought he was perhaps in his early thirties, average height, slim (not surprising, being leader at this kind of recreational centre) but with rather unkempt curly hair. Adam reviewed Brian's features and was reminded of someone he initially struggled to recall. After a short time it came to him: the image of a successful businessman called Paul, a friend of his stepfather, who had started life in Eastern Europe.

'Any problems or worries about this week then feel free to talk to me or one of my colleagues at any time.' His voice lowered. 'We don't tend to eat the students. Not unless we're extremely hungry,' said Mr Lambert. This poor attempt at humour raised a mild response from the group. It also subconsciously lifted their spirits.

Adam followed Jonathan inside and started to take note of their surroundings. Another old building: a converted stone manor house, this one with a slight tang of fustiness. The Peaks were well known for high rainfall and Adam figured the dampness must have permeated its walls.

On the opposite wall to the reception desk hung a picture of a young girl. At the side was a framed collage of letters written by students, all positioned at different angles and overlapping. Under the two frames were the words *Rebecca Johnson, we miss you*. Directly adjacent to these frames was a panelled white metal door that looked industrial. It bore a plaque that read *Sick Bay*.

'Right, let's get back outside. We'll walk around the perimeter first.'

Mr Lambert pointed to the front door, signalling the group to fall in behind him for the guided tour. Adam nudged Jonathan and gestured with his eyes at the picture.

'I know, I've seen it,' whispered Jonathan.

'What's that? Somebody ask something?' said Mr Lambert.

'No, we're all okay. Just wondering if we could leave our bags here,' said Adam, looking at Jonathan as if to say that's all I could think of.

'Yes, fine. Good idea.'

They followed the group out to the entrance. Two pillars supported a canopied porch either side of three worn stone steps that spread wide to a front car park. The walls were dark grey Derbyshire stone blocks that gave a flat surface, broken only by ornate mouldings surrounding Georgian-style windows. The walls ended at the top in a parapet closed off by wider solid copings. The edge of the roof was not generally visible apart from glimpses where high lead-lined openings allowed rain to flow into cast metal hoppers and then into ornate rainwater downpipes.

Adam could see Mr Lambert in front and to the left pointing to the football pitches, a rugby field and a running track. They walked anti-clockwise around the building passing part of the school that looked very much like it had been added at some point, with columns of brickwork enclosed by painted glazed panels and a flat roof. It also had its own entrance. They continued their anti-clockwise journey along the back. A fenced-off area consisted of an Astro Turf court and adjacent to that were four tennis courts. The group continued to follow Mr Lambert. He and Graham were now deep in conversation that Adam believed might well have been Graham expressing admiration for the establishment. The group started to drift apart with Chloe, Adele and Jason at the front and he and Jonathan further back.

'Come on, let's keep together,' shouted Mr Lambert, as they continued further around to the left side of the main school entrance. A large structure stood completely independently from the old school building. In the main it had a smooth, stone-coloured surface covering approximately one third of the frontage. However, centrally located were glazed panels that rose high joining a band of windows around the top. Through the glass at the front and top, Adam could see thick wooden columns that looked like they'd been made up of many strips pressed together. The columns became wider at their highest point and appeared to bend over supporting the roof. The whole building sat within a dense wooded area and a warm orange glow from the internal lights reflected onto the canopy of trees through the windows.

'This building is our sports hall. In here is the main hall with badminton courts, squash courts and trampolines. In fact, all the usual gymnastic facilities. Oh, and that fenced-off area at the back is where our Ronald is planning a pool. They're carrying out soil tests.'

Adam looked through the wire mesh fencing where a steel tripod with a central spine disappeared into the ground. Around it were scattered discarded plugs of soil.

'What is that odd part of the building on the right-hand side of the school, sir?' Chloe asked.

'That's a local health centre. There's a doctor's surgery, some treatment rooms for minor injuries and a small sick bay facility for the school. We do make use of it occasionally. It helps stop bugs spreading through our small community,' Mr Lambert advised, and continued quickly. 'Now, between the sports hall and the main school building there's another entrance. This is known as the "dirty boot entrance" where any soiled shoes must be left before entering the main school. Do I make myself clear on that point?'

The group murmured their understanding and advised that this policy existed at their own school. They continued inside. Mr Lambert guided them around, showing them the dining area, common rooms and their respective dormitories.

MONDAY 13 JULY 2015

Two minibuses parked in a limestone car park near Longshaw Estate, a part of the National Trust. Adam jumped from the van first, holding open the sliding door as wide as it would go to enable the others to exit more easily. As they grabbed rucksacks from the back, Adam watched Mr Lambert who was looking anxiously at a blue Skoda parked in the corner.

'Everything all right, Brian?' asked Graham.

'Yes, fine. Let's go to the left down that trail,' said Mr Lambert, indicating a sign post on the path that read *Burbage Brook* that pointed along a well-trodden route heading along the edge of a peak. Purple heather covered the ground stretching to the right. Adam looked left. The rocky floor fell away to a valley. Between them and the babbling stream below, odd twisted trees grew from the bracken-covered slope. The path continued along the top, but they were led downwards by Mr Lambert, negotiating the rocky surface and using the crawling roots as footholds to maintain balance. He heard a scream and turning round he saw a girl from Park View being helped back to her feet.

'Chloe, watch out on the loose rocks,' said Adam.

'Yes, I know, and it's only going to get worse. Remember the itinerary of the day was "boulder hopping down Padley Gorge". Can you imagine coming back up here with wet shoes?'

Adam looked back at the others.

'You guys okay?'

'Fine, but can Jason join you or Jonathan?' asked Chloe.

'I'm all right. It's you that needs support, Chloe,' said Jason.

Adam laughed, more to himself. It was typical of her to worry about Jason.

'Mr Lambert seems somewhat distant,' said Adam quietly to Jonathan.

'He's not looking after the Park View group, is he?'

'No, he has left them completely behind. Looks like Graham's held back to support them. Did you see Mr Lambert stare at that car in the car park? He looked unnerved by it.'

'I think, Adam Brant, your imagination is getting carried away. But I don't think much of Mr Lambert.'

They reached the stream where the water ran around, and in some cases over rocks that protruded from the gravelly bed, and waited for everyone to catch up.

'Right, we're going to follow the stream, and for the more adventurous amongst us, literally hop from one boulder to the next working our way down to Grindleford. There are some places where there is no option other than to travel via the stream's boulders. Let's go then,' said Mr Lambert.

Before anyone could object, he was off. Adam and Jonathan climbed onto the rocks and commenced jumping from boulder to boulder. Others followed their lead. It wasn't long before shouts and screams were heard from a few who had slipped off and found themselves submerged in the icy cold waters.

The journey continued for over an hour before Adam saw Mr Lambert veer to the right of the stream and wait. When the last of the group had caught up, they followed a limestone path that parted the foliage, rising away from the valley basin. The scars of the task were evident in the panting red faces, ruffled clothing and the many stains both wet and muddy. There was clear relief at reaching the end but it was mixed with apprehension as most reflected in the knowledge that they still had to return.

'Well done, everybody. That's the hard part completed. I always believe going back uphill is easier along the stream. We have a short walk up this hill and along the top to a little railway café and we'll rest there a while before venturing back to the minibuses.'

The timber-clad, single storey cafe sat among trees and was sandwiched between the railway line and the road. At the front were wooden picnic tables on stone slabs, creating a courtyard area beyond which the natural ground fell away.

'If anyone wants a drink,' said Graham, pointing to his bulging rucksack overflowing with a variety of juices.

'Oh gee, thanks, sir,' replied Jonathan, and continued. 'Mine's a pint of lager or better still cider and blackcurrant.'

The group gave a collective giggle at this remark, all except Chloe.

'Chloe, are you ok?' Adele asked.

'I twisted my ankle on one of the boulders, not too badly, but I'll go back along the footpath.'

'I'll go with Chloe,' said Jason. 'I slipped off the rocks more often than not and grazed the side of my leg.' He lifted his trouser, showing them the swollen red patch that looked quite sore.

'You should get that checked,' said Adam.

'No, it's fine, but I'll walk back with Chloe.' He glanced around as though making sure the Park View group couldn't hear.

Chloe watched Adam disappear off down the path towards the valley basin. She certainly felt better after their short and enjoyable stop, but decided, for Jason's sake, she would stick to the high level path.

The alternative stone path gave a lofty view of the valley

below. Chloe could see the little knot of people behind them now as their route was fairly level and without obstruction. A whiff of the foulest odour drifted across their senses.

'What the heck is that?' said Chloe.

'I've no idea,' replied Jason. Looking into the distance they could see something dark lying on the ground with a mass of flies circling it. 'It's a dead sheep,' said Jason.

'That's absolutely disgusting. Don't look at it, Jason.'

But the young boy's curiosity was far too piqued to miss it. They struggled to keep their distance from the carcass as the opposite side of the path dropped off very steeply. The sheep's legs and head were still very much intact. The body, however, had been subjected to what appeared to have been a vicious attack. The ribcage gaped around raw meat with most of the organs missing. Blood had flowed freely across the grass, staining it dark red, almost black. The intense smell caused Chloe to retch and she regretted her earlier snacks at the café.

Chloe and Jason were well ahead and upon reaching the car park they sat silently, perching on a couple of strategically placed rocks, the scene they'd witnessed still fresh in their minds. Chloe now wished she'd taken the keys to the van from Graham. In the distance they caught sight of a dark figure that looked familiar – a tall man walking along the footway that continued across the moor. He was carrying a sack slung over his shoulder and in his hand was a clear plastic bag. Chloe struggled to make out the contents, although it looked dark red in colour. At first he appeared to be heading towards them, but then he changed direction and veered to the left. Chloe instantly felt isolated and vulnerable with only a twelve-year-old boy by her side.

The time dragged as they continued to wait. The rustling noise of wind through the trees became more noticeable. Chloe felt an amazing sense of relief as she heard the sound of the group returning and grinned widely on seeing Adam.

'Well, that makes a change... not my normal greeting.' Chloe didn't say anything, but she struggled to remove her pleased expression.

'What's up? I'm not flying low, am I?'

'No. I'm just glad to see everyone,' replied Chloe.

Sounds of laughter and the shrill of adolescent hum filled the hillside as the group tried to create a human pyramid with lads at the bottom, girls forming the next layer and Jason attempting to climb on top. It ended in a heap of human entanglement. The sun remained bright, although the sting had gone. A little heat still warmed the air, creating a glorious sky of orange where it met the hills.

Chloe and Adele were fascinated with the identical twin girls from High Peak School, Louise and Lisa Holloway. They were indistinguishable from one another. The twins were one academic year below them, as was the general rule, with High Peak School housing the third-year students. Peg Low housed first years, Park View had second years, Dale had fourth years and Water Mill currently had the fifth form. However, soon they would be moving up one. Water Mill would absorb a new intake of young pupils. Chloe deliberated over the twins' ages and concluded that there was not actually a full calendar year difference between the Holloway twins and themselves.

'Do you often find you're thinking the same thing even when you're apart?' she asked.

'Sometimes, but that could be because we know one another so well,' replied Louise, who tended to be the communicator for the pair.

Louise had an equal fixation on Chloe's wiry, tightly curled hair and porcelain complexion. She was also interested in the fact that Chloe and Adam were twins. They had a connection, a bond that she had not yet come across – twins of a different type to her and her sister.

'Are you mistaken for one another?'

'Leave them alone. You're so invasive at times, Chloe Brant. I'm sure they're sick of such questions,' said Adam, as he and Jonathan joined them.

'It's okay,' said Louise, 'we're used to it. The teachers here can't tell us apart, so we generally wear a contrasting colour on our clothing. I wear blue and Lisa wears red. It might be as little as a hair bow or a belt.'

Chloe looked at Louise, struggling at first to find the blue item. Louise noticed the examination and leaned back wriggling her feet. She was wearing navy blue striped training shoes; Lisa's were red striped. Chloe wondered whether their parents could tell them apart, but felt that Adam may indeed be right, and decided to change the subject.

'That big block to the right side of the schoolhouse ruins the whole look of the place, don't you think?'

'That's a health centre for the local villages and our school's sick bay. It's really just a couple of rooms with twin beds; I think the whole building is owned by the Academy,' Lisa replied.

'Early last year we caught a bug. It was quite nasty, and you know how these things go around, so we spent some time in the sick bay –' Lisa advised, but before she had time to complete her sentence Louise cut in.

'We were very well looked after.'

'Yes, very well,' reiterated Lisa.

'I thought this was supposed to be a healthy place,' said Adam, stating what should have been the obvious. Somehow this statement seemed to close the conversation and the twins retired, suggesting they had a big day ahead of them.

TUESDAY 14 JULY 2015

The clear blue sky and the sharp cool breeze were a contrast to the lukewarm evening of the previous day. The rock face in front of Adam rose several metres high. The structure changed in length from a very rugged face with lots of ledges to a particularly smooth one with few indentations capable of carrying the tip of a boot or small fingers. On the right the natural stone rolled out at the top giving the students the challenge of an overhang. A range of seven different climbs had been marked out with coloured pegs along the top and bottom respectively.

The students were up and facing challenges of varying degrees of difficulty. All the necessary climbing paraphernalia had been distributed as they helped one another with their protective clothing. The Dale group was joined again by the class from Park View. Adam had completed all the climbs and was poised waiting for another turn. Mr Lambert had been directing and controlling the proceedings from the lower level. The colleague he had introduced as Miss Harper was stationed at the top helping the students unclip and then directing them down the path that led around the back. Adam felt uncomfortable in her presence; she seemed to struggle to communicate effectively with the group, as though preoccupied with something else. She wore dark green tracksuit bottoms and a woolly jumper. She appeared quite thickset for her height with red, shoulder length hair. She had decided now to focus on Adele more than the others.

'Come on, Adele. Try this route. It's got a slight overhang that can be avoided if you move more to the right halfway up!'

'I'd rather not. These belts dig in too hard and I don't feel strong enough for those climbs.'

'Come on! Have a go! You'll get a sense of achievement from this one,' she bellowed from her lofty position.

'Not if I fall off.'

'I can hold you from the top.'

'Okay.' She reluctantly gave in. 'But only if Adam holds the rope from down here like Mr Lambert is doing for the others.'

'That's fine. I totally understand.' she said, a little too loudly.

Adam looked at Adele, shaking his head as her face contorted at the innuendo. Adam figured she trusted him far more than this woman, and from what he had seen she was not that good at climbing. Adam admired how Adele remained in control enough not to retort as he watched her walk up to the rock face and place her feet through the relevant holes of a harness. Adam pulled up the harness, tightened the buckles and connected the carabiner through the loop at the front, then attached the figure of eight. She smiled at him, her eyes conveying a sense of trust that made him feel warm and fuzzy inside. Mr Lambert looked over and nodded his approval after checking what Adam had done.

Adam grabbed the front of the harness with both hands and lifted Adele off the floor. With her legs dangling she held his shoulders for support and gave a short squeal.

'Sorry, just wanted to be sure,' he advised with a half-hearted grin. Adam then placed the opposite end of the rope through his figure of eight and pulled it through and around his body indicating to her to go. He continued pulling the rope, taking up the slack as she climbed slowly but steadily to the halfway point and then stopped, unable to see where to go next.

'There's a crevice just to your left, nearer to your head. That's it.' Adam shouted from the floor. That's great. You're doing great.'

'AAHHHHH!' A fierce, high-pitched scream bounced off the cliff face as a boy fell. Adam glimpsed his arms and legs waving as though he were attempting to manipulate air. Thud! There was a delayed sound like a drum being struck below his level of vision. Onlookers moved instinctively away from the falling mass. Adele panicked, losing her grip and sliding down. Adam, losing concentration just for a split second, gripped hard on the rope as it ran through his gloved hands. He altered the angle as he should have done initially and the moving rope stopped along with Adele's downward momentum, although she remained dangling like a rag doll uncontrollably flailing about.

A crowd gathered around the young boy.

'Adele, try to grab hold of the rock or the rope. It's okay. I've got you,' Adam shouted. 'I'll lower you down slowly. Just stay calm and you'll be fine.' She pulled herself up, holding tightly to the rope while he lowered her down. 'Sorry, Adele.'

'Fraser! Fraser! Can you hear me?' said Mr Lambert. There was no response. Adam turned, looking through the students. He could see Mr Lambert bending down and putting his hand gently on the boy's chest, trying to sense any movement. At the same time, he inclined his head over the boy's mouth. The group around them was transfixed. Could he hear anything? Was there a breath? Miss Harper came running down the path towards the scene.

'He's breathing. Phone for an ambulance.'

'I've already done that, sir.' Jonathan pushed through the crowd and passed his mobile phone to Miss Harper. 'They want to know our exact location.'

Through the newly formed wider gap Adam could see the twisted shape of the boy's body. His leg and arm didn't conform to normality. Held tightly in his hand was his helmet. Blood trickled from his nose.

FIVE

INSPECTOR RUMCORN

TUESDAY 14 JULY 2015 – 14:00

Dale group sat in stunned silence inside the common room at the end of the dormitory corridor on the top floor, Level D. The silence seemed to cause a ringing in Adam's ears and visions of the boy's twisted form on the floor wouldn't leave his head. Jason was the first to break the silence hanging in the air.

'Well, I think it should be closed. This place is jinxed.' He looked hard towards Chloe. 'I don't understand why he fell.'

'I don't either. We're not supposed to unclip until we're safely away from the edge,' said Chloe.

'Oh, so it was his fault! Is that what we're saying now?' Adele winced, the movement clearly causing pain from the abrasions on her cheek.

'Adele, no one is blaming anyone,' Chloe replied, sympathetically looking across at her. 'Curiosity... you know what young boys are like.'

'Young boy in the room, Chloe, and we're not stupid!' said Jason.

The door opened and Graham entered.

'Fraser is in intensive care. He hasn't regained consciousness and will be operated on shortly. That's all we know. Let's remain positive. I'm advised we are all to be interviewed by the police. An Inspector Rumcorn is here and wants to speak to everyone who was at the scene.'

Adam wanted to get it over with and was keen to offer to go first, although by the time he got to the office where the interviews were being held, it suddenly didn't seem such a good idea. Graham accompanied him, advising him not to worry. He left him with a female police officer outside what was now being called the 'incident room'.

'Hello, I'm Debbie,' the policewoman advised Adam. 'And you are?'

'I'm Adam, Adam Brant', he replied, as the woman indicated four plastic chairs against the wall, one of them occupied by a timid-looking boy. Debbie made a note, which he assumed was his name, on a clipboard, and then disappeared into the incident room.

The boy sitting next to him was rocking slowly and looking straight ahead, staring at the wall. Adam assumed he was from Park View School. He vaguely recognised him and thought hard about what to say, but struggled. After all, what could he say? 'Are you all right?' Well, that would be silly. Of course he wasn't, or perhaps, 'Can I do anything to help?' But what could he do? The conflict in his head became overwhelming, so he decided to say nothing and just sit quietly and wait. The time began to drag as he too sat staring at the walls. School notices stuck up with Blu Tack suddenly became more interesting. They informed students of forthcoming events: events that now seemed insignificant.

Moments later Graham reappeared with Chloe, and although they remained in silence, having his sister next to him made everything feel much more bearable. Suddenly the handle turned and clicked as the door latch disengaged. When it opened, it allowed light from the opposite window to fill the narrow corridor and two silhouetted figures were visible. One was a boy who Adam definitely remembered as being with the boy who fell. He was clearly upset. His companion was the policewoman, Debbie. Debbie guided the last occupant away from the office, talking as she did so, and then watched him leave. As she returned, Adam saw her smile at the small group and this gave him a certain amount of comfort.

'I believe you're next,' she said to the other small boy sitting next to Adam. He rose slowly, following her into the room. When the door closed again it banged loudly, making Chloe jump. Adam looked around at her with a half-smile as they shuffled along one seat.

When it was his turn, Adam first saw a man of athletic build, perhaps in his mid-thirties. He watched him pace from the window to the desk seemingly deep in thought. His dark hair was cut in a current style, short on one side but long on top, sweeping over and leaving a neat parting. Impeccably dressed, Adam thought, although not wearing a tie. His white shirt and dark grey flecked trousers with shiny, black, patent leather shoes made him look smart but casual. As the man turned towards him, he immediately noticed his intense green eyes that appeared to reflect the room's light like precious stones. Adam struggled to prevent himself from staring. His face had a chiselled, worn appearance with a defined chin line.

'Please have a seat,' said the man, gesturing to a chair as he perched on the edge of the table in a more informal manner.

Seated at the side of the table was a plump, older woman with dark hair and an over-powdered face, wearing a purple scarf wrapped around a black woollen jumper and a checked skirt. She radiated warmth.

'I'm Detective Inspector Peter Rumcorn and this is Mrs Chivers from Social Services.'

She interrupted the inspector's speech.

'Now, there's no need to worry, dear. The inspector just wants to get a clear picture of what happened this morning.' Her tone became softer as she continued. 'We do realise it may well be distressing.'

'Please, just take us through this morning's events,' said Rumcorn.

'At what point would you like me to start?' asked Adam.

'Well, at any point you like. Did everything seem normal?'

Adam went through the events, who he was with and where he was standing when he heard the scream and saw the boy fall.

'Fraser, the boy's name is Fraser Johnson,' interjected Rumcorn.

Adam looked at Rumcorn. Something inside him tingled, but he couldn't understand why.

'Please continue, Adam,' said Rumcorn.

'Jonathan, my friend, immediately called for an ambulance. Adele slipped, but I held onto her. I remember seeing two boys just prior to... Fraser falling.' He paused at that point, swallowing hard, and Mrs Chivers nodded encouragingly and he continued.

'The boys walked down from the hill along the path which led to the top. It was the safe way back and everyone used it. The boys passed in front of me back to their group. I'm sure that one of those boys just previously left this room.'

The inspector appeared to make some notes and Mrs Chivers smiled again encouragingly.

'Can you remember who was at the top when Fraser fell?' asked Rumcorn.

'Miss Harper, she was, but I was watching Adele, so I didn't see, well, anything.'

'Can you remember hearing anything? Shouting or raised voices before Fraser fell?'

'Sorry, no. Nothing,' replied Adam.

They thanked him and asked that he return to the dormitory lounge. Should he remember anything else, however insignificant, he must not hesitate to get in touch. Contact details would be posted around the school. As Adam left, he passed Chloe. She looked tense, so Adam smiled and mouthed, 'You'll be fine.'

Adam returned to the top floor lounge.

'However we thought this week would go, no one could have predicted this. I just can't believe it. Everything seems so unreal. This morning we were all having breakfast, perfect normality, and now this.' he said, when the five of them were all back.

'There is something I learned from Louise. You know, one of the twins.'

The group turned, all eyes and ears focused on Adele.

'Go on,' Adam encouraged.

'Fraser, the boy who fell. Well, his full name is Fraser David Johnson. His cousin was Rebecca Johnson.'

That was it. He now realised what had made him so uneasy when Rumcorn had said Fraser's name.

'Louise said that Darren Cooper, a lad in her class, had told her Fraser seemed upset, more so after some incident with Miss Harper.'

'What kind of incident?' Adam asked.

'They had some sort of, well, Darren wasn't sure,' replied Adele.

'Like an argument?' Adam enquired further.

'No idea! Just that Fraser had been agitated after an encounter with Miss Harper.'

'How does Darren know Fraser? He's not from this school.'

'I asked that and apparently Fraser and Darren live around here, went to the same junior school and stayed friends,' said Adele.

'I wonder if Inspector Rumcorn knows about this? Did Louise say?'

'No,' replied Adele.

Inside the interview room, Inspector Rumcorn paced up and down, hands in his pockets, momentarily looking through the window but not really noticing anything on the other side. Deep in thought, Rumcorn felt a sense of unease about the whole affair, yet on the face of it, it was nothing but a tragic accident.

'Debbie, can you see whether Miss Harper has returned from the hospital and is available to be interviewed?'

PC Amott disappeared, returning some ten minutes later with Stacey. Her eyes looked swollen and her bedraggled hair hung loosely around her shoulders. She was still wearing the tracksuit bottoms and woolly jumper that she wore on the climb.

'I have told the other officers everything I know,' Stacey said, prior to any formal greeting.

'Hello, Miss Harper. I'm Inspector Peter Rumcorn,' Rumcorn replied slowly and methodically. He continued. 'I'm sorry to take you through the events again. However, we do have to be sure everything has been covered, particularly under the circumstances.'

'Where do you want me to start?'

'What's your role here at the school?'

'Er, well...'

There was a short pause, as Stacey initially seemed surprised at this question. Rumcorn looked enquiringly at her, but remained silent.

She continued, 'I'm a teaching assistant and support Brian with the activity centre.'

'How long have you been at the school?'

'About four years now.'

'So, roughly since the time of the fire here?'

Stacey looked stunned and confused.

'I started at the school just after that.'

'Right, and did you know Fraser well?'

Rumcorn had moved now and was perched back on the edge of the desk, a point at which he was elevated.

'No, not really. He was from Park View School, not here, and I don't often go there. I'd come across him a couple of times, that's all.'

'And what was he like?' There was a short pause that seemed longer than it actually was as Stacey appeared to deliberate.

'He was quite a normal boy.'

'And what would that be?'

'Inquisitive, he was known to be bright; tended to keep to himself.'

'Did you like him then?'

'As I have said, I didn't know him that well. I suppose he was nice enough, just like all the other boys here.'

'But you prefer the girls.'

'I wouldn't say that. They're easier to deal with, I guess. More understanding, perhaps. What's this got to do with this morning's accident?'

'So what did happen this morning?'

'Well, like I said in my earlier statement, Brian and I took the students to Black Rock for a climbing session. They helped carry the equipment to the rock face.'

'Who was Fraser with?'

'I'm not sure. I don't really know their class. I think I remember seeing him with that small lad with long, straight blonde hair and painfully thin. Um, Billy I think he's called. When Fraser was in the school, I saw him with Darren Cooper, who resides here.'

'Didn't he have any friends from his own school? Did you suspect some bullying by his peers?'

'No, nothing like that! I'm told he knew pupils that were based here. I believe he lived near them, so he sometimes mixed with them, that's all.'

'Okay, so you were at Black Rock.'

'We set up the various climbs, meaning Brian and I. Brian tutored from the bottom and I helped, generally at the top.'

'Then what happened?' Rumcorn pursued.

'Fraser came up the easy climb, no problem, disconnected himself, and walked off down the path. No, actually the first climb he did, I walked towards him. When he reached the top he waved me away and shouted, "No, I'm all right", so I left him to it.'

'And then what?'

'Well, there were other students coming up that I helped, and then I saw Fraser coming over the top for a second run on a more difficult climb. I was initially above Adele from Dale School. Fraser stood on the top and I felt guilty about not helping him the previous time, so I...' Stacey paused. 'I went towards him, but again he waved me back and said no he was all right and could manage. He unclipped his line, sort of looked at me, and just stepped back. I've no idea why. The next thing –' Stacey swallowed hard, 'was that awful scream.' Her bottom lip was quivering visibly now.

'You've not had any dealings with Fraser before or spoken to him about anything whilst he's been on this trip?'

'No,' she sobbed.

Mrs Chivers looked at Rumcorn. Nothing needed to be said. The interview was over. Rumcorn nodded at Debbie and she led Stacey away.

Adam paused outside the incident room door. He then took a deep breath before knocking without much conviction, but the voices he could hear inside the room stopped and there was a distinctive 'Come in'.

He entered the room and he saw that Rumcorn and Debbie were alone. What he assumed to be statements were scattered over the desks and photos were stuck to the wall: pictures of Stacey Harper, Brian Lambert and group photos of the two classes that were at the climbing session earlier that day. Seeing himself and his friends displayed here in what appeared to be no particular order felt unnerving.

'Hello, it's –' Rumcorn prompted.

Adam thought his memory would be fogged by the many pupils he had liaised with that morning.

'Adam, sir.'

'Yes, of course. Come on in.'

He walked across and stood behind a chair placing his hands on its top, as though this physical barrier offered some kind of protection.

'How can we help you, Adam?' added Rumcorn.

'My friends and I felt we had to mention that Fraser might well be related to a student who sadly lost her life in a fire here some five years ago,' said Adam.

'As a matter of fact, we were aware of the connection. They were cousins; however, I'm really pleased you came to us. No one else has thought to bring this to our attention. Not even the staff here,' Rumcorn replied. Then he continued, 'Is there anything else you can tell us? Do you know Fraser?'

'No, sir! I don't know him, but there is…' he paused, 'something.'

'Adam, don't worry. I'd rather know all the rumours, true or otherwise, and decipher things myself. So please go on,' Rumcorn encouraged.

'We believe Fraser was perhaps aggrieved by something. Apparently he seemed very upset, especially after some incident with Miss Harper.'

Adam let go of the chair with one hand and stood much more relaxed. He felt a weight had lifted now he had imparted this information, and the detective appeared grateful.

'Do you know what the incident was about?' asked Rumcorn.

'No, I'm sorry.'

'Please don't be. Did you witness this conversation?'

'No, a student that resides at High Peak School told a friend in my class. Apparently Fraser was quite agitated.'

'Which class are you in, Adam?' Rumcorn enquired.

'We're just known as 4GAB or Gabs. Our tutor is Graham Alan Bates from Dale School.'

'Do you know the name of the pupil at this school who witnessed this – shall we say – event?'

'I believe his name is Darren Cooper.'

'Thanks, Adam. I appreciate you coming to us with this, and please, if you hear anything else then let me or Debbie here know, won't you?'

'Okay,' Adam replied, and he left the room hoping Darren Cooper would not be upset at being approached. He felt like he wanted to find Darren and at least warn him of the possible conversation that would be coming his way. However, Adam also felt sure that Rumcorn would be discreet.

SIX

ISOLATION

WEDNESDAY 15 JULY 2015 – 17:00

Adam wandered into the dining room with Adele. The smell of cooked food wafted around the school making him realise just how hungry he was. Stew and dumplings were being served by the hostel duty group. Adam led Adele to a table away from those that were already occupied, in particular by school staff. The remainder of their class spotted them alone in a corner and joined them.

'It's so tedious here now they've stopped all the activities,' said Jason.

'Graham has said that anyone who wishes to go can leave tomorrow morning. Anyone who wants to remain can do so, as there may be some activities on Friday. But they're not sure yet,' said Adam.

'Well, I'm definitely going then,' said Jason, and he got up and went over to Graham.

'You have that look, Adam. Come on, what's on your mind?' asked Jonathan.

'I think we should split up tomorrow and do some digging.' He looked over at his sister who shifted uneasily in her seat and continued. 'Chloe and I have discussed a plan. I will remain here and visit the village. See if I can get any information on Rebecca.'

'Hold on. What's this got to do with Rebecca?' Jonathan asked, looking confused.

'Everything. You know I wanted to find out more about her, and I think what happened yesterday is linked to her accident, depression or whatever, if you know what I mean.'

'Murder,' said Jonathan. He turned to look at Chloe. 'And what are you going to do in this plan?'

'Chloe is going to return to Dale School and home,' said Adam, 'to see if there is anything in the library or –'

Chloe cut him off.

'Adam wants me out of here. He doesn't think it's safe, especially if he's "digging around". Is that not the truth, Adam? Well, is it?'

Adam looked appealingly at Jonathan. She was right. That was exactly why he wanted his sister to leave High Peak, but he was not about to openly admit it. He hoped Jonathan could read his appeal.

'Absolutely not, Chloe. We need to split up. You're smart and can find out about Rebecca from records while I roam around here asking the locals. You've said it yourself. It's boring here.'

'Okay, I'll go with Chloe,' said Jonathan. 'Adam's right. We can do some research.'

'I'll stay with Adam. Someone has to look after him,' said Adele.

Adam suspected Adele shared his sense of protection of Chloe but felt that, overall, this offered a solution.

'That's settled then,' he said.

'Has anyone seen the Holloway twins?'Chloe asked.

'I heard they've been taken ill. Some virus or something,' said Jason.

The group was startled by his reappearance. His statement stopped all conversation and there was a moment of silence. Adele looked at him sternly.

'Jason, you're not making that up, are you? This school doesn't need any further problems.'

All eyes were on him.

'No! I overheard Mr Lambert and another member of staff talking about them.'

Chloe looked panic-stricken.

'They'll close the school for sure.'

Adam sternly interjected.

'We have to find out.'

'Find out what exactly?' Chloe asked, looking sideways at Adam, who was staring ahead in a total world of his own.

'Find out if they're ill.'

'Okay, and exactly how do we do that?' Jonathan asked.

'I guess we'll just have to ask.' They all looked apprehensively at Adam, who then continued. 'There's nothing wrong with being inquisitive or having concerns about friends, is there?'

'We know where the sick bay is. No harm in going to see them, I suppose,' said Chloe.

'I'll go with you,' said Adele.

After the meal, Chloe and Adele made their way to the front of the school with its large impressive lobby. The solid but oddly metal sick bay door with its brass furniture held a strange sense of foreboding.

Chloe plucked up some courage and tried turning the handle, but the door remained firm. Not to be put off so easily, she knocked hard. A tall, thin, elderly man emerged from the front door on their right. He had grey, bushy eyebrows and an angular face with gem blue eyes. He looked down with a frown at the two girls. Chloe instantly recognised him as the person she'd seen in the distance on their Padley Gorge walk. There was no mistaking his features. She felt herself start to overheat as a feeling of panic spread through her.

'Yes, can I help you?' the strange man asked.

'We heard our friends have been taken ill and are in the sick bay... the Holloway twins?' said Chloe. She wondered at first whether he'd heard her as there was a pause. He appeared to be deliberating a response.

'Ah, I'm Dr Kovac. There were a couple of students admitted, so no doubt they are the twins to whom you refer. Please rest assured they'll be out in a day or two. We have a policy of isolation at the school when pupils are admitted to the sick bay. It's important that any bugs are contained. We wouldn't want the whole school infected. I must therefore request that you return to your classes or scheduled activities.' His voice was deep, with a slight eastern European accent; his manner was abrupt and cold.

'Right, okay. Well, thank you,' said Chloe.

They left. Once out of view they increased their pace, eager to inform the others of their encounter.

Outside, Adam and Jason passed a football between them. Jason kicked a little too hard and it sailed passed Adam, hitting the side wall of the health centre and landing in a garden bed.

'That's the sick bay', Adam said quietly, as though someone might overhear him. There was no one in sight and a thought occurred to him.

'Stay here a minute,' he told Jason.

Picking up the ball from amongst the plants, he carefully yet methodically continued towards the ground floor windows. Directly in front of the building was a path that encircled the whole centre. He turned and walked as casually as possible along the slabs, glancing sideways into each window. His eyes struggled to focus on items within the dimly lit interiors of each room as he tried to catch a glimpse of the twin girls.

Thud! Thud! Thud!

Adam visibly jumped with shock at the unexpected noise. Behind him, Jason had followed but had found he could barely see over the windowsill. In frustration, he'd begun jumping up to see. Adam glanced round and gave Jason a stern look.

'Sorry,' Jason whispered.

Adam continued his journey. Many of the glass panels were frosted, and he thought they were most probably treatment rooms or storerooms. As they circumnavigated the block, Adam began to feel certain that any beds must be on the first floor.

One remaining window at this level initially looked empty, but as he turned more fully, the shadow he cast allowed him a clearer view. A light oak desk butted up against the window with a computer perched on top and Dr Kovac sat engrossed at the screen, tapping away on a keyboard. Suddenly, and for no apparent reason, he glanced up, making eye contact with Adam. Adam guessed instantly who it was. He had all the characteristics that Chloe had described. The doctor appeared to explode as he jumped back, his body turning with a flailing, aggressive gesture. Muffled expletives rang out, stemmed only by the glass between them. Adam forced a wide smile, mouthed an apology and pointed to the football. Without looking back, he quickly left.

Jonathan walked slowly towards the communal staffroom. He was unsure why Adam was so concerned about these two particular girls. They hardly knew them, or anyone else at this school for that matter. Maybe the girls had now gone home and the doctor had forgotten. They were probably just resting somewhere, not wanting to be disturbed.

Jonathan reached the door and hesitated, going over in his mind what reaction might face him. He plucked up the courage to knock.

'Come in,' came an unfamiliar voice.

Once inside he immediately felt alienated and insecure as if thousands of prying eyes were on him. The air was hot and clammy. Brian Lambert and Stacey Harper were huddled in a corner. Their familiar faces did nothing to alleviate the sickening feeling in Jonathan's gut.

'Hello, Jonathan. What's up?' Graham came out of nowhere.

'Hi. I've borrowed this CD from Louise... Louise Holloway, but I can't find her to return it. Just wondered if anyone knew where she was.'

Most of the people in the room looked bewildered by the question. Stacey moved forward.

'Yes. Well, actually both Louise and her sister Lisa have been taken rather poorly at present and are isolated in the sick bay.' Pausing briefly, she continued. 'Oh, it's nothing to worry about. Just one of those bugs that goes around. I can give Louise the disc though, no problem.'

'Oh, don't worry. We'll get them a card; take them some grapes. You know, cheer them up a bit,' Jonathan replied.

'No, I'm afraid that won't be possible. Rules. We don't want this to spread and get out of hand.'

'Surely one of us could visit? Jonathan pleaded.

'Come on! What is this place? Colditz?' said Graham.

'I'll see what I can do,' said Stacey.

Chloe returned to the same sick bay door in the main entrance foyer. Graham had advised of an agreed visit that he'd arranged, and added how proud he was of his tutor group making friends and showing such compassion. In her hand was a CD of the latest chart hits along with a 'Get Well Soon' card that she'd made. She also carried a bag of grapes and two oranges that were clearly visible, and hidden within the depths of the bag were two chocolate bars. Whether the High Peak staff believed their little white lie was a concern. If the twins had been asked then surely this scheme was on shaky ground. Chloe tried to remove doubt from her mind. So what if they just wanted to see their new friends. No real harm done. Chloe knocked hard on the door. No one answered. She was about to knock a second time when Miss Harper appeared.

'What happened to... er?'

'Jonathan?' said Chloe.

'Yes, Jonathan.'

'We thought it might be better, more appropriate for the twins if a girl were to visit.'

'We?'

'4GAB class,' replied Chloe.

'Quite.'

Miss Harper pushed a panel to one side to reveal a keypad. Chloe tried to look disinterested as she strained to come to terms with the security. She watched from an angle, and knew the number from the pattern: a standard nine digits with zero at the base, just like her phone. Miss Harper had picked out the corners of the square. Not smart security, however, the staff equally did not need to remember the numbers, just the sequence.

Miss Harper went first. As they entered, the increased light levels hurt Chloe's eyes and then a combination of heat and disinfectant made her nose and throat tingle. They walked through a lobby, up an internal staircase and into a corridor leading to two separate smaller rooms. The twins were in the end room with two beds. In the corner was a further door that Chloe thought might well be a toilet. Both girls were fast asleep. As she walked towards them she noticed a clipboard hanging on one of the beds.

Standing at the foot of the other bed was a man in a white overcoat and black trousers. He had short hair and a finely trimmed moustache that travelled down to his chin. He was scribbling notes on a similar board. Miss Harper introduced him as Nurse Stephen Plant. He looked surprised to see them and forced an uncomfortable smile.

Miss Harper said, 'I'm sure they'll sleep for quite some time.' After a pause she continued, 'Just leave your gifts and I'll pass on your regards.'

'I'd rather just sit with them awhile. I've heard that even when you're asleep you can sense a presence,' Chloe replied, and without stopping she walked towards the first bed.

'Oh well, if you must, but don't disturb them. They need their rest,' Miss Harper said in a rather deflated manner.

Nurse Plant requested Miss Harper come over to him and they engaged in a conversation that Chloe couldn't hear, resulting in Miss Harper storming out the opposite door. The male nurse approached her.

'Know them well, do you?'

'No, barely at all.'

She didn't expand any further, hoping this stranger would leave. He didn't seem to want to go, but appeared to be deliberately finding jobs to do around her. Sensing that his presence and gaze appeared to focus on her chest, she felt sickened. Sadly, it reminded her of being at home and of her stepfather. She had never spoken about that.

At an opportune moment she pulled up her neckline and announced, 'Seen enough, have you?'

It had the desired effect. He walked away and busied himself elsewhere.

Looking at the twins, she was surprised to see how pasty and drawn they'd become, so different to how she recalled them just two days earlier. The heat of the room overwhelmed her and she opened the nearest window. The cool breeze trickled in and brought some relief. Just as Chloe felt she might as well leave, Louise opened her eyes.

'Oh, hello! I'm Chloe. We met the other day. How are you?'

At first the twin looked puzzled, perhaps, Chloe thought, from the deep sleep or maybe because the teachers here, including the doctor, had been so reluctant to allow any visits. She smiled widely.

'Not bad at all now, thanks. This has all come on so quickly.'

'It must have done. It only feels like five minutes ago we were on the field having a chat.'

'Thanks for coming to see us. They're normally not so keen on letting students visit.'

'That's okay. I've brought you a couple of magazines and some fruit.' She lowered her voice, 'And some chocolate. Fruit's just not the same!'

Chloe struggled with a desire to ask which twin she was, and then noticed just below her bed the training shoes with the blue stripes.

'Thanks. Can I ask a favour?'

'Of course, Louise,' replied Chloe, her confidence swelling after she wasn't corrected.

'Please, can you let our parents know that we have been poorly, but that we're fine now,' Louise explained.

'No problem, but won't the school have told them?'

'The nurse said they struggled to get in touch with them, so I'm not sure they do know.'

'Okay, but won't you be out soon anyway?'

'Well –' Louise looked uncomfortable. 'Well, apparently the doctor has insisted we give –' She paused. '– samples before we're allowed to leave and as we haven't eaten much...'

'Right, well as I said, no problem,' Chloe confirmed, understanding the sensitive nature of the situation. Chloe took a pen and paper from her pocket and made a note of the contact details and deposited the two chocolate bars in the drawer of the bedside table. Chloe thought Louise looked stressed, possibly at being so isolated and she assured her that they would visit again soon.

Nurse Plant must have felt the cooler air and came bounding over. He immediately closed the window.

'I'm sorry. That was my fault. I thought Louise and Lisa were too warm,' Chloe explained.

'Oh, doctor now, are we?'

Miss Harper reappeared.

'Ah, Louise, you're awake. I hope you've told Chloe how well you're being looked after.'

'Er, yes, Miss Harper,' Louise replied, somewhat hesitantly.

It was clear the visit was over, so Chloe made her exit. Once back in the main foyer, she felt very worried about the weird scenario and the strictness surrounding the twins' isolation. She turned to walk away.

'Just a minute.' Miss Harper's voice shrilled through the air and panic set in. Miss Harper held out her hand with the two chocolate bars. She bent down close to Chloe's face and whispered, 'Not good for them'.

Chloe's stomach flipped and she felt physically sick. She hoped the information she'd obtained remained in her pocket. No more was said and Chloe walked away, but she felt Miss Harper watching her every step like a hawk.

THURSDAY 16 JULY 2015 – 01:01

Adam's watch alarm was bleeping and he rolled over breathing deeply with a slow exhale. Then he fell into a deeper sleep.

'Come on, Adam,' said Jonathan, shaking his shoulder. 'This was your idea, remember.'

He stretched and got up. The girls were to meet them on the second landing. Adam hoped he wouldn't have to struggle getting them up. If caught wandering about the school at night, they would be in serious trouble, but that would be nothing compared to the consequences if found in the girls' corridor.

Adam and Jonathan were both armed with a torch, soft trainers and a compact rucksack. They carefully left their room, avoiding the noisier spots on the floor. However, it didn't seem to help massively as the cold vinyl echoed their every step.

The double doors at the end of the landing proved an equally noisy obstacle to navigate. Once away from the sleeping areas Adam felt relieved, but he knew not to feel complacent. He spotted the girls, as an external orange car park light created two dark shapes silhouetted against the high walls of the central landing.

'You okay?' Adam whispered to Adele.

'Fine,' came the reply.

Chloe just smiled and led the way, as Adam followed through the building to the ground floor entrance and to what they now knew was also access to the surgery as well as to the first floor sick bay. The door looked menacing and strong. Chloe pressed 1-3-9-7 in a clockwise route around the electronic keypad.

A motor whirred somewhere within its frame and Adam turned the handle. If the door was alarmed, things were about to get nasty. The contingency plan was 'run', and although they'd stayed in their pyjamas, they had their running shoes ready. Next, find the nearest toilet and hide until considered safe, then lope back to bed. It was not much of a plan but it was all they could think of.

The door opened noiselessly and they entered. It led to a stairwell that was bare and dark. Some moments passed as their eyes adjusted. They turned and went up the stairs to the first floor as Chloe had advised. Chloe and Adele would need to wake the twins. Adam and Jonathan were not so well-known to them and would probably have scared them.

Adam watched from a distance as Chloe carried out the deed, gently shaking them awake and whispering their names. The girls looked unwell. He was quite surprised at the change, even though Chloe had warned that their illness had affected them. The girls awoke and looked somewhat shocked at first, but then appeared grateful to see their visitors. Chloe made the introductions.

'Hi again! This is Adele. I'm sure you remember, and this is my brother Adam and Jonathan.'

They nodded respectively.

'We've brought cheese and lettuce sandwiches, crisps and apples,' said Adele.

'And we have some books... girly ones,' said Chloe.

'How did you manage to get past Nurse Stephen? He's normally at the desk just above the landing, asked Lisa.

'There's no one there,' replied Adam, opening the door and peering out.

'He was supposed to be here all night last night but only turned up just before Nurse Jane took over. I don't care though. I don't like him.'

'That's not the point if he's supposed to be looking after you,' said Adele.

'What time did he return yesterday?' asked Adam.

'Not entirely sure, but I think it was about half-six.'

'Well, lucky for us. Oh, and I've tried contacting your parents, but sadly there was no answer. I left a message. Hope that's okay,' said Chloe.

'That's fine. Thanks, Chloe,' said Louise.

The girls were talking quietly together and Adam felt a little in limbo, so he decided to explore, closely followed by Jonathan. They used their torches to nose around. Adam caught a glimpse of Chloe as the door closed behind them with little more than a tap.

He thought he heard her say, 'I wonder where they're going.'

An old bookcase held some rather dated looking science books, and a grey melamine-topped coffee table had been left untidy with used mugs, plates and crockery scattered across its surface. Two chairs with wooden frames and soft cushions caught his attention. The torchlight revealed the quite garish colours of orange and green. At the opposite end of the wide corridor was a door leading to another stairwell. The right hand leaf was held open with a fire extinguisher. Adam shone the torch around the landing to reveal a metal-framed staircase with a dark wooden handrail. The temptation to explore became too much and Adam continued down the stairs, followed by Jonathan.

The ground floor opened into a waiting area with seats just like the couple upstairs. They were positioned around the perimeter with a back-to-back configuration in the centre. A wire rack hung on one side, housing a variety of magazines. The space had a familiar air to it, one that always hung around medical waiting rooms. Adjacent to the wooden counter was a solid metal panelled door that exactly matched the entrance to the sick bay, complete with electronic keypad. Adam's curiosity and raised excitement for danger was now at a peak.

'I wonder if it has the same numbers,' Adam whispered enquiringly in Jonathan's direction, waiting for some sign of approval. Jonathan responded by raising his eyebrows.

Slowly and carefully Adam pressed the combination 1-3-9-7, then turned the handle and pushed. It remained solid with not even the slightest movement. He pushed harder, putting his weight behind it, but still nothing. They were heading back to the stairs when Adam stopped. He thought about the pattern on the keypad. Perhaps this was similar... but not corners... maybe middle numbers. He turned back to the keypad. He now looked more closely. They looked worn or was it grime? He pressed 2-6-8-4 in the same clockwise direction.

'Just a wild stab in the dark,' said Adam, with little real hope.

'That's what I'd get if my dad caught me,' replied Jonathan, and Adam struggled to suppress a giggle as he turned the door handle and started to push. It flew open, crashing against a wall. The noise echoed in their ears, seemingly lasting forever. Fear swelled within him like an inflating balloon about to pop. His heart pounded and he fought the instinct to run. Silence and stillness resumed and a dark passage now lay before them.

There were six doors off this corridor: three on the right with the first two revealing Yale-type locks, and the third looked like a door to another stairwell. The access straight ahead was a fire exit and Adam's instinct was that it would more than likely open onto the car park. This left two doors on the left. They entered the first door, somewhat surprised that it was open. It was a small room or lobby with white cupboards from floor to ceiling on one side and two stainless steel sinks centrally positioned on the other. Above the sinks were taps with large arms projecting over the basins, allowing the user to access the water hands-free. He continued, slightly more reluctantly, through the second door, directly opposite, which opened into a room that was beyond clinical. The strong odour of cleaning fluid hit them as they entered. Smooth white walls reflected the torchlight. A central island housed an array of instruments you would have expected to see in a school science laboratory. Standby lights revealed two fridges with secure padlocks rather oddly attached, and to the right was an array of shelving at a higher level. Adam shone his torch along the worktop to the left that revealed Petri dishes, many with a mould-type growth spreading and trying to escape the lids of their containers. On a bench by the fridge was a metal-framed glass cabinet with an expensive looking padlock. Inside the case were a further two Petri dishes, each one clearly labelled YPX1.

They moved out quietly, closing the door. There was no discussion, just an acknowledgement that something felt weird. Yet a lab within a health centre was perhaps not so strange. They had to do it. They had to continue to the last door along the main corridor. Adam turned to Jonathan.

'I think this is the doctor's room where I surprised him from outside his window,' he whispered.

'Right,' Jonathan replied.

Adam opened the door and they went in. Cool and eerie, the room held a fusty smell. A desk and a chair sat under the window and a treatment bench was situated against the adjacent wall, partly concealed behind an old privacy screen. Shelving on the left was full to capacity with medical books. On the floor was a large patterned rug attempting to offer some warmth to the bland, stark interior. Nothing of real interest.

Adam silently whispered to Jonathan, 'Let's go!'

Jonathan didn't move. Adam looked at him then down at what Jonathan was now focusing on. Centrally located on the desk was a computer. The small light beneath the screen was green. He took a step towards the desk and gently touched the mouse that sat idly on a mat displaying an image of the school. The screen burst into life. Adam momentarily looked away, shocked by the brightness.

'Maybe someone was working late and forgot to shut down,' Jonathan suggested, then looked worried . 'Whoever it was could have gone to fetch something and they could be back at any minute.'

'I don't think so. There are no lights and it's mostly locked,' Adam said, looking at Jonathan whose face told him he remained unconvinced.

'They've all gone home,' he said, although he himself felt the desire to be elsewhere and preferably under a warm duvet. Still, something had made him touch that mouse. After his initial fear, he returned his attention to the screen. It showed a list of names and adjacent to each was a number. Adam scrolled down to H for Holloway.

'Look, Jonathan! Louise and Lisa Holloway.' He moved the mouse, which caused the cursor on the screen to hover over Louise's name, and then pressed Enter.

'We really shouldn't be looking at these,' said Jonathan.

'You're right, but they shouldn't keep people in isolation either. Who's to say if they've even told the twins what's wrong with them,' replied Adam.

Patient Record and Analysis of Bacteriophage

Patient No.: 2102
Date of Exposure: 13/07/15
Bacterium Name/Type: Streptococcus C
Phage Mix Batch No.: S12106
Date Bacteriophage Administered: 15/07/15

Notes:

- Bacterium found in patient confirms matches.

- Lytic activity moderate compared to batch S12105, review batch process, check for impurities.

- Although successful recovery time, this may in part be a contaminated result, as patient may have gained some immunity from last year's trial. Patients existing killer cells show some capabilities on the new strain.

- Stomach balance not effected, no other bacteria were affected by the phage mix.

- Draw off new phages from passed streptococcus c bacteria, feed on strain received from MP and retest lytic rate.

'Well, I bet that whatever you expected, it was definitely not that!'

'That, Jonathan, is a massive understatement. I don't know what bacteriophage is, do you?'

'No, but now I think we should get out of here,' replied Jonathan.

Adam read the headings on the form.

'They look very odd, don't you think?' He turned to face Jonathan, who looked horrified.

'This doesn't have Louise's name. It just has a patient's number and why have that heading? "Date of exposure" and "Bacterium found in patient" confirms matches?'

Adam looked further down the form.

'It also says something about last year's trial. Didn't one of the twins say they were ill last year?'

A fuzzy feeling of fear rippled through Adam.

'Yes, Adam. Can you copy this?'

'There's no printer here.'

As he looked around the desk, he caught sight of the telephone wire and data cables.

'Hold on, just a minute.'

Curbing his desire to run and not stop, he closed the patient record window and, underneath, discovered spreadsheets full of patient numbers and covers containing the name 'La Maison de Pharmaceutical'. He was now visibly shaking. He quickly accessed his online hard drive and started copying the 'Patient Record' file.

'Adam, come on. We've got to go!' Jonathan said, quietly but firmly.

'Wait! We have no idea what has been sent and I have to cover my tracks, delete any activity, and we don't even know if it has transferred anything yet.'

Noises came from the floor above: shuffling, a door opening loudly.

'End it now,' Jonathan hissed quietly.

Footsteps bounded down the stairs then along the corridor. Dr Kovac's door flew open and his tall, thin shadow occupied the empty frame. As his swift movements changed to a slow methodical appraisal of his room, the muscles in his neck started to relax. Some moments passed before he flicked on the lights, making him wince with the intensity. All was well. What had caused that silly feeling in the pit of his stomach? Was he getting too old?

That stupid Nurse Plant wasn't here. The two girls had been left alone. That was irresponsible, unforgivable, against school policy and his better judgement. He would be having words with Nurse Plant first thing. Hopefully he could get rid of him this time, but he had to be careful; he knew too much. It also upset him that he had left the computer on and the surgery door open. Retirement! That's what he needed; that's what he longed for, and soon. The samples Stacey had handed him from Rebecca held the key. He shuddered at the memory, but convinced himself to reflect on the logic that something good could quite possibly have come from such a terrible event. He now had the solution for YPX1. Just a relatively small amount of work on the new bacteriophage mix and his quest would be complete. His working life could end; he just needed careful closure. He left after locking the surgery, being meticulously careful this time to make sure everything was turned off.

Moments later Adam and Jonathan moved out from behind the screen in Dr Kovac's consulting room. They went carefully back up the stairs and rejoined the girls who had taken refuge in a toilet cubicle off the twins' room. They both looked shaken.

'That was close,' said Chloe.

'You have no idea,' replied Adam.

'Where did you two go?' asked Adele.

'Later!'

SEVEN

THE VILLAGE

THURSDAY 16 JULY 2015 – 08:00

Mr and Mrs Holloway entered High Peak School. They approached the reception area, which remained empty at this hour, but saw a boy they recognised.

'Darren!' called Mrs Holloway, with an edge of panic to her tone.

'Oh. Hi Mrs Holloway.'

'Where are the twins, Darren? We had a call from a girl named Chloe.'

'Er... Chloe? I don't know anyone called Chloe.'

'She said the girls were taken ill and are in the sick bay.'

'Yes, I've heard.'

'Where is it, Darren? Can you take us there?'

Darren pointed from where they were standing.

'It's there, Mrs Holloway.'

She turned immediately and rushed to the door, frantically pulling at it.

'It's locked, David.'

'Darren, how do we get into the sick bay?' asked Mr Holloway.

'There's a bell at the side and a combination lock, but I don't know the code,' said Darren.

Mrs Holloway's finger continued stabbing at the button.

'Hello, can I help?' asked Stacey, walking towards the strangers.

'Where are my children?' said Mrs Holloway.

'Louise and Lisa Holloway... we're their parents,' Mr Holloway added.

'Ah, Mr and Mrs Holloway. I'm Stacey Harper. We've been –' Stacey started, but Mrs Holloway interrupted her.

'Why are my children locked away?'

'We've tried to get in touch. The girls are fine; they're being very well looked after. The local doctor on site has taken good care of them, and we have a nurse with them.'

'You have not answered my question.'

'I assure you they're not locked way. We have to secure the building, you must understand, for their safety.'

'Just open this door now!' demanded Mr Holloway.

Stacey pressed the combination and entered the lobby, then turned to allow access. She looked at Darren.

'Go to your lesson, Darren.' Stacey then turned to Mrs Holloway and continued. 'As I was saying, we have been trying to get in touch with you both.'

The Holloways followed Stacey upstairs to the sick bay. There was no sign of a nurse. Mrs Holloway watched with concern as Stacey began roaming around opening doors and shouting, 'Stephen!'

'He must have just nipped out. He sometimes has to get supplies,' said Stacey.

Mrs Holloway ignored her. Relief and concern filled her upon seeing the children as the twins smiled emphatically back.

'We'll be making an official complaint and we're all leaving now,' Mr Holloway announced, as the family prepared to make their way out of the sick bay and back towards the main entrance.

'It must be a shock. I can't even start to imagine how worried you must be. But please let Dr Kovac deal with the girls. He is very good with these cases and they're both well on the mend,' she pleaded, following the retreating parents. Then added, 'The girls are fine now. They were due to go back to school today anyway.'

'We'll be seeking a second opinion. The twins leave with us immediately!'

'Chloe!' shouted Louise, and Mrs Holloway saw her daughter pull a girl out from amongst the crowd that had now gathered in the main entrance: a girl with naturally frizzy hair held down with a wide black band.

'Mum, this is my friend Chloe,' said Louise.

'Hello, Chloe. I think we have a lot to thank you for,' said Mrs Holloway.

'Oh, no, it's nothing really. Please let me help the girls pack,' replied Chloe.

Outside in the car park, Mrs Holloway was waiting when she saw the girls emerge from the front entrance. She walked up and took some of the bags from Chloe, then watched as the three girls hugged their goodbyes.

'Chloe, thanks again,' said Mrs Holloway. As she got into the car she glanced across and saw Stacey and Chloe regarding each other and Stacey wearing a fierce expression. Chloe turned back to her and must have read her concern.

'It's okay, Mrs Holloway. I'm leaving today.'

'Come and see us. Come and see us soon.'

'Thanks, I will,' replied Chloe.

At midday, Adam and Adele approached a young boy sitting on a log at the edge of the wood behind the school. Adam had missed the commotion that occurred earlier, but Chloe advised him on every detail before leaving with Jonathan, Jason and a few others on the Dale School minibus, complete with a subdued Graham Bates at the wheel. The boy looked small for his age. Adam knew he attended High Peak.

'Hello. Darren, isn't it?' said Adam.

The boy looked up and leaned away slightly.

'Yes,' he replied.

'I'm Adam and this is Adele. We go to Dale School and we're here on refreshment week.'

'So... you were at Black Rock on Tuesday,' Darren said.

'Yes, yes, we were. I'm sorry your friend got hurt.'

'Did you see what happened?'

'No, not really. I only saw Fraser fall,' said Adam.

Darren looked down and fiddled with a twig.

'I want to go and see him, but they won't let me.'

'Seems a common thing around here,' said Adam, sitting next to Darren on the log. 'Have you known Fraser a long time?'

'For as long as I can remember. We went to the same junior school. He lives in the next village to me and Clive.'

'Clive?'

'Clive Ross. He's in my class here at High Peak. We live on the same street. He's a prat though, not like Fraser. I liked Fraser. I mean I like Fraser,' said Darren.

'Someone said you saw Fraser involved in an incident with Miss Harper?' said Adam, wondering whether this may well be too direct.

Darren looked up at him and then at Adele and then he started rubbing the twig with his thumb.

'Not really an incident. It was the day you all arrived. Fraser was in the main entrance and when I walked in he... well... he seemed frozen to the spot and was glaring at Miss Harper. Just one of those weird moments.'

'She's a weird person. I'd glare at her,' said Adele. 'Was she wearing something awful?'

Darren smiled, and looked deep in thought.

'Er... I don't think so, but now I think about it, she was carrying something. A case that looked quite bulky. Yes... I think that's what Fraser was looking at.'

'Darren, can you help me get onto the school's computer here?' asked Adam.

'I suppose so. When did you want to do that?'

'How about now?'

Darren took them to the computer room located next to the tutor classrooms and after advising his personal password he left them.

'Let's see what we've got,' said Adam, logging onto the system.

'A bit sneaky using someone else's password, Adam Brant,' said Adele.

'Well, let's just say it's better to stay below the radar. It's a gut feeling. We stand out. We don't belong to this school.'

'So you believe we would be in more danger than Darren?'

'What Jonathan and I saw looked suspicious to me. If it's true, then yes, that's exactly what I believe.'

He clicked on a link, keyed in his password and started downloading the stolen patient records.

'Well, we have that report I looked at in the surgery and also the first page to some document that looks basically like a title page.'

'What's the title?' asked Adele.

'La Maison de Pharmaceutical.'

At the bottom of the page, Adam noticed a thick black line.

'We should call Rumcorn.'

'With what, Adele? This report is basic. It's written using "Word". I could easily have done it and a title page. Plus, please don't forget we shouldn't have been in the surgery,' Adam replied. He continued. 'What is Bact-er-io-phage?'

He clicked open his search engine and typed in 'Bacteriophages'. A vast number of links erupted on the screen:

Browser

Bacteriophages were named by a bacteriologist called Felix D'Herelle.

Bacteriophages were discovered in 1915 by Frederick Twort & Felix D'Herelle, amongst other scientists at the time.

Bacteriophages are viruses that multiply within a bacterial cell until it bursts, thus destroying it.

Phage therapy is the use of *bacteriophages* to treat pathogenic bacterial infections. Phage therapy is more widely used in Russia, Georgia and Poland.

'That's pretty amazing stuff. It says here Felix D'Herelle's work included discovering how viruses are transmitted and is regarded as fundamental to the eventual understanding of DNA. His work and achievements were pretty much groundbreaking. How come I've never heard of him? We get to hear about Newton and he just stood under the wrong tree; Einstein and his theory of relativity, light travelling through a vacuum or something. It doesn't seem to cut the mustard compared to this guy.'

'I guess not all scientists are recognised as much as they should be,' replied Adele.

'You would have thought that kind of discovery and its significance would be more talked about though, don't you think?'

'Yes, I agree, but I'm not quite sure what all that means for our

High Peak health centre,' said Adele.

'No, not the easiest to understand either, but it looks like these are viruses which eat bacteria,' replied Adam, covering his eyes with his hands and rubbing his forehead. 'I'm sure I've heard the term "phage" before.' He continued searching for linked information. 'Pathogens – I remember something about them from Mr Miller's lessons. Aren't they what cause disease? I recall something like we have tiny killer cells that patrol for pathogens and digest them if they can, therefore keeping us healthy.'

'Okay,' replied Adele.

In a slow manner, Adam's mind processed his thoughts about what someone at the health centre was doing recording this kind of information: a doctor most likely or perhaps a nurse.

'This does kind of feel dodgy,' said Adele.

'Really, let's just think about this for a moment. This is a health centre, right, and all this report really states is a record of a patient's health. We don't know what the rest of it means and it could be perfectly legitimate,' said Adam. 'Odd though that there are no names on the report. These patients are just known as numbers, yet I know that I clicked on Louise Holloway's name and it took me to this report.'

'That could have been an error. Not all programmes work,' said Adele.

Adam kept searching. He found a large diagram of a bacteriophage. It had a spider-like body with several spindly legs and a long scrawny neck leading to an oblong-shaped head. Between the tentacle-type legs was a stinger. The notes read: *Once the legs latch onto a cell the stinger will dive down piercing the cell wall and delivering its nectar*.

'Yuk, you're kidding. Those things could be inside us. Well, gross!' said Adam.

'Well, these little blighters are not necessarily bad for us. They're all part of the balance of everything, Adam: yin and yang. You know, every action has an equal and opposite reaction and all that jazz. If these nasty-looking bugs invade our bodies and fight bad little critters, then they're on our side. I, for one, am all for them.'

'They look revolting.'

Adam printed off the report and front cover. Looking at the headings and back at the definitions, it could be taken in different ways. Was someone administering the students a disease? Surely not. Or merely recording when the bugs were first discovered? Or simply noting when the patient was admitted.

Adam paced around the room.

'Looks to me like someone at the health centre is doing something – creating or using these bacteriophages.'

'You sound like you know what you're talking about, but we don't know anything. We really need to call Inspector Rumcorn,' said Adele.

'Exactly! We don't really know anything. I feel everything that has happened started with Rebecca Johnson. We need to find out more about Rebecca.'

'I beg your pardon. Why? Why go looking for trouble? If we get caught with this report – if nothing else it's against privacy laws,' replied Adele.

'Send it to Rumcorn,' said Adam. 'Send it anonymously, print the envelope, and then post it. We can go into the village right now.'

'High Peak village! You must have gone mad. Why there?'

'Because, my dear friend, I'm sure that's where we'll find out more about Miss Rebecca Johnson.'

'Look, if something sinister is happening, and I'm not totally convinced but for argument's sake let's assume it could be, then you want us to go right back into the lion's den?'

'Like you said, it may be nothing, but what else are we going to do?'

'Yes, well, I'm not keen on falling off a cliff or dying in a fire,' replied Adele.

Adam ignored her and continued enthusiastically.

'Let's call Chloe and Jonathan. We'll fill them in.'

'You're bonkers!'

THURSDAY 16 JULY 2015 – 15:00

Adam and Adele walked down the access road then turned left up the hill towards St Peter's Church. Adam thought everywhere looked so peaceful, odd how he felt so uptight. He turned to look at Adele. Even in her raincoat, which had several scuff marks from their rock climbing day, Adam felt a warmth towards her, closely followed by a sense of frustration.

'Adele, do you really think I'm bonkers?'

'No, not really,' she replied.

Her eyes locked onto his then she frowned ever so slightly, as though she had read his thoughts.

She continued, 'But I think Jonathan may be right.'

'What do you mean?'

'Rebecca could have been depressed, taken her own life. I think you struggle to understand or accept differences in other people.'

'Burning yourself alive would not be a decision any normal person would make Adele. How can anyone understand that?' He unzipped his coat a little feeling hot. 'Anyway, what would have made her so unhappy?'

'Oh I don't know, how about our school's ethos to do so well?'

Adele replied with a slightly sarcastic tone.

'Our class sizes are generally so small, we would know if someone in GAB was not happy.'

Drizzle started and Adam looked up feeling the tiny cold and wet droplets on his face, wishing they could wash away his anxiety.

'No, Adam we wouldn't. People hide their feelings. They don't talk about what might be hurting them deep down, possibly in their private lives.' Adele stepped back towards him, grabbed and linked his arm pulling him forward to continue walking. 'I love you like a brother Adam, I understand you better than you think.'

Adam looked right as they passed the old schoolhouse. He knew she was right, but he did not want to reply. He studied the path to the old school as it turned around what was left of a boundary wall. The overgrown access road to the hall was not much better than the hillside path that forked off it and continued on up behind. The drizzle turned to rain as Adam stopped and looked at the church.

'Maybe the Johnson family are buried here,' said Adele.

The thought struck a chord in Adam's mind.

'Let's have a closer look in the church,' he announced.

'I was only joking, Adam.'

'The vicar may remember something and I'm certain he'll be more approachable than the villagers.'

They walked through a single wooden gate. On either side of the gate butted grey Derbyshire stonewalls encircling the churchyard. Dark clouds gathered above, and as they continued along the old path overgrown with moss and weeds, it started to rain more intently. It was no longer a light sprinkling but a heavy deluge, like pebbles hitting their bodies and penetrating their clothing. Their so-called waterproof jackets did very little to resist the sheer force of the downpour.

Adam vocalised his displeasure at suddenly being wet through and joined Adele sheltering under an ornate porch majestically overhanging a dark wooden door with wrought iron hinges. Adam turned the handle, lifting the latch and pushing hard. It opened slowly, giving access to a huge, dimly lit entrance.

'Well, someone's in.'

'They don't lock churches, Adam,' said Adele.

They walked in, their wet shoes squelching on the well-worn concrete floor, disturbing the silence. Adam felt a weird sense of unease. Adele followed him, closing the door with a louder bang than anticipated and making them both jump involuntarily.

'Sorry,' she whispered.

Adam took in their surroundings: stained glass windows rich in colour but allowing little natural light. The roof was held high with hand-cut stone grotesque gargoyles supporting large oak beams. Strangely it felt colder inside than out.

At the front near the pulpit a small elderly woman was arranging flowers. Their entrance was unnoticed and Adam wondered whether she was somewhat deaf. She wore a long, padded grey coat, bottle-green trousers and brown suede boots. Adam approached her.

'Er... excuse me.'

The woman looked up with a warm smile. She had tight curly grey hair and piercing blue eyes. Her lined face looked like it could tell a hundred stories.

'Yes, young man,' the lady replied in a slow, well-spoken manner.

'I wondered whether the vicar was around.'

'Not today. Getting married, are you?'

Adele struggled to restrain a large grin as Adam stumbled with that last question.

'No! No! I'm, that is, we're doing a school project on,' he paused, 'Rebecca Johnson... the student who died in a fire at High Peak School.'

'Terrible, terrible,' said the elderly woman.

Adam wondered whether she meant the loss of life, the fire or the fact that they were writing about it.

'We feel she ought not to be forgotten.'

'Absolutely. Quite so,' the lady replied with bounding vigour.

'We wondered whether the vicar could tell us more about her and the effect it has had on the community,' Adam said, now starting to gain a little confidence.

'Oh, I very much doubt it.' The lady visibly paused and then continued. 'Nice girl.'

Adam was again struggling. Did she mean the vicar or Rebecca?

'Who's nice?' he asked.

The lady stared. Adam thought she appeared to be looking through Adele, focusing somewhere beyond.

'The school keeps itself to itself; they have very little to do with us.'

Adam sensed not anger but resentment in her voice, so he decided not to pursue this any further.

'Thank you, anyway,' he added.

'Try Mrs Forshaw,' she said.

'And where can we find her?'Adam replied, surprised at the outburst.

'She's our postmistress. Rebecca used to help her in the shop.'

Once out of the church, they saw that the rain had subsided. Adam led the way around the corner of the churchyard and on towards the village.

The post office was little more than five metres wide with one door and a window that looked like it belonged to a domestic dwelling rather than a business. The iron plaque high on the wall displayed the words 'Post Office' and was dated 1919. It had been serving the villages here and providing contact with the outside world for almost 100 years. Adam could well imagine that this quaint village probably adorned many of the Derbyshire Peak District guidebooks. Its stone-built run of community stores gave the impression of a way of life that many deemed as locked into a time long forgotten. Clearly, little had changed since the time the plaque had been cemented into position.

The village was beyond quiet. No one was around other than the two of them. The air was filled with the mouth-watering scent of freshly baked bread. It made him feel hungry. He could well imagine that this tiny facility delivered to many of the local bed-and-breakfast establishments, along with the campsites scattered around the area.

Adam turned the shiny brass door handle and pushed. The stone threshold gave witness to years of traffic; its surface at the centre was worn away. The door swung on its arc and something pinged – an intense and unexpectedly loud note. An old-fashioned bell fixed to the frame had rung out alerting the owner to a customer. The floor inside was made of small, square quarry tiles reflecting a reddish glow from a surface sheen achieved after years of regular cleaning. On the right, a thick, dark wood counter spanned the length of the oblong-shaped room. Fixed firmly on top of the counter was a glass screen held together by an aluminium frame.

Very few items appeared for sale. Immediately on the left was a freestanding display unit with postcards, greeting cards, notepaper and envelopes. Further along the left wall were three shelves, carrying a range of books that didn't look new. On the wall behind the counter was an antique clock. It broke the stillness as it emitted a melodic noise that seemed to echo off the walls. The place felt cold and uninviting. An odd thought crossed Adam's mind that maybe the shop was closed and the owner had forgotten to turn the sign around and bolt the door.

They heard a shuffling from the other side of the counter and an elderly lady slowly emerged from a dark corner. She moved with a swing-like motion. A feeling of guilt flooded him at disturbing her, more so as they had not intended to actually purchase anything.

'Can I help someone?' said the lady. She was tiny, well below five feet. She had bright white curls and wore gold-rimmed spectacles perched halfway down the bridge of her nose. Her face looked tired. Her cheeks sagged lower than her chin.

There was a pause broken by Adele.

'Are you Mrs Forshaw?' she asked.

'Indeed I am! How may I help you?'

'I'm from the Jameson Academy and my friends and I are writing a project at school about Rebecca Johnson. We feel she should be remembered.'

Mrs Forshaw clutched the counter. Adele looked at Adam, searching for support, and then continued.

'And... we wondered whether you could tell us what she was like.'

'I see,' said Mrs Forshaw.

'We've been told that she liked coming to the village and spending time in the community,' said Adele.

Adam thought Adele was floundering. Somehow it didn't feel right. However, this was the only route they had and probably their last chance. Adam watched how Adele looked intently at the old lady with puppy dog eyes.

'Can you help us, please?' she said.

The final plea must have touched a nerve somewhere and the old lady moved forward, her body pressing against the counter.

'I'm not sure exactly what you want to know. She was a delightful girl and don't let any of the others at that school of yours suggest she was weird, because it simply isn't true.'

'Yes, agreed. We've heard the same rumours. Did she come to the village regularly?' asked Adele.

Adam remained silent. Adele was doing great now on her own and he was not sure Mrs Forshaw even knew he was there.

'Rebecca was one of the few that actually did. The students tend to stay at the school and go home at weekends. Many of the village people are employed there, of course. It provides good employment and those that do work there, get to know some of the students. I'm not like some around here who opposed the Academy and tried to prevent it from even opening.'

'We've been told Rebecca helped here in the post office,' said Adele.

'I went to school with Annie Mann. She married Alan Johnson and, of course, became Annie Johnson, and Auntie Annie to Rebecca. So, you see, I knew her from the time she was born. Annie and I always kept in touch. In answer to your question,' the lady inclined her head slightly, looking over her glasses at Adele. 'Yes, Rebecca loved coming to this shop and enjoyed pricing the second-hand books and tidying the cards.'

'Did she ever talk about her life at the school?'

'Not so much. However, she never said she wasn't happy there. I certainly believe she had no desire to move elsewhere. In the main, when she was here she loved to listen to Annie and my stories of how we lived and the things we got up to.'

'I'm beginning to see how smart she was and mature for her age, Mrs Forshaw.'

'When you've finished your project, could you send it to me and to Annie. I'm sure she would also be grateful. She took it so very hard. Rebecca was more like her daughter.'

'Absolutely yes,' Adele replied.

Adam could sense Adele's guilt. He knew that if she promised something she would see it through and he would definitely help.

'I know I perhaps shouldn't, but as a friend and not in the capacity of postmistress, please take this,' and Mrs Forshaw pushed a slip of paper through the gap meant for envelopes, money or small parcels. Adele slipped it into her pocket. At that point the door opened, the reliable bell pinged, and they were joined by a beefy-looking man of medium height with glowing red cheeks.

'Well, thank you, Mrs Forshaw. We appreciate it,' Adele said as she started to leave.

'She's buried in High Peak cemetery. Annie said High Peak was where she had been her happiest and so this is where she should rest.'

Adele looked back and saw the lady was visibly shaking, possibly she thought, resisting imminent tears.

'Thank you. I'm sorry to have caused any distress,' Adele said.

Mrs Forshaw nodded.

Once back outside, they breathed in the fresh air.

'Well, that was hard,' she said, and then added, 'I didn't see that coming.'

Adam posted the letter to Rumcorn in the box attached to the front of the post office and they headed back. On the way, Adam turned down a track leading past the church and its cemetery.

'Oh, Adam, I really don't think I can. Not now, perhaps not today.'

'Then you wait here and I'll take a look.'

'No, no, I'll come with you. I know I'll regret it later if I don't.'

They came across a small metal gate and entered it, walking away from the church and following the line of the wall.

'I think she would be towards the end as it wasn't that long ago and I can't imagine that many people have passed since. It's not such big population around here, if you know what I mean,' said Adam.

'I guess so,' agreed Adele.

Along what Adam assumed to be the back were bushes that had grown together and now formed a hedge line, along with the odd gap. They searched, reading many headstones, but none appeared to be the right century, let alone the right decade.

'Looks like they don't use this cemetery anymore. The locals must be cremated or buried elsewhere.'

Adam watched Adele skirting in a square formation, as though invisible shields were preventing her travelling in straight lines.

'Adele, what are you doing?'

'I'm not keen on these places and there's no way I'm treading on someone,' she replied.

'I don't think they'll complain.'

'Say what you like. Think of it as a respect thing.'

She disappeared around the back of the hedge.

'Come on, Adele. Honestly!' said Adam. He needed all the help he could get or it could take all afternoon.

'Come back, Adele. Please, I need your help!'

'She's here,' Adele shouted from over the hedge.

'Really?' said Adam, somewhat surprised. Adam went to her through a different gap in the hedge. And there she was, the headstone newer than all surrounding it, and it simply read:

> Rebecca Johnson, died 2010, aged 13
> Best daughter, best cousin, best friend

Adam and Adele looked at each other.

'Well, that's different,' said Adam.

'It's nice though, isn't it,' replied Adele. 'I wonder what caused those three circles?'

Adam looked down directly into the centre of where Rebecca must have been lying. There were three clearly defined circles. The well-established grass had been cleanly cut by something; just smooth brown soil showed. Around the area were tiny grey flecks. The circles were no more than 75mm in diameter and around 50mm apart. They formed the shape of a triangle.

'Maybe someone has planted some flower bulbs?'

'But we're beyond spring and there are no flowers.'

'Do you think it's some kind of sign?'

'What do you mean, like from Rebecca?' asked Adele, grabbing Adam's arm.

'No, silly. I mean like a cross, some sort of religious emblem.'

'Well, looks a bit weird if you ask me.'

'Have you got your phone?' Adam asked. She was squeezing him tightly now. 'To take a photo of it.'

'Use your own phone,' she replied.

'My batteries are practically dead and yours is much better at taking photos.'

'Adam, I'm not roaming around a cemetery taking pictures of graves. No way.'

Adam looked at her, repressing an urge to laugh, but he could see that she wasn't going to change her mind.

'Okay, well, let's look up any symbolic signs that look like this when we get back.'

As they left, Adam noticed a small pile of concrete left by the base of the wall, no more than a shovelful and barely noticeable between the blades of grass partially covering it. Its colour made it stand out from everything natural around it.

'It looks like someone has been repairing the wall,' said Adam, although he couldn't see any evidence of maintenance. 'Have you looked at the note Mrs Forshaw gave you?'

'Oh no, I forgot about it.'

Adele took it out. It bore the name and address of Rebecca's aunt.

'Feels like we have permission to go and visit Annie Johnson. Mrs Forshaw clearly wants to see a story written about her friend's niece. I feel bad about that,' said Adele.

Back at the school, Adam took out copies of the papers he and Jonathan had obtained from the doctor's computer.

'Let's have a look, Adam,' said Adele. She took the sheets from him.

'La Maison de Pharmaceutical.'

'Have either of you deciphered the words along the bottom of the sheet?'

'We didn't see any words,' said Adam.

'Well, I think there are words at the bottom. It's not just a line. It looks like there are tiny letters.'

Adam leaned in closer. Adele was right. Now that he looked really closely at it, there were actually small letters that were clearly not English.

'Reçu pour deux cent cinquante mille euros, melanges de phage,' she read in French.

Adam looked at her, clearly struggling.

'This looks very much like a receipt to me.' She paused. 'A receipt for a mixture of phage.'

'What's the matter, Adele?'

'The receipt is for a payment of 250,000 euros!'

EIGHT

PATTLE COTTAGE

FRIDAY 17 JULY 2015 – 08:30

Deep in the bowels of a relatively newly constructed office development, Detective Inspector Peter Rumcorn had managed to secure a position close to the window. The natural light and view across the countryside gave him some pleasure in contrast with the impersonal space he worked in.

He was perplexed with his morning mail: a plain envelope printed with his name and address – if you can call *Derbyshire Police, Ripley* an address. Nevertheless it had found him. He had opened it with care, complete with sterile gloves. Something had made him suspicious. At one time a secretary would have opened the mail then recorded the item before passing it to the appropriate person or agency. Now it was different. The changes, he had to admit, were not really the result of cuts to funding as many would claim. Most of what he now received could be stored on his computer, available at the touch of a few keys regardless of where you were in the building or anywhere in the world for that matter.

Rumcorn carefully pulled two sheets of A4 paper from the envelope and one smaller odd-sized piece. The first A4 sheet appeared to be a report entitled *Patient Record and Analysis of Bacteriophage*. He scanned it. It itemised patient number against exposure to bacteria and symptoms witnessed, showed phage mixes and something called lytic activity. Some of the terms sparked a distant memory, but he struggled to recall exactly what. At the bottom were recommendations and general comments. Rumcorn turned to the second page. This seemed to be virtually blank with the exception of a title boldly located at the top that read *La Maison de Pharmaceutical* and along the bottom, a thick black line.

'Debbie,' Rumcorn called off to his right.

Debbie looked up from a report. She had a kind face with a fair complexion and was some ten years younger than Rumcorn.

'Yes, sir.'

'What do you make of this?' he asked, passing across the A4 sheets along with a fresh pair of latex gloves. 'How good is your French?'

He silently read the smaller note that simply read: *Taken from High Peak Health Centre.*

'Interesting, don't you think?'

'It doesn't make a lot of sense to me, sir, and there's no patient name, so it's not going to help unless we can find out who number 2102 is. And my French is not great, although I can get by on holiday. Is this some sort of test, sir?'

He ignored the question.

'It's very odd,' Rumcorn said, showing Debbie the third sheet and continuing. 'Someone obviously believes this is important enough to send to us.'

'Where was it posted?'

'High Peak village.'

Debbie typed in 'bacteriophage' in a search engine.

'It looks to be a method for curing bacterial diseases.'

'I thought that was antibiotics,' said Rumcorn, and continued. 'I think we need some specialist advice, certainly before we go and have a chat with them at High Peak Health Centre.'

'Sir!' Debbie announced, more to get Rumcorn's attention. 'This first sheet with the title "La Maison de Pharmaceutical" – I can't make out the writing along the bottom.'

Rumcorn pulled out an old-fashioned magnifying glass from his drawer. He held the convex glass over each word, reading them out to Debbie.

'Reçu pour deux cent cinquante mille euros, melanges de phage.'

Debbie typed them into a translator box on the internet.

'Receipt for 250,000 euros, phage mix.'

'Well, that's no insignificant amount of money,' said Rumcorn. The hairs on the back of his neck started to prickle.

'So, a young boy has a near-fatal climbing incident and three days later we have an anonymous note.'

Rumcorn rubbed the palm of his hand up and down his forehead, his concern clearly visible.

'I've checked this morning, sir. There's no change. Fraser is still in intensive care. He survived the operation but there's no way of knowing how he's been affected, at least not until he wakes up.'

'If he ever wakes up,' replied Rumcorn sadly.

'We also have a girl who lost her life in a fire in a not completely non-suspicious event.'

'Let's get forensics to check these papers. There may be some prints. Take some photos of the report and we can go and see the police physician to see what she makes of them.'

FRIDAY 17 JULY 2015 – 10:00

Graham Bates pulled the minibus into the driveway of Pattle Cottage, Hockerton.

'Thanks, Graham. You're a star.'

'Right, yes, well, I have a few errands to run and then I'll be back.'

The crunch of tyres on gravel had announced their arrival and the Holloway twins ran outside to greet their guests.

'Hi, Louise. Lisa, how are you?' asked Chloe, as she and Jonathan alighted from the bus.

'We're fine,' replied Louise.

Chloe looked at them and smiled. She felt awful for them. She was worried the school had neglected to provide them with proper care. She brushed the thought from her mind and forced herself to focus on the here and now. It struck her again just how alike they were. She was mesmerised by their symmetry and then felt awkward for a different reason.

'Sorry, well, I just find you both so fascinating... oh, that sounded a little weird.'

Jonathan changed the subject by turning around and speaking through the now open bus window.

'Okay, Graham, we'll see you later.'

Graham looked over at the cottage porch where he saw Mrs Holloway waving.

'Right, see you in a few hours. You have your phone, don't you?'

'Chloe has. Stop fretting,' said Jonathan.

They walked off through a painted metal gate. The Victorian cottage had grey stone walls and cream wooden windows. Chloe felt the whole place radiated calm. The overall effect was of a quintessential English country home. It didn't look overly lavish, rather simple and traditional. To the right of the front door was a cast metal sign that read *Pattle Cottage*.

Stepping onto the front porch, Chloe felt as though they were stepping back in time. Ornate coat hooks hung in the entrance lobby. The twins led them through to the kitchen. Central to the space stood a solid wooden table and six chairs. The only storage was along the rear wall fitted from floor to ceiling with cream-coloured cupboards and drawers with patterned white porcelain handles. To the left was a cream range cooker. Chloe turned to look at the wall opposite the range, hearing a ticking noise. She spotted a wooden wall clock, dated 1895, with writing just below the centre of the dial. Chloe drew her breath, exhaling slowly.

'This is a gorgeous house.'

'Thank you,' said Mrs Holloway. 'Why don't you go on through while I rustle up some lunch?'

Chloe and Jonathan followed the twins to the main lounge and Chloe whispered to Jonathan, 'I still don't know which is which. It's embarrassing.'

Lisa turned around and wriggled her predominantly red-check hair band. They both looked at Louise and sure enough she had a blue-check band.

'Sorry,' said Chloe.

'Stop apologising,' said Lisa, smiling at them both. 'Our brother struggles to tell us apart at times, so you've got no chance.'

'Right, sorry.'

Lisa screwed up her face, bringing her eyebrows together and trying to look stern but failing. They all burst out laughing.

The twins led them up a narrow, wooden, twisting staircase, across a very small landing and into a medium-size bedroom with two beds and two wardrobes. It was quite compact for both of them, but Chloe thought it was a small price to pay to live in such a house.

Along one wall were a number of beautifully pencilled drawings. Chloe thought some of the people depicted in the drawings had clearly lived a long time ago, judging by their clothes.

Perhaps a hundred years. However, one portrait of a more recent figure, she recognised, as her memory took her back to their first day at the High Peak Activity Centre and the entrance foyer with its pictures and commemorative plaque for Rebecca Johnson. This particular picture was far more disturbing as it looked as if Rebecca was crying.

Lisa picked up on Chloe and Jonathan's fixation with her drawings.

'They're my sketches.'

'They're really good,' said Chloe.

'Is that Rebecca Johnson?' Jonathan asked.

'Yes, I copied it from the picture in the entrance lobby at High Peak,' said Lisa.

'I don't remember her crying in that picture.'

'She wasn't. It just sort of... well, happened.'

'What do you mean?' replied Chloe, curiosity piqued.

Lisa retold the story of the night the twins and Darren were working in the study and how she had accidently smudged the drawing.

'You must have touched your phone accidently. I think we all got a little over-excited,' said Louise.

This caused both Chloe and Jonathan to give a half-hearted laugh, but Lisa remained solemn.

'You can say what you like. I didn't go near my phone.'

The air was a little tense, so Chloe broke the mood.

'What about the other drawings? They're wonderful. Do you know who they are?' she asked.

'When we moved into the house my dad found some old papers and photos stuffed in a cupboard – the one off the stairs. Did you see it?' asked Lisa.

'Yes,' replied Chloe. 'On the right as the stairs turn back on themselves.'

Louise continued, 'Well spotted. It's the only loft-type space in the house. Anyway, amongst the items were letters and photo postcards dating back to the early twentieth century, around 1916.'

'Wasn't that during the war?' asked Chloe.

'Exactly. At that time the Pattle family owned the cottage. There were five of them living in the cottage at one time.'

'Thus "Pattle Cottage",' said Chloe.

'Wow! It must have been a tight squeeze,' said Jonathan.

'Absolutely. Dad did some research on them, William and Elizabeth. They had eight children. Three of them lived here and there was quite an age range. Three of the sons joined the army.'

'I've a feeling this is not going to end well,' said Chloe.

'Not great. The first son who joined as a volunteer was Harry. He returned a few months prior to the start of the war on medical grounds. Not sure what they were though. He lived a long and full life. The others were not so fortunate. Bill or William Jr fought in France and in 1917 was gassed in the trenches. That's him there, third from the right.' She pointed to the drawing and continued, 'He survived the war and was brought back to the Norfolk War Hospital. Some of the letters and postcards were from him to his family here at the cottage. My dad says William must have never recovered from the gas incident. Sadly, he died when he was just thirty-one.'

'Tragic. And what happened to the third son?' Chloe asked.

'I'm afraid Jonas lost his life in the trenches. His name is on one of the panels at the Arras Memorial in France. We really have no idea how lucky we are.'

'Too right. I can't imagine how horrific it must have been,' said Jonathan.

'I researched some of the awful things they had to deal with in the trenches as I want to do something in the medical field when I'm older,' said Louise.

'If it's what you want, you'll no doubt succeed,' replied Chloe.

'I hope so. In those days the soldiers suffered so much as the mud, damp and rats spread diseases like typhoid, trench foot and dysentery. All could have been curable if the scientists had known about antibiotics a little earlier. Sir Alex didn't discover penicillin until the mid-1920s and it wasn't until the 1930s that it was made more readily available.'

'They say these bugs are now beginning to resist antibiotics, which is scary,' said Jonathan.

'Exactly. We'll all need people like Louise to find a new solution,' said Chloe. 'Will your parents allow you back to High Peak? Sorry, I er... didn't mean to pry.'

She'd been burning to know this long before they'd set eyes on Pattle Cottage. But now that she'd asked the question and looked at the faces staring back at her, she regretted her question.

'Random, Chloe, and not so subtle,' said Jonathan.

Louise looked across with a smile.

'Yes, well, at least we think so. Ron Jameson came to see Mum and Dad yesterday and apologised for the whole thing, although it was the health centre's fault and not the school's really. Ron was so angry with them. Apparently the school has been paying the health centre whenever any student is admitted to the sick bay and they've been contracted to look after us. I'm not sure Ron knew about the strict policy of no visitors. Nurse Plant has been dismissed. He was supposed to have been there, but as you know, he'd slip off and didn't return. I think he has a drinking problem. Apparently the school and the health centre now have a new policy procedure that's implemented when any pupil is in the sick bay and now the doors aren't kept locked. I still think it's good to have the facility close to the school though.'

'I think they have it there because they can use it as part of the advertisement for the outdoor centre. It looks good to have such facilities. I bet the centre brings in a lot of revenue,' Lisa added.

'I'm sure you're right,' replied Chloe. 'So your parents are still considering?'

Lisa looked inquisitively at Louise. Chloe picked up on the request.

'What?' she said.

'It was a close thing that we ever went to High Peak School in the first place,' said Lisa, pulling at her hair and dragging her fingers through its length. She continued, 'Our brother Martin went before us and he's doing really well now at university.'

'So why is there concern about sending you?' asked Chloe.

'Martin had a friend at High Peak. A close friend. Rebecca Johnson.'

Chloe felt shocked and desperately hoped she didn't show it.

'What? Your brother knew Rebecca?' she said, a little too fast.

'That's what she just said, Chloe,' said Jonathan.

Lisa fiddled more tensely with her hair.

'So obviously that put them off sending us there. Martin was devastated when she died. He didn't talk about anything much for weeks afterwards. I'm sure they were, you know, boyfriend and girlfriend.'

'We don't know that, Lisa,' said Louise.

'We know that he was fond of her... more than that,' replied Lisa.

'Did he speak about her? Eventually that is,' Chloe asked, now feeling a deep sense of inner concern. Her stomach had that knot, but she wasn't really sure why.

'No, he never spoke about Rebecca to us, but we overheard him in the garden once talking to one of his classmates, Catherine Banks. She visited him one day in the holidays after the accident.'

Lisa was still pulling at the strands of her hair and glancing at her sister. 'Catherine mentioned that he and Rebecca, well, apparently they did homework together.'

'That's not so unusual,' said Chloe.

'No,' continued Lisa, 'but they weren't in the same class and she also said, "I know the way you felt about Rebecca".'

'It does sound like they were close,' Chloe said tenderly, reading Lisa's emotions. 'Did Catherine say anything else?'

'I think Catherine was worried about something, something about Rebecca's diary. The other girls in her class said she had one but that it was lost or had disappeared,' said Louise.

'Do your mum and dad know about that?' asked Chloe.

'I don't know. I'm sure Martin wouldn't hold back anything that was important,' said Louise, as she sighed and paused. 'Then Catherine gave Martin a letter. She said one of the girls in Rebecca's dormitory had found it, a letter written by Rebecca, one she had not got around to posting. She may have written it the night she died.'

'What did he do with it?' Chloe asked.

Lisa looked down.

'He was crying and said he couldn't open it as he thought it may have been a suicide note.' Lisa had tears in her eyes and she hastily wiped them away. 'He thought she'd been acting oddly in the last few weeks and blamed himself for not telling her how he felt about her.'

Chloe felt saddened and conflicted. She wanted to change the subject to make Lisa feel better, but she also wanted desperately to know more.

She tentatively and quietly asked, 'Did Martin ever say what he did with the letter?'

Louise answered, 'He posted it.'

'Well, then, it couldn't have been a suicide note as they would know by now and I believe, up to now, no one knows what happened, so it could only have been an accident,' Chloe surmised.

Lisa wiped her eyes again and smiled at Chloe.

'Sorry! I get upset just thinking about what Martin went through... such a shock for him.'

'It's not surprising your parents were worried about you going to High Peak School,' said Jonathan.

'Yes, and I can't imagine the conflict when Mum and Dad discovered our year at the Jameson Academy actually placed us at High Peak.'

'If only you'd been a little older, you would have been at Dale School with us.'

At that point Mrs Holloway called up to them, 'Come and have some lunch.'

Chloe looked at the twins.

'You all go down. I just want to call my brother. He's still at High Peak School and I'm worried now.'

Chloe looked down and then felt Jonathan rub the back of her shoulders.

'He'll be fine,' said Jonathan. He turned and looked directly at the twins. 'Come on then', he said, before squeezing Chloe's shoulder. 'We'll see you downstairs.' And they left.

Chloe looked up at the picture of Rebecca on the wall. It really did look like she was crying. Her stomach churned as she dialled.

Inspector Rumcorn and Debbie drove into the car park at High Peak Health Centre, pulling up in front of the school that they had become increasingly familiar with over the past week. It had been sunny in Ripley, yet here, among the peaks, the clouds were winning the battle to obscure the sun.

The two plain-clothed officers made their way inside and approached a small, painfully thin female receptionist with long, straight black hair and pointed features. Rumcorn wondered whether she was suffering from some form of illness.

The receptionist smiled politely at the newcomers and said, 'How may I help you?'

'I'm Detective Inspector Peter Rumcorn and this is PC Debbie Amott. We're here to see Dr Bence Kovac.'

'Ah, yes, please take a seat. I'll let Dr Kovac know you're here.'

Turning around, Rumcorn reviewed the chairs, their light wooden frames with multi-coloured cushions of orange and green: a 1970s design. He wondered whether they'd actually been there from that early period and the styles had gone full circle. He watched Debbie take a seat by an iron-framed staircase with dark wooden treads and handrails. He remained standing and wandered around viewing the various notices as the doctor emerged from a large metal door.

'Hello, Inspector Rumcorn and –' he paused, looking at Debbie.

'PC Debbie Amott,' she said, completing his sentence.

'Please come through.' Dr Kovac guided them along a corridor and into his consulting room. 'How can I help?' he asked, pointing to chairs adjacent to his own.

Rumcorn took out one A4-sheet that had been sent to him earlier and passed it across to Dr Kovac. Rumcorn watched him intently to gauge his reaction. He thought he witnessed the narrowest amount of tension at the edges of the doctor's eyes, but only for a fleeting moment. Rumcorn remained silent and waited as the doctor looked straight back at him with no further hint of stress or surprise.

'What do you make of it, Dr Kovac?'

'Well, it looks like a record sheet or part of a document from a phage therapy trial.'

'So you're familiar with this practice?'

'Well, I'm familiar, of course, with some of the terminology. We sometimes support the students from Derby University,' the doctor replied. 'Students there study bacteriology and may create a thesis around their particular research. This could be their work or it could be from another university.'

'Doctor, we've carried out some initial enquiries and are advised that there are no such human trials being conducted at the present time, nor indeed have there been for the last few years,' Rumcorn iterated, still intently watching the doctor and wondering whether there might be some break in his composure.

Dr Kovac looked unfazed.

'It's more likely this report would be referring to animal tests. There are a number of universities and laboratories around the country that undertake such work, on mice, for example, and I suspect the patient number refers to Mickey Mouse.'

Rumcorn was unsure whether this man was now taking the piss, but he showed no sign of his annoyance. He would not give him any such satisfaction.

'Why come to me, Inspector? I'm sure the police have their own physicians.'

'We actually have reason to believe that this document came from this particular practice, so you'll forgive me if I'm not convinced by your suggestion as to who this actual patient may be.'

'Who told you that?'

'We're not at liberty to say at this current point in time,' said Rumcorn, now feeling he was back in the driving seat.

The doctor, although still not showing obvious signs of stress, was leaning further back on his seat and conducting the tiniest of rocking motions.

'It could very well have been a student, as I've said. One that was here on work experience.'

'Can you please give us the names of these students, and indeed any other persons that have been working here over the last, say, five years?' Rumcorn asked.

'I can't see how or why any of this is necessary.'

'Are you refusing to assist, doctor?'

'No, of course not! But I still don't see why it's necessary. Please feel free to inspect the health centre. We don't carry out any animal trials here.'

'Dr Kovac, we are not required to substantiate any line of enquiry that we see fit to follow. I must reiterate, we do have reason to believe this document came from here, so if you could let us have the information requested, it would be appreciated.'

'I can get Janice to forward the names of all past and present students. Is that all, Inspector?'

'No, not quite! What do you make of this?' Inspector Rumcorn passed over a second sheet of A4 with *La Maison de Pharmaceutical* boldly lettered at the top. This time there was a momentary widening of the eyes. 'Something the matter, doctor?'

'No, why do you say that? I've never seen this before.'

'I didn't ask that. I simply asked what you made of it.'

'Inspector, I don't know what this is. It's not a company I've ever heard of. What is it exactly that you want to know from me?'

'Well, we think this may be a receipt. There's a note across the bottom advising of a rather large sum of money in exchange for some phage mix.'

The doctor screwed up his eyes in an effort to read the bottom line and then put on his glasses.

'I don't read French,' he advised.

'It suggests this is a receipt for a quarter of a million euros,' said Rumcorn.

'Really!' the doctor exclaimed, and then after a further short silence, continued in what could be conceived of as a rather more helpful tone. 'You actually believe there is some substance to this accusation of a trial, yet there remains nothing in this document to prove such a practice is being carried out.'

'That remains to be seen, but such a trial would be illegal without the correct approvals, and it would be an act of some neglect were we to ignore it and not make enquiries. Don't you think, doctor?'

'Absolutely! I'm only sorry I can't shed any light on the matter. While I think about it, there are a couple of locums that have supported us here at High Peak. I'll make sure Janice includes everyone on the note to you, Inspector. Is there anything else?'

'No. Well, one thing. Have you always lived in the UK?'

'Ah, no. I'm originally from Hungary,' replied the doctor.

'When did you make the move to the UK?' asked Rumcorn.

The doctor, Rumcorn thought, appeared flustered before composing himself prior to answering.

'Er, it must have been just after I qualified as a doctor in the late eighties, early nineties. I studied late in life, making a career change in my late thirties to early forties. Prior to that I worked in the mines. Not a nice existence. I did not want to stay in that career. I'm sure you'd agree.'

'Yes, I can certainly understand that,' Rumcorn replied, but was internally pondering the reason given, as usually people joined the health profession, in his experience, because they had a calling, a need to help others – not to make life easier for themselves.

The doctor continued, 'In the nineties people were,' he paused, 'well, less sympathetic towards immigrants. I struggled to even get an interview. Once you were able to sit with someone face to face, then those initial barriers and prejudices, if you like, could be broken down.'

'Yes, I see. Well, thank you. We'll be in touch.'

MONDAY 3 APRIL 1989

As usual Vladimir left his son Boyan for the day with his late wife's sister, Alethea, and he travelled east from the city. The streetlights flickered off as the morning light became brighter. He moved fast, navigating cattle that appeared to wander aimlessly with little direction or care. He turned left into the Georgia Municipal Centre that was the only sign visible from the main road and pulled up by the guardhouse. The small glazed structure contained monitors flashing pictures of the entire complex's double ribbon of high security fences complete with barbed wire stretching along the top.

'Morning, Dr Orbelin.'

Vladimir looked intently at the guard, who nodded at him, his recognition and demeanour making it clear he needn't show his pass, despite this being against protocol.

'Morning,' he replied, as the guard pressed a button that lifted a yellow barrier allowing passage to an inner sanctum of secrets.

He navigated the labyrinth of internal structures, parking outside the laboratory's research centre. The building itself was a white square block of metal with little in the way of character or history – a modern tin shed with no outward expression of its internal use. He went through the lobby, swiping his pass on the unit adjacent to the opposing lift door, barely acknowledging the two guards sitting behind a console of switches and screens. As he approached his office on the third floor, he was surprised to see it open. He was certain he'd closed it and the cleaners had left long before he departed the previous evening. Sitting down, he instantly noticed the reports and notes from yesterday were missing. He got up and tore open drawers, frantically searching the filing cabinets. Then sitting back down again, he regained composure and pondered for a short time before going to check the cultures he was working on inside the sealed room.

Vladimir viewed the moving YPX1 through his microscope, its flagella propelling it helplessly around its sealed container. The sanitised room had powerful air conditioning, but the clothing required inside the chamber still caused overheating. There were rules imposing a restricted time limit. Vladimir had exceeded that curfew and then some. This was an environment in which he thrived, where he felt relief from his powerful thirst for knowledge of the molecular world and gained a feeling of achievement. The use of viruses to destroy bacteria was far from a new concept. In fact this knowledge had been around for a hundred years. A virus he had cultivated the previous day hadn't shown any attraction to the bacteria. It was a bitter blow. He cared not for himself but he thought about his son. Eyes were watching. He felt it more than he knew. The notes he would write about today's work would be fabricated descriptions that were far from what he was currently witnessing. He would need to consider a new future.

Later that day, he arrived home with his son to find a note had been pushed through his door. He placed it on the sideboard then continued getting Boyan ready for bed. Vladimir thought Alethea had been less rude to him that night. Perhaps she detected something in his mood or maybe she was concerned that she would end up a full-time foster parent for Boyan.

Boyan had initially been restless but when he was finally

asleep, Vladimir sat alone looking around his house. The empty chair was a constant reminder: a symbol radiating loneliness. There had been many times he and his wife would sit in this very room and plan. They'd imagine some adventurous journey, discuss their son, perhaps create a different path for their future and look forward to their ideas coming to fruition. It was a symbol – that chair. It was a statement of the emptiness growing daily. He wanted to go back and be with the one and only person who had made sense of his world. Then he remembered the note. His tired eyes scanned the folded paper with little interest, until he saw the sign: a bass clef.

8:30 - park corner (leave through the back and destroy this note). 𝄢

He went through to the front room, pushing papers and garments out of the way, and peered through the window as though he might see the person who'd delivered it. He spotted a car three spaces down from his. A lone figure was fiddling with something below the dash.

Ten minutes later he had only just made it. Leaving Boyan alone was against his better judgement.

'Vladimir, over here.'

He looked beyond the entrance to the park. On the left a small stone structure held equipment for the summer and behind that stood Daviti Isakadze.

'Is it really you, old friend?' asked Vladimir, grabbing his hand and using it to pull him close into a hug.

'You remembered!'

'How could I forget bass clef,' said Vladimir, struggling to wipe the grin from his face.

'What happened to us, Vladimir?'

'Women,' replied Vladimir.

'We shouldn't have let them come between us,' said Daviti.

'Don't let my parents ever hear you say that.'

Vladimir chuckled at the memory.

'I believe it was their ridiculous prejudices,' said Daviti, 'and these became the catalyst for our friendship blossoming: one of defiance.'

'I heard you'd moved back to Russia to study music,' Vladimir said.

'For a short while.'

'How did you find me?'

'I have some... acquaintances,' replied Daviti, avoiding the answer.

Vladimir eyed him with an element of suspicion.

'And the note? "Leave through the back"?'

'They're watching you. I take it you followed my instructions,' said Daviti, looking back along the road which appeared clear.

'I did as requested, but how did you know?' Vladimir asked again, confused.

Daviti changed the subject and said, 'I'm sorry about your wife.'

Vladimir looked down and nodded acknowledgement.

'I can help you, you and your boy,' whispered Daviti.

'Who are you now, Daviti?'

'I'm an old friend who wants to help.'

Vladimir looked directly into his eyes. They were cold, unreadable. Vladimir considered for a moment but had few options.

'You'll need to trust me completely.' Daviti warmly grabbed Vladimir's shoulders. 'The authorities here won't just let you walk away. You'll need to leave this place, disappear.'

Vladimir undid his top shirt button and struggled to look at him.

Daviti pressed him.

'It won't be safe for you to remain here. Think of your son.'

Vladimir lifted his head and stared again into his friend's eyes. They remained impassive but Vladimir felt trapped.

He said, 'I trust you, Daviti. Both my son's life and mine are in your hands.'

NINE

UNIVERSITY

FRIDAY 17 JULY 2015 – 14:00

Chloe and Jonathan sat on the Kedleston Road bus. Chloe silently contemplated the information Adam had given them. Open day was an opportunity for the Learning Academy to showcase its courses and generally promote itself. Aside from its academic reputation, this great establishment was located close to all modern amenities and perched on the edge of the Peak District National Park.

Chloe and Adam's mum was a friend of Professor Kim Bliss who managed the Life and Natural Science department at the university. After a brief conversation the previous evening, Professor Bliss was only too keen to meet Chloe at the open day and give her an overview of the courses on offer.

Walking up the sweeping curved entrance, Chloe thought the tall central building looked lost in the mist that hung low beneath ominous clouds. She felt a shred of annoyance. It was typical that this country would turn on such a dull morning just as they started the summer break.

'Not a great day to advertise the university,' said Jonathan.

'Don't be silly. Come on. Let's get into the main entrance, just in case it does decide to rain.'

The foyer was impressive: visible steel trusses soared many metres high, curving across and forming a support for the glazed, white panelled ceiling. Even on a dull day the light bounced off the internal walls, oddly alleviating any feeling of encumbrance.

Meet and greet staff warmly approached Chloe and Jonathan and advised them where to go to find the science department and Professor Bliss. Each was handed a map of the campus. They walked along corridors and up various staircases and began to feel quite lost.

'They should have issued us with a Sat Nav,' said Jonathan with a wry smile.

'Here we go. Look.' said Chloe, pointing to a double door above which was displayed the sign, *Life and Natural Science*. They entered a large room with several groups huddled around separate tables. The students were engrossed in conversation and reviewing literature, pamphlets, etcetera, that were scattered about.

Chloe looked around, taking on board the occupants before spotting Professor Bliss liaising with a group on the right-hand side of the room, and in particular with a girl with an assortment of studs protruding from orifices around her head. The two joined the group and listened as the professor's conversation enraptured the potential students. The professor was a middle-aged, rotund gentleman with thick-rimmed spectacles and wispy dark hair falling lightly around his ears and forehead.

'You will get a firm grounding in human physiology and anatomy, biochemistry, genetics, medical microbiology, human diseases, environmental health and global health. This will enable you to understand the basics of human disease, diagnosis and, of course, treatments.'

As the professor spoke, he looked around at the pupils, taking in their gaze and interest, disseminating information with ease amongst the gathering.

A tall lad with blonde hair asked in a somewhat high-pitched voice, 'What do we need in order to be accepted onto the course?'

Others in the group could be seen to struggle against the urge to giggle at his odd-sounding voice. The professor, however, either ignored the tone or didn't acknowledge the level of pitch.

'Good question. You would require 300 UCAS points, including forty from level three qualifications, A-Levels or a Diploma route, a minimum of five GCSEs at Grade C or above. These should include biology, and although not essential but certainly preferable, chemistry.'

Chloe and Jonathan waited until the group had completed their questions and were busying themselves with the paraphernalia that adorned the tables and walls around the room.

'Hello, Chloe. How are you?' said Professor Bliss, picking her out from amongst the throng.

'Oh, hi. I'm fine, thanks. This is my friend Jonathan,' Chloe replied, and Jonathan smiled and nodded appreciatively.

The professor continued, 'Hello, Jonathan. Are you both finding the items on offer here of interest? Although it's a few years off yet, one is never too young to have an interest.'

Chloe looked initially at Jonathan and then turned to the professor.

'I thought this subject would perhaps be for me. It's fascinating, the molecular structure of our cells, and to imagine finding cures for diseases.'

'I'm thrilled you're interested, Chloe. I have little doubt you would achieve the necessary grades.'

'I'm told there'll be a greater need for scientists in this field of research as antibiotics are...' She paused. 'Well, I believe they're becoming less effective?' Chloe emphasised the end of her sentence as more of a question than a statement.

'Well, you're quite right.'

'We read about the potential use of "phage therapy" that may help in the future,' Jonathan butted in, perhaps a little too keenly.

'It's a possibility. Is this the field you're both interested in following as a career?'

Chloe's stomach was doing overtime. She had gone over in her mind how they would broach this topic of conversation. As the question was put, she had never realistically considered it up until now. However, the subject was certainly appealing and extremely interesting.

'Possibly. Can you tell us a little more about it?'

'Well, Chloe, it's a very large area and some understanding of cells is required; however, this knowledge has been around since the late nineteenth, early twentieth century. Many different scientists were discovering cell structure and behaviour at the same time. One such scientist, Felix d'Herell, was fascinated by it. Interestingly, he was well educated but hadn't actually qualified or trained as a scientist. He discovered, and importantly recorded his findings of, viruses that could be transmitted from one host to another and that some viruses would devour bacteria. He named them bacteriophages. Felix wrote papers on the lifecycles of these phages. Quite remarkable for the period when you consider the equipment they had available at that time. Then, of course, once Sir Alexander Fleming discovered benzylpenicillin, a lot of the earlier methods of controlling diseases and infections went by the wayside.'

'Why was that?' asked Jonathan.

'The problem with bacteriophages, quite simply, is that they are very difficult to locate. Many scientists believe all bacteria will have a bacteriophage somewhere on the globe that would devour it, but finding it can often be practically impossible. They're found in seas, sewage, rotting matter and similar substances. Therefore, when Sir Alex discovered antibiotics that pretty much eliminated most bacteria, then it made sense to use that. It was much cheaper to produce. You were correct though, Chloe. Bacteria can return, beating and resisting the antibiotic. In fact, when Sir Alex gave lectures around the globe, he recited again and again: *Caution against the use of benzylpenicillin. Never use unless there is a properly diagnosed reason for it to be used, and if administered, never use too little or for too short a period. These are the circumstances under which bacterial resistance to antibiotics develop.* Unfortunately, we tend not to hear that which we do not want to believe. Sad, really, as we believe that "phage therapy" is much better for the patient.'

'Sorry, Professor. I don't understand,' said Chloe.

'A bacteriophage lives, as I said, to devour the bacteria you're trying to eradicate. These phages are cherry-picked, if you will, and therefore don't attack other bacteria which our bodies need and maintain all the time to keep us healthy. So, you see, patients receiving "phage therapy" treatment would show little if any side effects, whereas with antibiotics they are not so selective and destroy all types of bacteria, leaving a patient with potentially many different problems.'

'Wow! Fascinating, Professor,' Chloe exclaimed.

'Yes, indeed. The mechanics of the phage structure can be quite difficult to grasp, but once the principles are understood, like anything, it's not so bad.'

'Can you tell us where we can get information on this subject? The internet can be a little patchy, and not necessarily aimed at our level,' said Chloe.

'Yes, of course. I have some papers that help our students and I'm sure will guide you. I also have copies of some of the earlier reports you may find interesting, as they show the progression of our understanding.'

Chloe and Jonathan sat in a corner of the university café, papers scattered on the table before them.

'Professor Bliss wasn't joking about the complexity. Just reading the headlines here is hard enough: "Gram-positive and gram-negative bacteria, gram-positive bacteria taxonomy and cell structure virulence factors",' said Jonathan.

Chloe glanced up and watched him flicking over the sheets.

'Glass half-empty,' she replied and continued, 'it's just like all subjects. When you start looking into the explanations, it's not so bad.'

'Okay, but somewhat gross! How about, ah, yes here: "Bacteriophages resemble most viruses. Consider them like tiny spiders with long scrawny necks. These attach their legs around the cell of bacteria and then penetrate a probe or stinger through the cell wall thus injecting phages into the bacterium."' He paused. 'Chloe, can you imagine these tiny, well, spider things inside you? It's awful and it gets worse: "Following this transformation, new capsid DNA and enzymes are formed. Eventually the bacteria cell fills with new phages until it cannot hold any more and consequently pops in a process known as lysis, releasing all the new phages. I'm starting to feel sick.'

Chloe returned to rifling through the information, but chuckled at Jonathan's words. At that moment, in the centre of the university's café, Brian Lambert walked in casually with Ron Jameson and two others: one a gentleman and the other a woman, both formally dressed. They were quite out of place amidst the general public, students and staff milling around the university.

There was little conversation among the small group as they walked across to the serving counter.

Chloe continued reading.

'This advises how to collect phages. Listen! "Bacteriophages can be found in soils, sewers, seas and generally any decaying matter, either plant or animal."'

The memory of the dead carcass and the High Peak doctor carrying a bag of something red flashed through her mind. 'I bet that's what he was doing, collecting samples,' she said to herself. Then she returned her attention to the sheet and continued.

'"Centrifuge your drawn-off sample. The phage will collect on top and can be extracted. These need to be tested to determine which ones grow a suppression effect (lysogenic) or destruction effect (lysis) of the target bacteria."' She broke off the text. 'That's the one you were talking about that causes the bacteria to pop,' she advised, not looking at Jonathan. '"Discard the lysogenic phage and concentrate on the lysis phages by amplifying them on the cultures of the bacteria you wish to eradicate. These more powerful amplified phages must then be micro-filtered to remove all other impurities and mixed with your suspension medium."'

'Chloe,' said Jonathan.

Chloe remained focused on the script, either not hearing Jonathan or choosing to ignore him.

'Well, it's amazing what can be done with such small molecules. I'm not totally sure how some of that is managed, but the principle is fairly clear.'

She felt a kick under the table.

'What?' she said, looking up.

Jonathan nodded in the direction of the little knot of people rearranging coffee cups on trays at the serving counter.

'Oh, okay, well at least the doctor from High Peak Health

Centre isn't with them. I think they're all the heads of the Jameson Academy. Shall we go and say hello?'

'Er... let's just play it cool. If they notice us, then we'll say hi.'

Chloe continued thumbing through some of the reports Professor Bliss had given them. She pulled one to the front, not initially sure why she did so. Written in the nineties, it reviewed a discovered new strain of *Yersinia pestis*. The author had named this new strain YPX1.

'*Yersinia pestis*,' Chloe mumbled.

'Pardon,' replied Jonathan.

'*Yersinia pestis*. I'm sure I've come across that somewhere before,' said Chloe.

'Hold on! Yes, here in these notes it looks like some exam question Professor Bliss had given to the class,' he said, then continued reading aloud. '"*Yersinia pestis*, so named after Alexander Yersin, a Swiss/French bacteriologist in 1894 who discovered the bacterium better known as the plague or Black Death. The plague is now known to have been initially transmitted by fleas and not rats as originally believed. The rats were the unfortunate first recipient of the disease."' Jonathan stopped and looked at Chloe. 'What has made you focus on this? It's horrible.'

Chloe didn't answer directly but said, 'Does it give anything else about the plague?'

Jonathan looked down at the note.

'It just describes the three different types of bubonic plague, often manifested as a bite on the surface of the skin which, if not treated, turns into a lump. The parasite has blocking effects within the cells and, therefore, after the incubation period, if not treated, the infection will spread to the bloodstream. This then becomes known as septicaemic plague. Septicaemic plague has signs of dark blue or black patches on the skin, along with severe cold/flu-like symptoms. The third type is pneumonic plague. This is by far the most aggressive, where the infection is breathed directly into the lungs. It can have an incubation period of 1 to 6 hours with death following in less than 48 hours.' Jonathan looked up again. 'I suddenly feel sick again, and you didn't answer me. Why are we focusing on this?'

Chloe passed him the report on YPX1.

'So there is a new strain of *Yersinia pestis*. I still don't see a connection,' said Jonathan, as Chloe pointed to the scientist who had discovered the new strain.

Jonathan read the report.

'"A new strain of *Yersinia pestis* or plague, which shows a total resistance to any current antibiotic on the market has been discovered and identified by Vladimir Orbelin, a Georgian scientist/physician known for his research on phage therapy. Vladimir named the new strain 'YPX1' and it was discovered when Vladimir was treating villagers in Southeast Turkey. It is believed that he sadly lost his wife of 20 years to the disease following their visit to the area where he was commissioned to help."'

Chloe looked directly at Jonathan, who still looked puzzled.

'Chloe, what's wrong?'

'Just look at the picture of Vladimir.'

Chloe watched Jonathan look down at the small but well-defined picture of a younger man that she had recognised not as Vladimir Orbelin but as Dr Bence Kovac. There was no mistaking the features. Perhaps 25 to 30 years had passed or maybe the photo was older than when the doctor had made his discovery of the new strain of plague.

'We need to tell someone.'

'There's more. Read the bit below about Vladimir.'

Jonathan continued to read the article below where it

mentioned him being commissioned to help.

"'Vladimir, and his son Boyan, who was just seven years of age when they were both reported as being tragically killed, were believed to have been crushed in the chaos at Tbilisi, Georgia during an uprising for independence in April 1989.'"

'Looking at this photo, I'm sure it's him. He isn't who he claims to be. Don't you find that odd and, well, creepy?' said Chloe.

'You're missing the fact that he's dead.'

'Yes, exactly! Well, I don't like it.'

'Hello, Chloe, Jonathan,' said Ron Jameson. 'Are you looking at the courses on offer?'

'Oh, you startled me,' Chloe said, putting her hand on her chest and breathing out slowly. 'Er... yes Jonathan and I were just looking at this university. I know one of the professors.'

She looked over at Brian Lambert who was now looking at the papers on their table. She thought she saw a momentary look of shock on Brian's face, but it passed almost instantly. She gathered the information, stuffing it back into the folder.

'Sorry. We're going into a meeting now. So nice to see you. Perhaps catch up later,' said Ron.

The rain was light but unforgiving as it fell continuously on the outer layer of Chloe's coat. Walking back down the main drive from the university, her thoughts were focused on contacting Adam and Adele. She had taken a snapshot of the report containing Vladimir's picture on her phone and was deliberating the text to add prior to sending it.

Deep amongst the shadows and hidden from view, a powerful stranger watched. He observed the two students as they reached the main entrance and turned, heading towards the bus stop. He knew what he had to do. These two meddling young kids were potentially going to ruin both his and his brother's goal in life. If he had anything to do with it, they wouldn't manage to get more than a mile. The girl was now fiddling with her phone. He placed both hands deep into lined pockets wrapping gnarled worn fingers around two epipens. They were no ordinary medical supplies. He'd personally made them to a recipe not available from any chemist. They were full of a drug that would knock out a twelve-stone man in seconds and he wouldn't wake for at least five hours. As he thought about this, he wasn't totally sure how it would affect a petite girl.

It was just the two of them waiting patiently at the bus stop, a strangely deserted period for people to leave the university. Looking east towards the city, Chloe noticed the distant traffic leaving the city's ring road. Nothing seemed to turn in their direction, which was when she saw the elderly man, firm and well built, walking quickly in their direction, his eyes full of malice and intent.

'Jonathan, it's time to go,' she shouted, an inner sense of foreboding flooding through her very being. She grabbed him and pulled away from their three-sided enclosure. The confined space suddenly felt like a cage.

They took off west, away from the city, away from activity, but importantly to Chloe, away from their pursuer. However, this new direction took them away from the urban area and into a more rural setting. They reached a T junction in the road and Chloe looked at her mobile. The picture remained of the younger doctor, Vladimir Orbelin, and some of the accompanying article of achievement. She pressed 'Send'. She took a cursory look back and fear filled her. The man was now running. He'd considerably closed the distance between them. He was swift for his years and he was talking on a mobile. She suddenly felt a pull on her hand as Jonathan, equally keen to get away from their pursuer, took flight and yanked at her. Chloe tripped and stumbled. Instinctively she turned and grabbed his arm for support at the same time dropping her mobile phone. It fell, as if in slow motion, and she watched helplessly as it slipped between the gaps of an iron grate. The phone splashed, disappearing into a pool of water freshly formed from the morning's rain. However, all her attention was heavily focused on getting away from the stranger. They would need to pick up their pace. Without thinking, they both ran straight across the junction.

A screeching sound rang through the air; tyres across damp tarmac. Both their heads turned in shock and they were momentarily paralysed on the spot. They were stunned, waiting for the ultimate impact that never happened. Chloe placed her hands on the cold steel red bonnet, as though this act would instinctively save her from further harm. Her heart pounding and adrenaline flowing to its peak, she looked up at the man now getting out of the car and walking towards them. Relief flooded her offering a boost of hope before a covered cry pierced her like a knife. Horror washed over her as she witnessed their original pursuer plunge something into Jonathan. Immediately, she started screaming and began ferociously thumping their assailant. Hands closed around her mouth and wrapped around her body, a vulgar annihilation of her personal space by a known human perpetrator. She wriggled and squealed as hard as she could, fear reaching a level she had never known was possible. She could see Jonathan's movements of protest subside. Slowly they came to a stop and his limp form was dragged sideways.

'How could you?' she mumbled between the plump fingers that pressed hard against her lips. There was a sense of movement to her right and a sudden pain swelled from her thigh. She fought against the onslaught of nothingness, but it was too powerful, too strong.

TEN

CIVIL WAR

Rumcorn sat in his front room, notes and reports scattered all over the floor. His encounter with the doctor had made him most uncomfortable. He was sure that something was happening at the health centre, but proof was what he needed. He went over all the original investigation files. It felt strange looking at the previous reports and now, knowing the school, the health centre and the area, he could piece together all the corridors, rooms and the general look and feel of the place. This gave him a detailed overview of the event, like watching a programme or a film in his mind's eye. Five years ago all the staff and students had been interviewed by Detective Inspector Roland Cooper and Rumcorn felt like history was repeating itself.

The fire alarms had gone off early one Monday morning around 1.30 am. The school had immediately carried out its evacuation procedure. The teachers had done their duty as fire marshals, ensuring the dormitories and corridors of each wing were empty before leaving the premises themselves, and then conducting a roll call at the assembly points. On dormitory Level B a storeroom had shown signs of smoke, and even at that early stage, orange flames had been witnessed under the door. Miss Claire Blount, a young drama teacher, had banged and shouted on the door and after no audible response other than the crackling of an established blaze, she'd left without opening it. The whole process was well-recorded and, by all accounts, it had taken only twelve minutes, thirty-five seconds to complete the evacuation.

It had become clear that one student was unaccounted for after the registers had been taken, and that was Rebecca Johnson. The fire brigade had arrived just seventeen minutes after the linked alarm system was activated and only Brian Lambert had remained inside the building looking for Rebecca. However, he was not able to get close to the area of the fire.

The fire brigade had struggled to control the blaze at first. They'd confirmed in a subsequent report that the cause was a naked flame in the cleaner's store cupboard located in the girl's dormitory wing on Level B. Miss Blount was now known to have left the school, and indeed the profession, after suffering from depression. The account mentioned that Miss Blount had reported a strong smell of bleach along the corridor as she'd marshalled students from the building. This memory now meant she had flashbacks whenever she came across that distinctive smell, which psychiatrists had directly associated with the trauma.

Rebecca was found in the very cupboard in which the fire had started. The fire brigade's report had confirmed that they had found the remains of an old-fashioned, winkie-style candleholder that had undoubtedly been the source of the fire. The fire's ferocity was explained by the presence of a cocktail of cleaning substances. The report seemed to suggest that one of the containers in the storeroom might have exploded, thus placing the accelerant of the fire generally around the small space. Another contributing factor had been the small window at the back left slightly open. It was a warm period in July and the open window was believed to have been an oversight by the cleaner, although she had denied leaving it open.

Rumcorn reviewed the files more than twice. Two names appeared more often than the rest in the list of interviewees, those being Martin Holloway and Catherine Banks. The report, written by his predecessor, Rowland Cooper, had surmised that Rebecca had been rather an odd girl and far more comfortable in her own company, as asserted by the teaching staff and most of the pupils but not by Martin and Catherine.

Martin in particular had shown a heavier grief at the loss of his friend. He was adamant she wouldn't have taken her own life, and Roland had noted that the two perhaps had a much closer relationship than anyone else at the school had known. This had been difficult to prove and Martin was either not admitting it or struggling to do so, even though it didn't show any particular relevance to the case. Catherine, remaining loyal to Rebecca, would not admit that they had been a couple. Neither had accepted Rebecca as being odd and they didn't believe she was suicidal – in Roland's words anyway. Catherine had mentioned a diary that had belonged to Rebecca, but its whereabouts were unknown. The teaching staff had denied any knowledge of a diary.

Rebecca had allegedly either been hunting for something, was hiding, or just preferred this particular space, which was beyond anyone's comprehension. Sadly, the intensity of the fire was such that very little remained to identify Rebecca. Foul play could neither be proved nor eliminated, and it had been logged as unresolved. Rumcorn felt an increasing sense of concern surrounding this whole case and a determination to look into it in far more detail.

Rumcorn had just started to drift off when the shrill of his phone brought him starkly back to the present.

'I've located Martin Holloway and Catherine Banks, sir,' said Debbie. 'They're studying at the same university. Catherine is enrolled in History Art & Design and Martin in Business Management. All the educational establishments are on summer break. However, both Catherine and Martin have remained in Brighton working: Catherine as a waitress in a local café and Martin works part-time in a local recruitment agency. The two share a flat just off the central area opposite the seafront.'

'Well done, Debbie. Looks like an early start tomorrow.'

'I'm off tomorrow, sir. It's Saturday and the study period for sergeant exams. You approved it last week.'

'That was last week.'

'Really...' After a further pause, she changed her tone. 'Sir, have you found anything useful in the files?'

'No, unresolved,' he said, feeling agitated at the lack of success. 'I'll see you at five then.' And he clicked off the call.

SUNDAY 9 APRIL 1989

Vladimir took his son and travelled north by train through Georgia from Rustavi to the capital, Tbilisi. As he left the concrete-framed station, with its ribbon windows arching centrally above the main entrance, he spotted Daviti in the distance but didn't acknowledge him. They remained apart as he travelled on foot to Rustaveli Ave, a main thoroughfare of the capital consisting of a wide pedestrian pavement sandwiched between trees and three-storey stone façades of old buildings with shops and cafés at ground level. Once there, he joined the throng of marching protesters: thousands of people flowing like a river.

Vladimir was sure they were being watched and he felt nauseous. He held onto his son with difficulty. A small brown leather bag held their essentials, as well as a tiny molecule of bacteria – one which he remained resolute to kill. He'd brought little else. As the moving crowd came to a halt at a wider section of the avenue he felt claustrophobic – tightly contained amid a mass of people – his people. The crowd began singing national songs. He could see groups dancing, and as it grew darker, candles were held high. Zviad Gamsakhurdia stood at a rostrum conducting the gathering as if it were an orchestra.

'I thought you said there would be trouble, Daviti?' Vladimir mumbled to himself.

Then it happened. An instantaneous cacophony filled the air: large vehicle engines revving, screaming and shouting. People were running in all directions, which made no sense. Soviet forces mingling with the peacefully marching protesters started physically battering them, not with clubs or rifle butts, but with spades. The spades looked odd, the edges glinting in whatever light was spilling around the scene from streetlamps, the moon or candles that had somehow remained lit. Two soldiers surrounded Vladimir, their faces resolutely denuded of emotion. Then they simultaneously raised their spades high in the air, bringing them down forcibly with intent to kill.

Daviti shouted at Vladimir, 'COME ON! IT'S TIME, MOVE!'

Vladimir opened his eyes. He was still on the ground, cradling his son, but there was no pain anywhere. No feeling of physical trauma, only shock.

'What's going on? What happened?'

'It had to look convincing. Now, come on! We don't have much time if this is to work,' replied Daviti. 'Your attackers were not soldiers; they were part of our movement, but we knew what was planned. Sadly, what you thought was true, for some really was.'

They disappeared from the mayhem and jumped into a car far from the cacophony that was now becoming fainter. A part of him wanted to return and help the injured; after all, he was a doctor.

Their tired eyes stung as they travelled by road through Turkey in an old brown Peugeot hatchback that sounded rough. Its engine struggled as they climbed through the mountainous region towards Istanbul. Vladimir sat in the back and his son lay across him, adding to the discomfort. But Boyan was asleep and for that Vladimir was grateful. The driver was a complete stranger: a short stocky man with jet-black hair and a bushy moustache who said his name was Doug. But Vladimir seriously doubted that was true. He didn't trust him; he trusted no one. Doug had a habit of constantly smoking roll-up cigarettes. He would continue steering with his knees as he constructed the sticks. Vladimir partly admired his ability to multi-task, but it made him more than nervous when this creative activity coincided with vehicles going in the opposite direction or adjacent to cliff edges. For the two of them, this ride had cost 1,400 lari, which was close to one month's wages. If things had been different, he would have been in a limousine for that much money.

Vladimir listened intently to a news bulletin that broke across the music on the badly crackling car radio. The reporter advised of a tragedy that had occurred in Georgia. There had been 150,000 peaceful protesters. Now twenty were dead and thousands injured. The newsreader struggled as he reported that the dead included women and teenagers. Two of the victims were believed to be a scientist called Vladimir Orbelin and his seven-year-old son. Fires had started and many bodies were impossible to identify. Mikhail Gorbachev was said to be horrified and claimed he hadn't sanctioned any such action by the army.

A new sense of fear and revulsion rippled through him. If they had found bodies, then who were they? What was going on? Vladimir felt sickened. He should have stayed to do what he could to help the injured. He thought about Daviti and how he had known about what was going to happen. Then he looked down at Boyan. He gently caressed his hair, pushing the lose strands behind his ears as the boy slept. They were on the run. There was no going back and a sense of isolation washed over him.

The high-pitched sound of seagulls told him they were close long before he could actually see the sea. These birds would no doubt flock to the port picking up any scraps cast from the hive of activity. When the car slowed and then stopped at a busy junction, Vladimir opened the door, and pushing Boyan in front, they exited the vehicle. He nodded at Doug who looked somewhat confused and, Vladimir thought, pissed off. He kicked the door shut and disappeared through the crowded streets.

They entered a bland, concrete-faced building off a side street, where a middle-aged lady, wearing jeans that were far too tight, showed them a dingy room. Through a dirty window he could see docks in the distance, with the Black Sea on one side and the Mediterranean on the other. People, like nomads, wandered around the landing, eyes watching this smart man with a young boy in tow. Vulnerability flooded him. He knew they would have to get up early and vacate the room regardless of lack of sleep.

Early the next day the two slipped away into the morning darkness, continuing their journey, mostly by train, through Bulgaria, Rumania and finally into Hungary. Walking through Budapest, holding tightly onto Boyan's hand, he felt pleasantly surprised at the warmth. They located the bed and breakfast with ease. Its light stone, majestic façade penetrated the skyline several storeys high. The roof offered accommodation with pleasant dormer windows breaking the plain of grey tiles. Looking lower down, many windows had black iron railings around quaint balconies. This was a far cry from Istanbul.

He knew Hungary was going through a similar political change to his homeland, but their transformative journey away from communism seemed less hostile. Georgia had suffered a terrible massacre and at the same time Hungary was pulling down the barbed wire fences, making an easy passage through to Austria and on to West Germany. He came across families escaping East Germany through Czechoslovakia into Hungary as they were allowed to pass into neighbouring, currently communist countries. Then they travelled back via Austria to West Germany, which all seemed quite bizarre, but the Berlin wall stood in their more natural path. He believed Hungary would soon become a totally independent republic. It presented a stark contrast to Georgia which contained a large percentage of newly settled people who wished to remain under Russian rule. He actually believed it could manifest into full civil war. This convinced him more than ever that he had done the right thing. He and Boyan were better off getting far away from such hostilities.

He was now Bence Kovac. 'Bence' meant 'to conquer' and somehow he felt that fitted his renewed passion to start afresh. The name 'Kovac' was fairly common and had originated from families of blacksmiths. Boyan would be known as Gellert Kovac: 'Gellert' meant 'being at the top', sometimes referred to as 'a spearhead'. The meaning of Boyan was similar – being on high or noble – but names never translated that closely and Boyan did not like being called Gellert. Vladimir knew they had no choice.

FRIDAY 17 JULY 2015 – 23:00

On the opposite side of the peak, adjacent to the basin of a natural stream, a mist rose around a medium-sized, Tudor-style detached house that stood alone from its neighbours. Black-stained boards clung to the gable, no longer held by their original iron fixings.

However, between the boards sat a layer of render that stuck in part to the brickwork beneath and remained steadfast, at least for the moment. The owner-occupier clearly had no time or inclination for maintenance: his skills and focus lay far from such tasks. The driveway was strewn with leaves of autumns past and when wet became another hazard.

Bence turned the wheel of his blue Skoda then jabbed the brake too hard, bouncing over the edge of the pavement, and only just managing to stop before hitting his own front wall. He got out and slammed the car door, glancing across at an old red hatchback parked behind his hedge. The soles of his shoes kept sliding on the unkempt paving as he marched up the drive. His milky blue eyes fixed sternly on his son and Stacey Harper who stood on the porch.

'I've just got your garbled text message about students,' he said, his forefinger pointed across at the parked car, 'and I know whose car that is. You've no idea what he's capable of.'

'I was at the university and... and they knew, they know who we are,' said Brian.

'What have you done, Boyan?' Bence was now prodding his finger into his son's chest. It had been a long time since he had used that name. The sound of it brought back images of Lidya.

'I haven't done anything,' he replied defiantly, raising himself up towards his father.

Bence breathed heavily, his face now barely an inch from Brian's.

'Don't lie to me!'

'I called Uncle David. He always knows what to do.' Brian's face twisted into a snarl. 'Stacey told me what you did to Rebecca.'

'David is not your uncle, you damn fool! You stupid damn fool! And what do you mean what I did to Rebecca? Perhaps it was her fault right from the start.' Bence jolted his head towards Stacey. 'Did you go poking around in my lab when I wasn't there? You were always clumsy, but not clever enough.'

Stacey's eyes narrowed.

'I'd only been at the school five minutes and you asked me for help. Help to move a dead girl to a storeroom because you were going to save the world. I'm a pharmacist. You said you would help me get my degree. Showing kids how to climb is not my idea of fun. I still don't understand your work. You're just a bad teacher. And to think I helped you get those samples from Rebecca's grave.'

'Oh yes, yes, I forget myself. You're Miss Too-good-to-be-true. Perhaps Fraser wasn't an accident. Perhaps he too was one of your victims!' said Bence. He parted them both as he pushed past and entered the house, slamming the door behind him and leaving them locked outside.

Bence moved through the hall and shoved the living room door open, causing it to hit the wall. Inside the front room, a coal fire flickered, radiating a low singular direct heat out to two occupants.

Bence stood, filling the doorframe, and for the second time that night he asked, 'What have you done?' It was a question to which he felt he already knew the answer, but it seemed too awful to contemplate.

'We have done exactly what was needed,' replied Daviti in a calm, calculated voice as he sat passively. His long fingers drummed the arms of a green velour chair.

Bence regarded his old friend with pure loathing. He breathed in deeply, swelling like a frog about to croak.

'Oh, you really think so, do you?'

'Absolutely! But we need to resolve the situation carefully and plan properly. You know I don't like spontaneity. It creates mistakes.'

'Well – let – me – tell – you, I've already had the police banging on my door. They've got hold of some of my research trial documents. Do you really believe this act will eradicate that?' said Bence.

'We've been through difficult times before. I saved your life remember. You trusted me then; you have no choice but to do so again. I will sort everything. I always have.' Daviti leaned back and placed his hands on top of his rotund belly.

'They were onto us. Somehow they found out. I admit I have no idea how, but thanks to your son's tip off, the two students... now they're silenced or soon will be. All will go back to normal and you, Vladimir,' Daviti paused, turning round slowly to face Bence, 'well, you must complete your work. Remember your vow to Lidya.'

Daviti turned back to look at his brother, Levan, silently standing by his side, a beefy man with thick stubby hands clenched into fists.

'I don't use that name anymore. I've moved on. Why haven't you, David?' He emphasised the name as though this might hurt. 'And you, Levan, I haven't seen you since we were children,' said Bence, looking at the man next to Daviti. 'Still being controlled by your brother like a puppet. Always the bully.'

'We do what's needed for the cause,' replied Levan.

'No, no, no, you all remain deluded. But this is preposterous! What about the students? Have you no morals at all?' said Bence, repulsed at the account that had just so casually been offered to him with no remorse whatsoever. 'You teach these students music at Dale School. You surely know them.'

'Morality, Vladimir. You lecture me on morality, yet you initiate suffering on the students. I understand, Vladimir... and not many do. We carry out brave acts above all to achieve a better world.

You, Vladimir, are no different to me,' said Daviti.

'I don't kill, Daviti... minor ailments, short-lived... to save hundreds, possibly thousands.'

'You're blind, Vladimir. You've just confirmed my argument. We're the same.'

'This is so wrong. You must surely see that.' He stared deeply into Daviti's eyes, longing for him to show understanding.

'You were not so vexed when it was Rebecca,' said Daviti.

'How dare you! She had passed.' Bence's head went down. 'She was already dead.'

Daviti leaned forward and looked up.

'But it was your fault. They were your actions that killed her.'

'No! What are you saying?'

'Your work brought YPX1 to the school. If you hadn't brought it, she would be alive now.'

'That's not the same thing, and it was you, Daviti, who persuaded me to continue with my quest.'

'Yes, but you brought it here to this sleepy hollow, and now I believe you've almost succeeded,' said Daviti, punching his fist into the air. 'You must finish it, Vladimir! Surely you of all people can understand that. You should not let Lidya or Rebecca die in vain.'

Bence felt bile rising. He swallowed hard.

'Don't you dare try and justify anyone's death to me. The tests I carry out are not life threatening. They finance the quest. How Rebecca contracted YPX1 we may never know.' He looked down on Daviti. He would never have believed he could hate anyone so much. He had one mission left now. 'Where are they, the students?'

'Oh, they're quite secure. Let's just thank the conservative nature of villages for not allowing change.'

Bence darted off down the hall. He heard Daviti shout at his brother:

'Go and get him; bring him back here.'

But he was already through the front door. He flicked the latch and pulled it shut. It would buy him a few seconds. A fine rain hit his face as he slipped on the drive and cursed the leaves. Gathering himself he got to the car door then glanced back at the house and saw the gun pointing straight at him.

'Go ahead! I don't care anymore,' said Bence, as he got into his car.

Levan Isakadze started to pull the trigger. Smack! Brian shoved him hard, pushing him over. The bullet went straight into the rear tyre of the red hatchback. Bence's car revved too high and the wheels spun as he drove away. Levan remained on the ground and fired two well-aimed shots. Brian and Stacey fell like puppets that had had their strings cut.

ELEVEN

THE OLD SCHOOL HOUSE

SATURDAY 18 JULY 2015 – 00:30

It was cold, airless and damp. Something tiny in a corner of the room gave off the low flicker of a glow. The room was square with high windows that had virtually no glass remaining other than a few shards attached to their frames that refused to be dislodged, even after years of attack by local youths. The windows at the lower level remained fully intact, protected by strong wooden shutters. These now showed signs of weakness. Rotting in the corners and blackened, they were low enough to have been vandalised by the next generation of youths. How this wooden wrapping had not caught fire remained a mystery. The building, once the local schoolhouse in the early part of the twentieth century, perhaps held a mystic strength beyond general understanding.

A clouded realisation hit Chloe and it was one of fear and terror as she slowly came around. Cloth stretched tightly around her mouth, allowing only the narrowest of gaps for much-needed air. The cloth across her tongue forced her jaws apart. Her hands and feet were bound together, allowing little movement. Groaning and moving very slightly, she became aware that she was lying on her left side. Her left arm was completely numb. She fought desperately against being violently sick. Some internal instinct shouted at her very soul not to lose the contents of her stomach.

Chloe found strength from somewhere deep in her being and

159

wriggled in an attempt to move upright. The first two attempts failed, causing pain mixed with despair to flood her body. An inner voice persisted: 'Just drift back to sleep'. Chloe refused and on her third attempt she managed to roll into a sitting position, the effort creating an increase in lung movement that had another effect. As her heart pounded and her blood surged, an unimaginable pain rippled down her left arm causing a deep muffled cry that resonated around the room.

She was alone in the dark with the exception of the tiniest orange glow to her right. It gave a steady low light, and she thought perhaps a little heat, although it remained elusive. The air was musty and infused with a mouldy odour. Chloe's senses became more responsive as she became aware of a smell that seemed to emanate from the orange light. But the low light gave off something else... hope. A memory stirred and images flashed through her mind of her in a conservatory at home that her mother regularly cleaned with bleach. There were visions of a gas fire in the corner opposite her favourite chair where she would sit reading. Then, without warning, tears welled up in her eyes. They flowed and dripped onto the cloth. She sat still, calming herself. Her left arm started to tingle, feeling twice its size and imaginary tiny pins and needles were jabbing into her soft flesh. She closed her eyes again absorbing the pain.

In the dark, and with very little vision, nothing of the room could be understood. Was she alone? Time was ticking away, seconds, minutes, maybe even hours. It certainly felt like hours. Then a sudden muffled cry penetrated from the dark zone to her left. It was a sound that radiated around the room and caused a deep ringing whistle in her ears. She jolted in panic and instantly joined in the noise, screaming as she leaned away from the source of the sound.

Chloe's volume reduced but the source of the other noise changed almost instantly into a coughing then retching sound and finally a gagging noise. Fear flooded through her again. Was this Jonathan? Was he now suffering the same fate she had resisted? Through the gag she shouted 'Jonathan' as loudly as she could, but knew the sound was barely recognisable as anything other than a rumble.

She turned, looking at the orange glow, believing there to be a wall to its right. She shuffled backwards little by little until a cold, solid form hit her hands and arms. Chloe turned her head sideways and rubbed the rag tied behind her head. The movement caused dust particles to burst off the brick, filling her nose and mouth and penetrating her throat, but that seemed a small price to pay compared to the loss of a dear friend. She could hear him rasping and struggling to free himself from the rag.

Adrenaline flowed through her with renewed vigour, thrusting different angles of her head against the roughness of the wall until the fabric started to give.

'Jonathan,' she screamed at the top of her lungs. 'It's me, Chloe. Hold on! I'm coming!'

She was not sure whether he understood, as her mouth was so dry she sounded completely different. Chloe shuffled over to where the noise was originating and bumped into a body. She had no idea whether it was Jonathan, but it seemed most likely. Who else could it possibly be? He was wriggling and flailing.

'Jonathan! Keep still!' she shouted.

After a short moment he settled. Perhaps her message had sunk in or maybe his energy levels had depleted. She pushed her cheek against him. The soft, loose material and the familiar shape of his back told her what she needed to know. He was lying on his left side with his back to her, so she moved up fighting her own bonds.

She felt his hair tickle her nose. She found his gag and started biting down hard, twisting her head from side to side like a dog playing with its owner. It was not budging and she wondered whether it was too late. Jonathan was still: no sound, not even a murmur.

Tears engulfed her for a second time, flooding her eyes and stinging. A pain far deeper than any physical one pulled at every living cell she possessed, but something within her refused defeat. She pulled and raged with increased aggression and amazingly the bonding material loosened.

The room became silent.

'No! No! No!' she yelled.

She pushed at him, causing him to roll over onto his front. With an immense effort she raised herself and dropped on top of him, her chest landing with force between his shoulder blades. She felt the initial resistance as his body held her weight for just a fraction of a second, and then it sank as the air and the congealed blockage flew out, popping like someone had crushed a packet of crisps. A laboured inhalation of breath was followed by coughing and spluttering. Chloe slid back off Jonathan's frame, allowing him to breathe. She silently sobbed and the stinging increased, but she didn't care. He was alive! They were both alive!

SATURDAY 18 JULY 2015 – 02:00

Adam stared at the ceiling and then focused somewhere beyond the curtained window. He hadn't heard from Chloe since midday Friday when she'd explained about their visit with the Holloway twins at Pattle Cottage. He'd learnt the twins had a brother called Martin who knew Rebecca. She had possibly even been his girlfriend. Rebecca had written a letter – maybe a suicide note. She had been bright, inquisitive, but now she was dead and this made him reflect on his feelings for his sister. Chloe had been by his side forever. Then that other question occurred to him: how could he possibly cope if she were gone, passed away after some horrible accident or from a disease? Not being able to talk to her ever again. All that would remain would be memories. This new pain was a soft, dull emptiness, a longing that made him feel physically sick with immense sadness. Something deep inside his brain tightened.

He thought about Martin and how he must have suffered. He desperately pulled his thoughts back to the room and the challenge that faced him with a renewed passion for discovering more information about Rebecca.

Ping. One solitary note – the sound of a mobile – echoed around the space. He got up and walked across the dormitory, his feet sensing the vinyl's cold thrust penetrating upwards. His screen flashed a message from Chloe. He figured she must be up too, struggling to sleep. Perhaps her mind was also going over and over the events that had occurred. He touched the message icon and a picture appeared, grainy and a little out of focus. He figured she must have taken it on her phone. The image looked to be part of an article, with a photo of a young, finely dressed man wearing a contented smile. He looked familiar, and beneath the photo were scripted notes like a newspaper cutting. The print was too small to decipher. Adam pressed return and sent back a message:

Thanks for the photo. Hope you enjoyed the uni trip.
Adam.

As he got back into bed, the stressful thoughts about Chloe released, and then he mused on the photo she'd sent. The retained heat within the covers washed over him and he dozed off again.

SATURDAY 18 JULY 2015 – 08:30

The long drive to Brighton ended in a café just off the city centre. The streets were busy, especially for that early time of the day. Many traders were setting up shop and early commuters wandered about with intent to their specific destinations: a one-way movement with little assessment of the world around them. They took a seat at a table on a particularly wide pavement. The café frontage was deep red with an art deco appearance. The sun's morning rays gave gentle warmth. In the distance a green dome shone above the closer rooftops in a majestic far eastern manner.

A short, slim girl came over to their table. Rumcorn reviewed the brightly coloured dots that adorned her black trousers. Surely they were in defiance of the standard dress code. Her hair was dark and shoulder length with spasmodically placed bows of various colours. On each bow were cleverly sewn brooches of multi-coloured stones that twinkled in the light. On the left side of her chest was a name badge that simply read *Catherine*.

'Morning! What can I get for you today?' she said in a cheerful voice that had a richness to its tone.

'I'd like an Americano white coffee, please. No sugar,' said Rumcorn.

Catherine turned to Debbie.

'I'd like a pot of tea please.'

'Catherine?' Rumcorn announced.

Catherine turned to look at him, still smiling but weary. Not many people actually used her name although it was displayed for all to see.

Rumcorn continued, 'I'm Detective Inspector Peter Rumcorn and this is Police Constable Debbie Amott. We're from the Derbyshire Police.'

'Oh, has something happened? My parents?' Catherine asked anxiously.

'No. Nothing like that. Nothing for you to worry about. We would like to talk to you for a few minutes about Rebecca Johnson,' said Rumcorn.

Catherine looked surprised and somewhat confused.

Debbie added, 'I spoke with your manager here yesterday. Unfortunately, I couldn't get hold of you. Mr Langton said you would be here today and that you never missed a shift. Apologies for the way we've turned up, but we need to speak with you about Rebecca.'

'Okay, of course, but I'm working here all day. I get about half an hour around half-eleven just before the rush,' Catherine advised.

'Mr Langton has agreed to let you talk to us this morning.'

Catherine turned around as Kevin Langton raised his hand and nodded and then walked over to them.

'It's okay. I'll cover for you. There aren't many customers.' He took the order from Catherine's note pad and added, 'I'll bring you your favourite hot chocolate.'

'Thanks,' said Catherine.

'Please take a seat,' said Rumcorn.

'Why the sudden interest in Rebecca?' Then she visibly paused. 'Oh, wait, I remember Louise telling me about another accident at High Peak. Do you think they're connected?'

'Louise?' asked Debbie.

'Yes. Louise Holloway. Martin's sister.'

'Okay, well, not necessarily connected. We're looking over the case... quite routine.' advised Rumcorn, and continued, 'From your original statements, you had concerns over a diary that was missing. Can you tell us anything about that? What made you feel so concerned?'

'It was a long time ago. I was younger, perhaps too much imagination,' Catherine replied.

'It's okay, Catherine. You have nothing to worry about. We would welcome anything you remember about that particular event or anything relating to Rebecca. We know Martin was closer to her and we'll see him later.'

'No, no, you mustn't.' Catherine replied with heavy concern.

'Why not, Catherine?' Rumcorn enquired, surprised at this reaction.

'Sorry, but this whole thing affected Martin really badly. It took him an awfully long time to get over the loss of Rebecca.'

'I'm afraid we'll have to see him,' said Rumcorn.

'I can tell you everything he can, which is really not very much. Martin and I have no secrets.'

'Go on,' Rumcorn encouraged.

'All I mean is he doesn't know why she took her life or why she hid away that terrible night. He, well, he feels responsible, guilty... not that he is anything of the sort.'

'Why did he feel this way, Catherine?'

'Martin was very fond of her, wanted to ask her out, but never quite found the courage, and he and I believe she felt the same way about him. But he didn't ever tell her, never said how he felt. Do you see?' asked Catherine.

Kevin arrived with a tray of steaming drinks that released some of the tension. Catherine sipped her drink and wiped the corners of her eyes with a napkin.

Rumcorn continued, 'It's not likely that a young girl would ever take her life because someone had not told them of their feelings.'

'Exactly, it's absurd. I have told him that time and time again, but he still holds a deep regret and has never had a girlfriend since. I'm so worried about him, and will be especially so if you go quizzing him about Rebecca. He could fall back into depression all over again.'

Rumcorn listened, appreciating how much this girl, this young woman, cared for Martin. She was passionate, but he had to press on.

'What was Rebecca like?'

'She was lovely, really. Others just didn't understand her, that's all.'

'In what way did they not understand her, Catherine?'

'Well, Rebecca was not one who ever wanted to be popular, if you know what I mean. She liked to be on her own generally, quiet and reflecting on things, taking in the world around her.'

'Do you believe that's why other students and teachers thought her rather odd?'

'Yes, and her obsessiveness.'

'Her obsessiveness?' Rumcorn replied, more as a question than a statement.

'Oh yes... massive on that score. She would lose herself in whatever she was doing, homework or hobby, a real in-depth focus to be beyond thorough, go into a lot of detail, a lot more than was ever requested or expected. Mr Joins really admired her.'

'An inquisitive nature then?' added Rumcorn.

'Absolutely. She was heavily into statistics and probabilities, if I remember correctly. Typical of Rebecca. It was one of the subjects we were covering in our maths classes, but Rebecca went much further. One day Martin showed me some of her work.'

'Can you tell us what it was about?' asked Rumcorn.

Rumcorn watched her reflecting and fishing through her memory to an area of her past he believed she had tried desperately to forget.

'Rebecca created some quite stunning graphs, charts and

general diagrams, beautifully illustrated. She analysed statistics and probabilities around illnesses that had occurred at our school. She compared them with the other schools of the Jameson Academy and local schools in the area. I think she also looked at the community in general, you know, to determine trends throughout the year, that sort of thing. Mr Joins, who took us for maths and computer studies, had said it was a great piece of work, one of the best he had seen from a pupil at our level.'

'Catherine – the diary that was missing – how did you find out about that?'

'Rebecca kept a diary. She was always quite precious about it. I overheard one of the girls in her class saying how it was not on her bedside table. I guess she had it with her when, well, you know.'

'Is there anything else you can tell us about Rebecca or that particular night?'

'I was not on the same floor as Rebecca. I was in the opposite wing, so you see I never saw the fire or the smoke.' Catherine looked down and spoke quietly, almost a mumble in the guilty manner of one who felt she was betraying a trust.

'There was a letter. Heather Copland, who was in Rebecca's room, gave it to me a day or so after the fire. I've no idea where she found it. It could have been anywhere in their room.'

Rumcorn and Debbie said nothing, but nodded gently.

'It was quite a thick envelope, definitely her handwriting, that gave the address of her aunt in Chaddesden. Martin and I thought it might have been a suicide note. Knowing how she was, it would have been, you know, thorough.'

'What did you do with the letter?' Rumcorn asked.

'I went to see Martin. I cannot express how depressed he was over the whole affair, but I had to give him the letter. I can't now explain why I didn't just hand it in to the teachers, which would have been the obvious thing to do.'

'Do you know what Martin did with the letter, Catherine?'

'He didn't speak about it for years, but yes, he did tell me once. He said that it was not his to open, that as much as he really wanted to know what was in it and to read something Rebecca had penned, he couldn't do it. So he posted it. Do you really have to talk to Martin about all this?'

'Yes, I'm afraid we do. But rest assured, we will be sympathetic.'

'Is there any news?' Catherine asked.

'News?'

'Yes, about the boy, Fraser, I think Louise said.'

'I'm afraid not. He remains in a coma; however, the doctors suggest he is a fighter to have come this far, so we must remain hopeful.'

SATURDAY 18 JULY 2015 – 9:00

'Adam! Adam!' Adele was pounding him from the foot of his bed.

'What the hell are you doing in here?'

Adele looked scared, panicky.

'There's no one around this morning. Miss Harper's room is next to mine on the girl's corridor, but this morning, nothing.'

'That's ridiculous. There must be people about. What about the activity centre next door?'

'Darren said they don't open the centre during the school holidays.'

'The health centre?'

'Saturday, it's shut.'

'You're telling me we're the only people here in this huge complex? Are we locked in?'

'I don't think so.'

'I can't believe my rotten luck,' said Adam, getting out of bed and stomping out of the dormitory room.

'What's got your goat?'

'Are you serious? I'm stuck in a huge complex full of beds, showers, etcetera, with a beautiful girl who... who...'

'Who's not keen on boys?' replied Adele, her face going red.

'Exactly.'

'You really are horrid, Adam Brant! That's all you can think of.'

Adam turned around, peering back into the room he'd just left and totally ignoring her comment.

'Really, there's no one?

'I've not seen a soul,' she said, as he turned and left towards the toilets. She raised her voice. 'And make sure you're fully covered when you return from the bathroom. I don't want to see, you know. Yuk.'

'Great, just great,' he replied, walking off down the corridor.

They sat in the empty dining room eating toast and drinking tea, the warm liquid soothing a nervous sensation that had started niggling at his mind. The place being empty echoed oddly and he'd begun to imagine some strange scenarios, including Martians landing, but Adele turned on the radio and the outside world seemed normal. Then he remembered.

'Oh, I got a text from Chloe last night.'

He passed Adele his phone.

'You've had four calls from your dad.'

'Step-dad.'

'Why haven't you answered him?'

Adam looked sideways out of the window, avoiding Adele's gaze.

'I don't like the way he treats Mum. She shouldn't put up with him.'

'He could be worried about you.'

'He's not... I sent a text back and told them we were fine. Anyway, Graham will pick us up soon.'

Adele clicked on Chloe's text.

'Odd that there's no message with the photo.' She zoomed the picture so the writing became legible. 'A Georgian scientist Vladimir Orbelin has been commended for the discovery of a new strain of the plague, better known as the "Black Death". He has called it YPX1,' Adele read out loud.

Something about that sounded familiar to Adam.

'Did you say the plague?'

'I'm sure I've seen that person before,' said Adele.

Adam leaned closer to her and viewed the screen.

'Looks like Brian Lambert to me.'

'I'm not sure about that. It's not a great picture, but I can see what you mean, although the eyes remind me of the doctor that works at the health centre.'

'I think you may be right. He's a lot younger there though.'

Adam pressed call and it went straight to answer phone. Chloe's recorded voice rang out.

'Hi, this is Chloe. Great to hear from you. Please leave a message after the beep. Byee!'

'I want to get out of here, out of this place.' said Adele.

SATURDAY 18 JULY 2015 – 10:00

Rumcorn and Debbie arrived at the building that was logged as Martin and Catherine's address. The building's façade reminded Rumcorn of the 1960s musical *Oliver!* where Oliver had finally been taken back to his grandfather's house in a posh area of London. He looked across this three-storey Georgian property, all connected as one long building stretching virtually the length of the street. It ran in a very slight curve and stood opposite parkland. The property was surrounded by ornate metal fencing. The buildings were tired looking and in need of some restoration. However, he observed they were currently a mix of bed-and-breakfast hotels, student accommodation and privately run businesses, dentists and financial advisory services.

Once inside the main door, Rumcorn was surprised at how the house had been split into several flats by a financially savvy landlord. Neglect was apparent, showing a lack of investment, in particular around the central communal area. A door opened to his right and Martin Holloway stood before him. He stepped back and gestured to invite them in. This section itself at least had an air of freshness about it, and although this one block had been carved into many units, the rooms remained large with tall ceilings and characterful period features.

'Martin, we're aware of your depression around the loss of Rebecca, and it is with regret that we need to ask you a few questions about your friend. We wouldn't be here if it were not absolutely necessary,' Rumcorn advised with authority and understanding.

'I don't think I can tell you any more than Catherine has told you this morning,' said Martin.

Rumcorn lifted one eyebrow slightly. Martin continued:

'Catherine called me. She's a good friend, more like a sister to me, and sometimes a little overprotective.'

'Please, can you tell us anything about the project Rebecca was working on, the one that compared sicknesses or illnesses between the schools and the community?' asked Rumcorn.

'That was my fault, or at least in a strange way, it was. You see, I was the one who'd been off with a bug, something I'd picked up whilst at the school. It hit me really hard. I was off for about a week, although it felt longer. Rebecca...' When he mentioned her name for the first time his face fell momentarily, and he paused. 'Sorry... she was worried about me and had asked to visit, but it wasn't permitted. When I got back to school, she told me she wanted to start this project, that my being absent had given her the idea. Rebecca wanted to do something more practical, useful I guess, with the maths stuff we were learning. This gave the theory a realistic twist. Rebecca was smart, a lot smarter than anyone gave her credit for. She took all the information she could find to draw graphs and diagrams on averages, means and probabilities, and then compared them to the schools in our group and other schools in the community.'

'Can you recall any specific conclusions from her work?'

'I'm sorry, I don't remember, or maybe she didn't share that with me'.

'Your sisters, they were off ill as well, weren't they?' Rumcorn enquired.

'Well, yes, but I believe they were only in the sick bay, quarantined if you like, for a couple of days. It was a lot longer for me but the quarantine of course sent Mum and Dad off the rails... finding them there and not being told. I can't say I wasn't looked after whilst I was there though. I can't complain, and I believe Louise and Lucy were equally well cared for in the main. They are, thankfully, okay now.'

'I'm glad to hear it,' said Rumcorn.

'Martin, we have to ask about the night of the fire. I apologise, but we need to ask whether there is anything you can tell us, no matter how trivial. Anything at all would be helpful.'

'What's to tell really? The alarms went off and everyone evacuated. After the roll call the teachers were clearly agitated. I had no idea that Rebecca was the missing person at that point. We heard whispers that someone was unaccounted for, which became obvious when Brian Lambert went back inside the building, even though Stacey tried to stop him.'

'Stacey?' Rumcorn repeated.

'Sorry – Miss Harper. She started actually teaching at our school after the fire. They lost a few staff that struggled after... well, you know. We knew Miss Harper and Mr Lambert were an item. His living quarters were on our floor. The fire affected many of the pupils, not just me,' Martin said, as his eyes started to glisten and he looked away in an attempt to hide his emotions.

'One last thing, Martin... in your own time... the letter.'

'Yes. As Catherine has told you, I didn't open it. I posted it. Rebecca's aunt must have received it years ago. I've never heard anything. I remain in the dark, which I'm told is part of my problem, but I couldn't face going to see her aunt, and f-finding out what Rebecca's last...' He swallowed hard, his eyes now visibly showing tears. 'Her last note, reading her final words.'

'Thank you, Martin. Catherine is right. None of this is your fault and you're not to blame.'

Rumcorn's final words resonated. Martin half-smiled.

SATURDAY 18 JULY 2015 – 10:00

Adam and Adele gathered their belongings, complete with rucksacks, before walking towards the village. It started to rain, but the fresh, cool air filled Adam's lungs, giving him a sense of freedom. He looked up at the old schoolhouse where a voluminous cloud of smoke bellowed from the rear right-hand side of the old building.

'Must be local youths. Idiots!' said Adele.

Adam's phone rang. He stopped, took it out and looked at the screen. It was his stepfather. He debated internally whether to just switch it off, but after his earlier conversation with Adele, something made him accept.

'John.'

Adam's stepfather erupted as though he had the phone on loudspeaker.

'Adam, why haven't you returned my calls? Your mother's going nuts.'

'I'm good, thanks. How are you?'

'Don't get smart with me!' There was a pause, a strange silence. His stepfather's tone and volume changed, softened.

'Adam, is Chloe with you?'

'No.'

'When did you last see her?'

John's voice had broken and Adam struggled to understand, his head swam and an unnatural heat rose, tightening his chest, which made it difficult to answer.

'She left on Thursday with Graham. Why?'

'She didn't come home last night. Kim... Professor Bliss, said he saw her at the university yesterday, sometime after 4 p.m.'

Adam stumbled, deflated, and his insides churned. Moving sideways, he lowered himself down onto a dry stone wall, just managing to reach its edge in time before his legs gave way. John's voice now became harsher.

'We assumed she had gone back to you. We know what you two are like.'

'What the hell is that supposed to mean?'

'Adam, I'm going to come and pick you up. You need to come home now. It'll help settle your mum if one of you is back.'

'Have you called the police?'

'No! Have you not been listening? I thought she would be with you.'

Adam dropped the phone. He could hear his stepfather in the distance, but he didn't care. Chloe was missing and it was entirely his fault. Adele picked it up, but it was cracked and made no sound. Adam's focus returned to the smoke.

'I'm going to take a closer look.'

'Adam, not a good idea. Let's call the fire brigade.'

But he was already heading across the road, completely oblivious to anything else around him. He came to a fork in the track. To the left was the route over the moor; to the right the road stretched around, curving away some eight hundred yards to the old schoolhouse. Adele said nothing but followed him, and then he heard the sound of a car engine coming from the direction of the old school. He darted left, pulling Adele with him, and they crouched behind a hedge. He wasn't really sure why, but some instinct was telling him to hide and trust no one. He heard a splash as the car's wheels dipped through one of the many puddles, its contents spraying them through the gaps of greenery. He watched an old red hatchback pass by, praying it wouldn't stop. It didn't but continued its journey, disappearing towards the main road with its rear red lights springing to life in the distance. Then, with an audible engine sound, it vanished, turning left in the direction back the way they had just come.

Adam stood, wet but determined to go on. He looked around and saw Adele emerge, brushing down the fronts of her legs. Adam moved on, walking fast and looking intently at the old school as it came closer into view. Mud was sticking to his shoes, making every step harder. He reached the building's perimeter fence. His heart was pounding hard, so hard he felt it might burst from his rib cage. There appeared to be no signs of life, except for one of the old chimneys at the back. At one time it would have been the only source of heating for the school. Now it was alive again and poured a black cloud skywards. But something lower along the rear added to the plumage.

Adjacent to the path stood wooden gates held open by an unnatural lean, wedging them against the ground. Most of their spandrels were missing. Adam ran through the gates and across the moss-strewn tarmac up to the old school. At first he attempted to gain entry through the main entrance, pushing at the door, but it held firm. He turned and sprinted down the side and around the back. The windows were boarded up, the paint peeling, and moss lumped deep in any crevice where it could sustain a hold. Black smoke oozed from the top of the left shutter and joined the fray high above the roofline.

Adam moved to a door on his right and then felt an immense sense of impending doom. Abandoned on the floor was an elastic black hair band. He had seen it before. It belonged to Chloe. It framed her face as her image flooded his mind. A momentary thought about telling Adele on the other side of the building came and went. No time for that now as a surge of passionate determination possessed him. He turned the old brown door handle and attempted to shoulder-barge his way in. Shockingly, he met little resistance and stumbled forward into a corridor. Running along either side of the long narrow room at chest height were thick wooden rails. Fixed to these were curved iron coat hooks, with a symmetry broken by the odd one missing. Above some of these sat curling labels. Surprisingly, a misted name remained just visible from what would have once been a colourfully crayoned piece of work. It defied gravity, stuck with yellowed tape. The ceiling sat high with an ornate frieze enclosing the junction to the walls and circling the top.

A moulded arch gave passage to the next room, but Adam paused. He found a piece of wood and wedged open the external door, as the light levels were poor. He shouted for Chloe and Jonathan, but heard only silence in reply, so he pressed on through the arch and into what must have been a formidable hall or classroom. The floor was made of tiny wooden blocks, now uneven and with many missing. His feet were sticking to the wood in certain places, lifting the little blocks as the mud on his shoes gave suction. The school's desks had long since gone but chalkboards at the front and pictures still adhered to walls: pencil drawings of infinite detail had been remarkably preserved by the lack of light. Two large panel doors led off the room in front of him. On his left stood a central fireplace that had been covered over. The chimney breast had been used to create alcoves on either side, useful storage spaces with painted white wooden shelves giving easy access to many books. Adam moved across to the right-hand panelled door and something on the floor caught his attention. Something shiny reflected some light that passed from the archway he had just entered. On further investigation he found it to be a padlock, and from its condition it was clearly new, although someone had snapped it. The door in front of him had a barrel bolt fixed just above centre height, one that could be locked with the padlock.

He tentatively pulled back the bolt and pushed open the door, peering around as he slowly entered. Small high windows afforded some extra low natural light. This room was smaller, but could comfortably have held twenty or so students, maybe more. The fusty smell was different, and then it came to him. It smelled like vomit. Confirmation wasn't necessary: there on the floor to his right lay a pool of it and at its base and poking out was a black cloth.

In the middle of the opposite wall was another fireplace, smaller this time. The walls were bare brick, painted long ago. The floor was a hard, reddish quarry tile covered in dust and broken glass. He moved further into the cold, dim and empty space. In one corner he saw a Calor gas heater that had obviously not worked for many years. He touched the cold surface as though it might offer a clue; perhaps tell him where his sister was now. Between it and the fireplace he spotted another cloth and, by it, a rope that had been cut. He turned to leave, his legs feeling like lead. Across the floor, the light from the open door highlighted letters written in the dust. He crouched down, adrenaline pumping. The letter *I* then a gap of disturbed dust, then an *a* and an *m* were clearly visible – *I__am*. But what did that mean? Why would Chloe or Jonathan write that? How could that possibly help?

There was one room remaining. He walked around and stood facing it. Crackling and popping noises emanated from within and a flickering orange glow flowed across the gap at the bottom. Common sense told him not to open the door... it wouldn't be good. He turned and started to walk out, but a vision filled his head: the rope, the material, the padlock, Chloe's hair band and the fact that she was missing along with Jonathan. Rebecca found dead after a fire.

At the thought of his sister, a memory and immense pain clenched his whole body and ripped through his soul. His chest convulsed, making it suddenly difficult to breathe, as a picture clearly came to him of Chloe burning in the room he hadn't entered. Turning around on the spot, he ran back to the closed door, yelling her name. He flew at it, kicking the door around the handle with the base of his foot with such speed and ferocity that the door snapped open.

A surge of air caused an explosive force in the opposite

direction, taking Adam with it, along with a mass of flames. Adam's body bounced on the wooden blocks and the orange heat licked across the ceiling, instantly stripping paint and creating droplets of a hot substance like rain across the floor. Black acrid smoke billowed out in many directions, growing and gaining in ferocity.

TWELVE

HARRY LAMBERT'S TALE

SATURDAY 18 JULY 2015 – 14:00

The journey back for Rumcorn and Debbie was quiet; Rumcorn's mind reviewed everything as logically as possible. Rebecca had been gathering information on illness patterns, but he had to be realistic. This information had been seen by many. It was not something that could surely cause her harm, yet some striking events were unfolding, including illnesses and documents of trials on bacteriophage. He had evidence of potentially illegal trials that, albeit somewhat tenuous, was nonetheless compelling. And furthermore, Rebecca had died mysteriously. Five years had passed and evidence would be difficult to find. The letter may well be the key, but it had not come to light, and if it had suggested foul play, surely the aunt would have brought it to the attention of the police. Fraser, a cousin to Rebecca, now lay perilously on the edge of life. Was this coincidence? Rumcorn had never believed in coincidences; in his experience there was no such thing. There was one massively important factor – Stacey Harper had not been open and honest with him when questioned about the fire. She had merely stated that it was before her time, when in fact she had been at the school that very night. He did not like people who lied to him.

Traffic was heavy but, moving northbound on the M1, he was making good time when a high-pitched ring tone caused him to jump. Rumcorn glanced at the screen on his phone. There was no number recognition. He pressed accept.

'Rumcorn,' he announced his name apprehensively.

'Peter, how long before you get back?' asked Chief Inspector Wesley Hicks. Rumcorn instantly recognised the tone.

'We could be about half an hour, traffic willing. Is something wrong, sir?' He looked across at Debbie, who showed the same concern he felt.

'I'm afraid things have spiralled. It started with a call just after 10 a.m. this morning from a Mrs Simms. Her daughter Chloe Brant and Chloe's friend Jonathan Yates did not return home last night. They were last seen at the university yesterday evening around 5 p.m. Neither has any history of going missing previously. We've just linked them to the Jameson Academy, hence this call.'

Silence fell around the car as though the road noise had been switched off. He continued:

'I'm afraid there's more. At about the same time, we received calls about a fire and accounts of a possible explosion at the old schoolhouse in High Peak village. A young Mr Adam Brant has been injured – and, yes, brother to Chloe, he also attends the Academy. He's been taken to hospital with a girl called Adelina Martel, known as Adele.'

Rumcorn pushed a button that set off blue flashing lights below the front grill and within the rear cluster of indicators. The siren was loud but muffled within the car's interior. He increased his speed and vehicles moved over allowing him passage.

'I recall the names, sir. I'm sure they were at High Peak this week.'

'The most disturbing element, Peter, is that we have found two bodies. They were in the room where the fire had taken hold. At this stage we only know one to be male and the other female.'

Rumcorn was concentrating on the traffic that lay before him, but he felt numb. He could see Debbie had one hand over her mouth.

Hicks continued, 'Get yourself up there; you need to lead the team on this one. Sergeant Burns is handling things centrally here. Let's get this turned around and damn quick, Inspector. Is that clear?'

'Yes, sir.'

SATURDAY 18 JULY 2015 – 14:30

Rumcorn and Debbie walked into the hospital's accident and emergency unit. The sweet-smelling odour, a mixture of chemicals that involved polish and disinfectant fused with heat, smothered him. Rumcorn had never liked hospitals; he didn't know anyone who did, yet they were full of kind, thoughtful, clever individuals who dedicated their lives to helping others – quite a conundrum really. They walked up to a reception desk.

'Excuse me. I'm Detective Inspector Peter Rumcorn. I believe a young man by the name of Adam Brant is here, possibly being treated for burns?'

The young lady in a white tunic, with the most perfect green nails, looked at him and Debbie. Rumcorn took out his identity badge and held it up prominently as he continued:

'I urgently need to know where he is.'

'Yes, there were two of them. Hold on.' She looked through a file in front of her, slowly turning the pages. 'I'm afraid you're too late,' she advised with little emotion.

'What do you mean too late?' Rumcorn asked, the veins in his neck becoming more prominent.

'It says here they left. Discharged themselves.'

'They're fifteen. Is that legal?' asked Rumcorn, looking around the entrance foyer, desperately hoping to see them.

'We can't lock them up at that age. I remember them now. Quite determined he was... the girl less so. Now, she had some sense, but not him. Nothing was going to keep him here. He simply refused to listen to the doctors and left.'

'What was the name of the girl who was with him?' asked Debbie, glancing at her badge and then adding, 'Vicky.'

'Oh, er... Adele.' Vicky looked back down at the sheet. 'Adele Martel. Odd name, isn't it?'

'And have you any idea where they went?' asked Rumcorn.

'Not a clue,' she said.

Rumcorn felt that summed it up completely.

'Can you remember anything they said, Vicky?' He moved a step closer and looked intently at her. 'It's really important.'

'Well, he was determined to see someone... someone around here.'

'Someone in hospital you mean?' asked Debbie.

'I think so. Fry, I think.'

'Fraser.'

'Yes, that was it, Fraser. Do you know him?'

Adam opened the door to Fraser's room; he was shocked to see him awake and looking at a magazine about mountain bikes. His head was bandaged and he had a lead that disappeared into a machine at the side of his bed trailing from one of the fingers on his left hand.

'Hi, Fraser. I'm Adam and this is Adele,' Adam said, as he continued into the room and looked over at Adele who had moved to the foot of Fraser's bed.

'You look like you need this bed more than me,' replied Fraser.

Adam turned to the side to a small sink with a mirror atop it. He looked at himself for the first time. His eyebrows, lashes and some of the hair at the front of his forehead were missing. He had dust on his head and his face had tiny red and inflamed spots. His wounds had been treated with a white cream that remained on the surface and was clearly not meant to be fully absorbed. He turned and glanced back at Adele. Her dark hair was now somewhat tangled and showed dust particles that matched his. He focused momentarily on the backs of her hands where she had the same wounds and treatment. She had saved him by pulling him from the burning building and he felt a surge of guilt for her suffering.

'You don't smell too good either,' added Fraser.

Adam moved closer to Fraser so he could see his eyes more intently.

'We were with you at Black Rock that day you fell. It's a long story but some pretty bad stuff has happened since.'

'Has anyone been hurt, apart from you two?'

'We're not sure exactly. My sister and our friend Jonathan are missing.'

'I'm sorry.'

'Do you remember why you fell? Did Miss Harper...?'

'I...' He looked down and fiddled with the clip that was attached to his finger. 'I'm sorry, I don't remember anything about the fall.'

'Darren told us that you had... well, an incident with Miss Harper. Can you tell us what happened?'

'Will that help you find your sister?'

'I'm not sure, but I think this is all connected.'

Adam watched Fraser turn away; he was looking at the door, then at the window. His fingers were rubbing the clip again that was attached to them. He saw the pain of the memory.

Adele moved around to the opposite side of his bed.

'We think this may have something to do with your losing Rebecca.'

Fraser's eyes narrowed and his lips tightened.

'Rebecca's gone, Fraser, but my friends, Chloe and Jonathan, they still may have a chance,' she said. She ran her hand across her face adding to the black smears that already marked her cheeks.

'I went to see Rebecca on Saturday and that's when I saw them. They were doing or rather getting something... something from Rebecca.'

'What do you mean, Fraser?' asked Adam.

'I don't know. It was like a big drill. Two men were drilling into the centre of Rebecca's grave; it was horrible. They had no right! No right to touch her!'

'It's okay, Fraser, calm down. No one can hurt Rebecca.'

Adam watched Fraser's face lose some of the colour that had so quickly appeared and he worried how far he should probe. He recalled the vision of the three circles that he and Adele had seen – the cuts in the grass at the centre of Rebecca's grave. He knew Fraser was not remembering a dream or hallucinating. In fact, it explained exactly how they were formed. It reminded Adam of the machine he had seen at the back of the school. The circles were not symbolic; they were taking samples. He felt his emotions rise and struggled to continue. He knew he must.

'Darren said you had a run-in with Miss Harper. Can you tell me what that was about?'

'When I arrived at High Peak School on Sunday, those men, you know the ones I'd seen, they handed a case to Miss Harper. It must have had...'

Adam watched Adele move closer; she cupped Fraser's hands

with hers. She was visibly crying now, tears slipping down her chin.

'It's okay. Don't say any more. We know,' she said.

The door opened swiftly, and in flew Inspector Rumcorn followed by PC Amott. Adam looked straight towards the window, but the bed would have blocked his path. Then he recalled they were on the third floor of the hospital. He turned back to face Rumcorn, who was clearly out of breath. For a moment, his eyes looked determined, and his forehead furrowed, but after they had made eye contact, something changed. Adam wondered whether it was because he looked so terrible.

'I'm not talking anymore. I don't want to think about anything. Please, just leave me alone,' said Fraser.

'Adam. And I presume this is Adele?' asked Rumcorn.

She nodded.

'Shall we go outside? I think we need to have a little chat, don't you? And please don't run off. I can and will catch you. I would hate to put you both up for the night. The beds are not so great in my hotel.'

They all left the room and when Adam glanced back at Fraser, he had already turned away, staring at the cover of the magazine. Adam felt Adele grab his hand as they moved down the corridor. PC Amott told them to sit in a waiting area. Rumcorn pulled a chair around and sat directly opposite them. PC Amott started filling plastic cups with water and passed one to Adam and one to Adele.

'I think we need to make a fresh start. Do you remember me, Adam?'

'You're the inspector from High Peak,' said Adam.

'Yes, and this is Debbie, okay?'

'Right,' said Adam. He wondered whether Rumcorn was stamping his mark, making it clear who was in charge. Adam sipped at his water.

'Why don't we start by you telling me what happened at the old schoolhouse?'

The inspector sat back and folded his arms, his gaze not leaving the two students. He waited. Adam's mind swam with images of the old schoolhouse, the smoke, the padlock and the hair band. He recollected the call he'd received from his stepfather.

'I can sit here all day, all night if necessary, but I think your sister and Jonathan might not be so keen to wait around.'

Adam's teeth clenched and his breathing became more audible.

'That's why I'm here; that's why I went into that burning building; that's why I'm not going to stop. Not until I find them.'

'You're not alone, Adam. There is a big, old force out there, and if there is anything you know that can help us find Chloe and Jonathan, then I strongly suggest you tell us.'

'They've been missing since last night.' Adam's voice was breaking but determined. 'And no one knows where they are. I've read stuff on the net. The first 24 hours are critical, then at 30 hours the likelihood is... well, I'm sure you already know. Adam looked down, his body deflating. He looked at his watch. 'We are already over twenty-two hours'.

'I'm not going to give up, are you?'

Adam looked to the side. Adele's expression was painful.

'They were at the old schoolhouse, inspector. They were being held there, but now they're gone,' said Adam.

'How do you know that?' replied Rumcorn.

Adam fished around in his pocket and pulled out the padlock and the black hair band.

'I found these at the schoolhouse. I'm sure this is Chloe's.' He felt Adele squeeze his hand. 'And one of the internal doors had a new lock on it. This padlock was on the floor, broken. There was a pool of fresh vomit on the floor.'

Rumcorn took the padlock using a handkerchief and passed it to Debbie, who dropped it into a plastic bag. Then he did the same with the hair band.

'Why didn't you tell the police at the scene?'

'I ran into the other room, where... I knew there was a fire, but I had to make sure they weren't in there. Surely you can understand that? She's my sister.'

'That doesn't tell me why you didn't tell the police afterwards, Adam.'

'Something happened... a back draft I think it's called. I was blown several feet back as soon as the door opened.' He looked again at Adele. 'I can barely remember Adele pulling me out, and the journey here to the hospital is... well, just a blur.'

'So, Adam, to be clear, you never actually got into the room that was on fire.'

'No.'

Adam regarded the inspector with suspicion. It seemed an odd statement, and he thought he saw a form of relief in the inspector's eyes.

Rumcorn continued, 'Okay. Why come and see Fraser and not go straight to the police?'

'I didn't think. I just needed to know what was going on. I needed to find Chloe and Jonathan. Nothing else matters,' replied Adam.

He stared straight back at Rumcorn, then looked down and started rubbing the back of Adele's hand, trying to eliminate the wounds he had caused. Everything was his fault. Rumcorn leaned forward.

'What do you think is going on, Adam?' he asked.

Adam looked back at the inspector.

'I think Dr Kovac or Orbelin or whatever his name is has taken them. I think he's been doing things at the school for years... tests.'

'Orbelin, Adam. Where did you get that from?'

Adam thought for a moment, his mind spinning. Then things started to shuffle into place and he wondered how much trouble he might be in, but it was a small price to pay if it helped find Chloe. He pulled out his mobile phone and touched the screen that remained cracked across the bottom. After a few attempts it worked and he passed it over to the inspector.

'I received this late last night. No, actually it was early in the morning. It all happened so fast.'

The inspector looked at it, but Adam also felt he looked confused.

'What?' asked Adam.

The inspector passed the phone over to Debbie and that too went into a plastic bag.

'Adam, I'm afraid your assumptions are wrong. Debbie and I went to see Dr Kovac yesterday, after receiving a note and some reports. Can we say now that these were sent by you?'

Adam nodded.

'Good. Well, I appreciate the correspondence, thank you. As I was explaining, we visited Dr Kovac yesterday, late in the afternoon, and unless he has a rocket-propelled car there is absolutely no way Dr Kovac was personally involved.'

Adam raised his arms with frustration.

'Adam, where did you find the reports?' asked Rumcorn.

Adam explained about the night the four of them had visited the Holloway twins. He said how he had touched a computer and it had come to life. He didn't elaborate where he had been at the time.

'Miss Harper and Brian Lambert, they're clearly involved. They could have taken Chloe and Jonathan,' said Adam. Then he continued enthusiastically, 'And they were missing from school this morning.'

'Brian Lambert was at the university and in a meeting with several other people, and I very much doubt Miss Harper could have overpowered two fifteen-year-olds. You need to leave this to us, Adam.'

Adam's shoulders sank.

Adele leaned in close to his ear and whispered, 'Don't give up, Adam. We've come this far.'

'Adam, are these reports the reason Chloe and Jonathan went to the university's open evening, to understand the science that is written in the script?'

Adam nodded.

'I can't hear you, Adam. We need to be open and honest now, for Chloe.'

'Yes, Inspector Rumcorn,' he replied.

'I need you to tell me what Fraser said. You've got some things wrong, so this time let me have all the information, and then we stand more chance of getting things right. We have more experience on how to deal with situations than you can possibly imagine. Trust me on that.'

Adam looked at Adele. She nodded and smiled at him.

'It's okay. People will understand.'

He told the inspector about his trip to Rebecca Johnson's grave and the circles and how Fraser had explained what had caused the disturbance. He related how he had then seen Miss Harper carrying a case handed to her by the perpetrators.

Adele moved closer to Adam.

'She as good as pushed Fraser off that cliff. He must have been terrified of that woman.'

'Okay, do your parents even know you are alright?'

'I didn't want to speak with... no, Inspector,' replied Adam.

Rumcorn put his head in his hands and breathed in through the gaps.

'I can go back with Adam. I was going to stay with... with Chloe,' said Adele.

Adam watched the inspector straighten his back and close his eyes; there was a momentary pause, as though he was contemplating an inner conflict.

'Adam, Adele, thank you for being honest with us. I'm afraid I do have to tell you something that you may hear shortly on the news. We have discovered two bodies within the burning room you were trying to enter.'

Adam rocked backwards and forwards his head shaking. Adele hugged him, tears flowing down her face.

'It can't be, it just can't be. Let me go see her,' said Adam.

'Adam, we can't do that. We don't know yet who we've found. So let's stay positive, for Chloe, yes.'

'Okay,' Adam shakily replied.

'I'm going to personally take you back to your house, Adam. An officer has been and spoken to your parents, and advised the current situation.'

The sound of a minute jet plane whooshed from the depths of Rumcorn's pocket; he took out a device and delicately touched the screen's surface. Adam watched his eyes scan whatever information had been sent. Rumcorn got up and spoke to Debbie. Adam strained his ears to pick up what was being said, but it was difficult, especially as his ears were still ringing from the blast. It felt better to focus on anything to take his mind off the situation.

'I've received the inventory of Dr Kovac's ownership and there's another house not far from here. I really want to take a look.'

'Would you like me to wait here with these two?' asked Debbie.

Rumcorn looked around and then at his watch before replying.

'No, let's call on the way back. Can you get Burns to run a check on the name Vladimir Orbelin, the name on the article Adam received?'

They travelled back along winding roads that were becoming ever whiter from the dust cast by trucks carrying limestone. The heart of the surrounding hills was under duress as a new topography was being gouged out. More often than not, they found themselves stuck behind the lorries as they negotiated the bends adjacent to sheer rock faces. Adam felt uncomfortable when peering down the valley over the edge of a road.

Queensway Road Buxton contained a row of Victorian terraced housing made from smooth, engineered bricks pressed tightly together like Lego, creating no pattern. The walls were broken only by contrasting stone surrounds to the windows and entrance doors. Each door had a circular pane of stained glass. From the outside at least, all the properties looked fairly well maintained, showing a more caring neighbourhood of homeowners.

Rumcorn parked across from number eighty-two. He turned around, looking intently at the two teenagers in the back seat.

'Do you think they might be being held here, Inspector?' Adam asked.

'I want to chat with the occupier. We won't be long, so you two please wait here. Okay?'

Adam and Adele nodded.

Rumcorn knocked pretty aggressively, a combination of urgency and concern. He stood back a little, looking intently for any signs of life. A rather frail old man came to the door, opening it wide and showing no fear towards his unknown visitors. He had intense lines across a face that now sagged. His back was bent at the top, giving him a curved round shoulder and causing his head to project oddly forward. Rumcorn found it difficult to gauge his height due to his stance. He wore grey trousers that at one time would have been part of a suit and a cream buttoned shirt complete with a maroon tank top.

'What do you want?' he rasped breathlessly in a tone that suggested he really couldn't be bothered any more.

'I'm Detective Inspector Peter Rumcorn and this is PC Debbie Amott,' said Rumcorn, showing the gentleman his ID.

'Anyone can get one of those, you know. I was offered one just the other week,' he replied.

'You are more than welcome to call the local police to confirm, Mr...' He paused.

'My name's Lambert, Harry Lambert. Well, I've nothing of value anyway, so come in if you wish,' said Harry.

They followed the elderly man into what was the front room and Debbie closed the door. Rumcorn was struck by the fusty stale smell of the place and he saw Debbie wince. He could also smell a hot vegetable odour.

'I've just microwaved some soup, if that's what your colleague is scrunching over,' said Harry. Debbie went red. Rumcorn was not about to correct him regarding what he believed to be the true cause of her nauseous reaction.

Rumcorn scanned the room for signs of occupation by two teenagers, unsure what evidence might manifest itself. The place looked quite bare: a smooth off-white wall housed a 1970s square wooden box of a gas fire with white-lined elements that would glow red when turned on. This floated above a quarry-tiled hearth. Rumcorn could well imagine a wrought iron fire surround would have originally occupied this space with an open coal grate. On top of the fireplace sat black and white pictures of a younger man than currently stood before him. He was embracing a lady with dark buoyant hair wearing a paisley patterned dress that sat tightly around her neck with no hint of a cleavage. To the right of the fire stood a lonely, worn, red cloth chair, stained black in the middle, where the old man clearly spent most of his days. In the left corner, between the fire and the outside wall close to the window, sat an old television, its screen flickering as the news played.

'We would like to ask you a few questions about Dr Kovac, Mr Lambert,' Rumcorn calmly stated.

'Good man, good man,' mumbled Mr Lambert, then said, 'Did wonders for my lumbago.'

'Is Dr Kovac your landlord?'

'Yes, but he hardly takes a penny and is always wanting to help me, he is. But I don't accept, not anymore.'

'Would you mind if we take a look around, Mr Lambert?' he asked.

'Are you one of those housing inspectors? Not easy, you know, for us pensioners on our own, like I is. Do what you want. No complaints from me on this place. Ain't goin' to no court, not against a great man like the doctor.'

Rumcorn nodded to Debbie, who instantly took off on an inspection of the property. He had no warrant but the gentleman tenant had agreed to let them in and look around.

'I'm a police inspector, not a housing inspector, Mr Lambert.' Rumcorn waited and observed, wondering if this man was slightly deaf or losing his faculties. Perhaps a tired brain. Then he continued:

'Can you tell me how you met the doctor, Mr Lambert?' Then he added, 'The great man.'

The faded old eyes focused initially on Rumcorn's then looked away, dancing around his room as though searching for that memory or struggling to make a conscious decision whether to impart what he knew.

'Such a long time ago. We had an advert in the paper. You can't do that now; probably not right then.'

'What kind of advert?'

Silence engulfed the room. The old man was looking down.

'Mr Lambert, what kind of advert?' Rumcorn pressed.

'Well, one asking whether we could help them out. My wife couldn't conceive see, no eggs or something. She was desperate, desperate for a child.'

'You wanted to adopt?'

'She would have done anything, anything. A massive gap for her it was. Then Dr Kovac turned up.'

Rumcorn thought there was nothing wrong with this man's long-term memory, but he was looking around the room again, searching as though something was missing.

'Are you okay, Mr Lambert? Would you like to sit down?'

Harry leaned forward, slowly turned around, and then used his hands for stability as he lowered himself into the armchair.

'He told us how he wanted to start afresh from Hungary. Terrible troubles over there in them days. Lost his wife in the riots. You've no idea, especially you young 'uns. You don't know what hard times are.'

'The doctor brought you a child?'

'It wasn't like that. He was with his child, Gillert. Thought the world of Gillert, he did.'

'But you did adopt the child?' Rumcorn asked.

'We looked after both of them. They both lived here with us. Gillert went to school. The doc struggled to get a job. A good doctor he was... still is.'

'And then?' Rumcorn encouraged.

Harry looked up and with increased volume said, 'Too much prejudice in this world. Nasty people not giving a decent human being a chance.' Harry lowered his head, energy lost, then continued. 'He started doing well eventually. Can't keep a good man down. He wanted to move away up to High Peak to start his own practice. Gillert didn't wanna leave. This had been his home, see, the only place the lad felt safe. So, so it was hard for Bence. He didn't want to stay here, didn't want to upset the boy. He used to call him Boyan, made me laugh. I think the doc had had enough of hard times, so we adopted Gillert and called him Brian. He preferred it. Mrs was beside herself. She about cried for a whole day. The boy's done well for himself now. He always was a bright lad, just like doc. Broke his heart when Mrs Lambert died. Bence did all he could. Nothin' doin' though. When your time's up, there's no changing it. Bence always looked after us, always visited the boy, his boy.'

Rumcorn could see Debbie going through the property's back door. He knew she would check all the outbuildings and cast an eye over the garden. He mulled over the information he'd been given. Things had started to fall into place as the old man was talking. Bence had a son and they had come here originally from Georgia and not Hungary, according to the article he'd seen on Adam's phone. The doctor had settled here, lodging with these people who wanted a child. Clever. These people were far more likely to support him, but then he had become attached, perhaps more than he wanted or intended.

'So, Mr Lambert, this place at that time would have been your house.'

'Course it was, but I lost my job. Cutbacks – that's what they say, isn't it? We were struggling. Mrs Lambert was getting worse and I would have lost everything. Brian could have gone to live with the doc, but he didn't want to. Bence helped us. He bought the place. He said "Just carry on and pay what you can". That man is the best thing that ever happened to us, to me.'

Debbie re-joined them in the front room. She shook her head marginally, advising Rumcorn that she'd found nothing.

'Happy are you now?' said the old man, staring at the returning woman.

'Thank you, Mr Lambert. Sorry for any inconvenience we may have caused,' said Rumcorn.

Adam watched as Rumcorn, followed by Debbie, returned to the car, trying to read any indications that they may have found Chloe and Jonathan. He remained quiet as Rumcorn sat for a minute and appeared to be contemplating before relating to Debbie everything that the old man had told him.

Adam stared out the rear window, but very little of the scenery actually registered as they travelled back towards Derby. He reflected on what he now knew. Brian Lambert was actually the doctor's son, and Miss Harper was Brian's girlfriend. He was sure the doctor had something to do with his sister's disappearance. However, everything he heard about the doctor always seemed good. No one had a bad word for him. Nothing made sense. He leaned forward towards the centre of the seats.

'The doctor has something to do with all this. We know he has been doing drug trials on the students at the school, and I bet Rebecca knew.'

'Adam, please, you need to leave this to us,' replied Rumcorn.

'Come on, Inspector. It's my sister, remember.'

Adam sat back heavily. The phone rang. It was Sergeant Burns.

'Sir, I have a few updates.'

Adam watched the eyes of Inspector Rumcorn viewing him through the rear view mirror.

'Go on, Sergeant, but be aware that we have Adam and Adele with us, classmates of the missing teenagers.'

'Okay, sir. The two persons discovered at the old school house, they've been identified as Brian Lambert and Stacey Harper.'

Adam felt a huge mix of emotions. He hugged Adele who was visibly crying again. Then he felt guilt as he thought about the teachers he'd been with just yesterday. Then fear... his sister and friend were still missing. He leaned forward again, grabbing the sides of the seat, and looked straight at the inspector's eyes in the central rear view mirror and said, 'It's five o'clock – six hours left.'

'Sergeant, please continue.'

'Well, I've done a check on "Vladimir Orbelin" as you asked. He was a Georgian bacteriologist working with their government in the late eighties. His wife died after contracting the plague. We are advised that Vladimir used to travel around as part of his work helping with disease outbreaks behind the Iron Curtain. Apparently he was a great scientist, recognised as having discovered a new strain of the plague, one he named "YPX1". It was the strain that ended his wife Lidya's life.'

'You said "was"?' said Rumcorn.

'Yes, sir! Vladimir Orbelin and his son Boyan are believed dead.'

There was a pause. Adam looked around at Adele who was looking straight back at him. She was clearly also taking in what was being said.

Burns continued, 'There was some sort of an incident in Georgia during a riot in 1989. Russian troops declared martial law on 150,000 peaceful protesters demanding independence from the Russian state. It was quite a messy affair by all accounts. There was an eyewitness that gave a statement advising that he saw both Vladimir and his son murdered by over-aggressive troops. On that night, twenty-two people died and thousands were injured. It started a civil war that lasted four years.'

'Thank you, Burns. One more thing. You said "Boyan". Was that Vladimir's son's name?'

'Yes, sir. Boyan Orbelin, and we are getting bombarded by the authorities from Georgia following our enquiries about Vladimir.'

'Oh, really!'

'They have advised us that Vladimir had a close friend known as "Daviti Isakadze". They've been looking for this man Daviti and his brother Levan for many years and say they are dangerous. They suspect Daviti is involved in many plots against the West and is a fanatic of Communist Russia. But Russia, I'm told, doesn't appear to support his extremist tendencies, if you can believe that. I've sent the latest photo we have of him around all the necessary agencies and emailed you and Debbie.'

All went quiet in the car again, apart from the road noise, and deep in Adam's ears a ringing continued.

'Inspector, can we see the photo?'

'You're unlikely to know such a criminal, Adam.'

'Like we didn't know Vladimir, you mean, or his son Boyan?' replied Adam.

'Fair point.'

Debbie clicked on the link she'd received and held it up for the two in the back. Adam struggled to breathe; his insides burned. Adele had inhaled in a squeak, putting her hand over her mouth.

'That's one of our teachers. We know him as Mr Ingham,' said Adele.

'Oh my God,' said Adam, rocking backwards and forwards. 'He's got Chloe! He's got Chloe!'

'Calm down, Adam. We don't know that.'

'Yes, we do! Yes, we do!' Adam was still rocking and tears were flowing down his face.

'Adam, what do you know?'

Adam struggled to speak; mucus was clotting his throat. 'He's – got – Chloe. On the floor... in the old schoolhouse, scribbled in the dust... *I__am*'. The middle bit had been rubbed, must have been caught when they were taken from the room... don't you see... Ingham!'

SATURDAY 18 JULY 2015 – 18:00

Adam got out of the car and walked to his house still clutching Adele's hand and followed by Rumcorn and Debbie. Adam struggled to comprehend that it was still only early in the evening. It felt like he had been awake for two days. His mother appeared at the front door and stared at him silently for the briefest of moments before running across the drive and hugging him. She was smaller than him now and Adam felt uncomfortable. His mother's sweet scent filled his nostrils and mixed with the damp summer air. He could hear his stepfather's voice booming from within the house and getting louder as he moved towards the front door.

'Krissie, is that Adam? Just wait till I get hold of that little shit,' shouted John Simms, as he stormed out of the front door.

Adam watched his stepfather do a double take when he spotted the scene that unfolded in front of him: Adam's injuries, the number of people that stood looking back at him. Adam enjoyed seeing this man fold inwardly, somewhat embarrassed. But he knew once the crowd had gone and it was just them then this man would vent his anger on him. His mother broke off and went to Adele, then hugged her just as silently.

Inspector Rumcorn stepped around Adam and walked up to

John. Adam's admiration for Rumcorn went to a new level as he saw the detective stop and stand closer than would normally have been comfortable. He was about the same height, perhaps a little taller, but there was no doubt about who owned the space that separated the two men.

'I'm Detective Inspector Peter Rumcorn. I take it you are Adam's… stepfather?'

'We are his parents, guardians. Have you found Chloe yet?' replied John.

'As you can see, Adam and Adele have been through a lot today,' said Rumcorn, directly to John. Then he turned his back on him and addressed Kristina. 'Adam has helped us massively with our enquiries. I'm hopeful we will locate Chloe soon.'

Kristina put her arm around her son and looked back at Rumcorn.

She said simply, 'Thank you… for bringing my son home, Inspector. They can both stay here.' Then she led Adam and Adele inside, leaving John and the two police outside.

Adam was surprised. It felt odd. His mother was so calm, not firing questions. She didn't show any emotion: she was there and yet not really there. The last twenty-four hours of sheer stress and worry had clearly affected her. Adam heard the sound of Rumcorn's car leaving and felt a new pang of concern; the inspector's presence had made him feel safe, secure. The front door slammed and the noise of shoe on wooden floor echoed through the hall.

'Well, what have you got to say for yourself?' demanded John, hands deep in his pockets, his face turning a shade deeper as he stared at Adam.

'Not now, John. We have a guest,' said Adam's mum, looking across at Adele, and then walking around the breakfast bar and switching on the kettle.

'Oh no, oh no, Krissie! He's not getting away with it this time. He plays you for a fool. What did the inspector mean? "Adam has helped us massively with our enquiries." Was it your fault? Do we have you to thank for Chloe running away?'

Adam stood his ground.

'Chloe did not run away; she has been abducted.'

He saw his mother flinch and grab at the countertop in front of her, and he regretted his words. Adele went around to her and held onto her. He could see Adele's lips moving, offering words of comfort, but he couldn't hear what she was saying.

'Know that, do you? Sure of that, are you?'

'Why would you think she would run away?'

Adam thought he saw an infintesimal shadow of guilt in his stepfather's eyes.

'I've no idea why she's missing, but I'm sure you're to blame. You rub people the wrong way. Stick your nose in where it's not wanted. You're not my biological son. There's no way any of my particles would create such a toe rag.' John grabbed hold of Adam's shirt just below the collar and pulled him close. 'What have you done to my beautiful girl?'

Adam felt his breath, but his mind was churning images of the past, trying to make sense of something that was forming deep in his thoughts. He had never heard his stepfather talk so passionately about anything before. They had argued, but this was different, and it made him want to throw up.

'Oh, my God. Have you ever touched Chloe?' he said, shocked at his own statement.

John leaned back, twisting his body with his right hand flying around hitting Adam's shoulder and sending him sprawling across the floor.

'How dare you. I would never hurt Chloe!'

Adam staggered away, moving around the open plan kitchen diner so the table afforded some refuge, like a toddler would avoid a parent set on chastising its offspring. He was almost as tall as his stepfather but he was by no means as well built. Flab or not, he was no match for him. Adam watched his mother run around the breakfast bar and shove the man hard in his chest. He staggered back slightly, his arms regaining his balance.

'I've seen the way you look at her. Oh, yes. You may not have touched her, but I'm damn sure you make her uncomfortable. And to think I've ignored it for years. Just thought perhaps that I was wrong.'

His mother's face was contorted now and her tears flowed. John grabbed the chair at his side and threw it back against the wall.

'Don't be so ridiculous, Krissie. This is him. He's poisoning you with his lies, getting into your head like a disease.'

Adam's mother stepped closer to John. They were virtually nose to nose now, her face red and determined. 'They say people like you always blame others. It's always someone else's fault, and you've pushed me around for far too long, John Simms. You're pathetic.'

John swung again, this time connecting with his wife.

'You little ...'

Adam moved to catch his mother, managing only just to stop her from hitting the floor. He kept hold of her and looked up at his stepfather with more hatred than he believed possible.

'Get out!' said his mother.

'You can't throw me out,' John laughed, as though the idea was absurd.

Behind the breakfast bar, Adele had used her mobile to make a call; it was at this point the other three took note of her conversation.

'Yes, Inspector. I believe we are in danger.'

She ended the call and looked up, noticing the silence that enveloped the room.

'Get out!' Adam's mother repeated to John.

'This is my house too, you know,' replied John, in a more subdued tone.

'That's not true. Ben and I bought this house and years ago you signed a paper to that effect. Somehow, something made me not fully trust you. I was stupid not to listen to my heart then.'

Adam couldn't remember the last time he'd heard his mother mention his real father's name, but it sounded nice. It felt good. Then his stepfather moved around the table towards them, sending it skidding into the wall. He was growling at them – a madman about to pounce. The door burst open and Rumcorn yanked John upwards and away from Adam and his mother. Adam was even more shocked to see John throw a punch at Rumcorn, but the inspector dodged it and sent a powerful blow to his solar plexus that completely took the wind out of him. Then Debbie grabbed him in an arm lock and marched him out the door.

'Are you two okay?' asked Rumcorn, as he pulled Adam's mum up from the floor. 'Mrs Simms, would you like to press...'

'Yes,' replied Kristina.

'Okay. I'll ask a local constable to visit, so you can make a statement here rather than have to go to the station. We'll keep him overnight. I suggest you file a restraining order.'

'Thank you, Inspector.' There was a pause before Kristina continued, 'Please... find my daughter.'

Adam watched the inspector. He had initially turned to go, then stopped, wearing an expression as though fighting some inner conflict.

'What's the matter, Inspector?' Adam asked.

'When you discovered the reports at the surgery, was there anything else that could confirm what was going on? Anything that would offer proof?'

Adam's mum looked at him confused.

'It's a long story, Mum.' He looked back at the inspector. 'We saw a lot of documents relating to the patients. There were lists of numbers against patient names. When we clicked on the number, it took us to the document we sent to you.'

'Rebecca knew,' said Adam.

'What makes you say that?' asked Rumcorn.

'This all started with her. She was smart. She knew what the doctor was doing. She had a diary that went missing and...' Adam paused, thinking hard. 'What about the letter she wrote, that Martin sent to her aunt?'

'How did you know about that?'

'The Holloway twins – sisters to Martin – they're at High Peak School. They told Chloe.'

'Good grief, you should join the force, Adam. I sent officers to check on that, but the aunt said she'd never received a final letter.'

'But that's silly. We know Rebecca sent letters to her regularly. How would she know which was the last one?' said Adele. 'Why don't we go? She may be more open with me and Adam rather than the police.'

'No, I need you both here safe. No more heroics.'

Adam turned to face Rumcorn.

'Please, let us go. I can't just sit around here. If it were your sister, what would you do? And an old lady isn't going to hurt me or Adele, is she?'

'Adam, absolutely not.'

THIRTEEN

AUNTIE ANNIE'S LETTERS

SATURDAY 18 JULY 2015 – 19:30

Adam ignored the order. There was no way he would stop now, not until Chloe and Jonathan were safe. He and Adele cycled up the hill out of Breadsall village. Adam felt the burn. His head hurt but not as much as his shoulder. This hill was never easy. Its steepness at the very peak tested the most ardent of bikers. The fresh air was soothing as they continued along the tarmac known locally as Lime Lane. They turned right onto Morely Road; fields ran to their left with wheat that had been harvested, leaving a light brown blanket flowing far into the distance. They were separated by random hedgerows. One portion of land had been developed between the cleared vegetation. It contained a modern building surrounded on three sides by green football fields. He could see young children being coached and running on the spot negotiating balls around cones using their feet, their youthful lives untouched by drama, emptiness and pain. On the right sat large detached houses with majestic drives giving way to opulent front porches. The ground sloped marginally downwards, making this part of the journey more pleasurable.

It was some distance before the area became more urban with a pub on the left. They crossed a roundabout then entered the old village of Chaddesden. It was a mix of pretty cottages, some over a hundred years old, and a late 1940s housing boom. The individual well-proportioned properties had front gardens that had been created to welcome back the troops that had survived the war.

The cool wind blew over them as they pedalled swiftly. Signs advised a change in road name to Park Lane, and the houses started to take up a loftier perch on either side of the main road. Adam was in the lead and turned left into Park View Close, which was fairly short, curved to the left and ended in a hammerhead. Adam thought these must be sought-after properties as they all backed onto the park. The wooden gate to number fifteen was painted fresh mustard yellow, and along with the whole front, looked pristine in appearance with well-maintained borders in which blossomed multi-coloured flowers of various shapes and sizes.

The 1940s porch gave a recessed entrance with low walls either side in line with the front brickwork. Adam reviewed the front door then looked at Adele, feeling a fresh surge of nervousness well up from within. He didn't stop to reflect too long; it wouldn't have helped to dwell on this emotion and he continued with the act of pressing the doorbell. It chimed louder than he'd expected. Adele looked shocked. She was gripping Chloe's pink and purple designed, hard-backed note pad.

'Adam, move behind me and let me do the talking.' He looked at her quizzically and she continued, 'Because you've lost your facial hair, remember. You'll scare her. And keep that hat on!'

Adam dashed to the opposite side of Adele just as a short, elderly lady answered the door. She had speckled grey hair and a round wrinkled face with a beauty spot on her left cheek. At one time it must have been much darker and would have added a mystic sense of charm. Now it stood raised, light grey and cracked. She wore a woollen top that covered her neckline and a thick woven skirt falling below the knee. Oddly, Adam felt there was something almost regal about her.

'Hello. Apologies for the intrusion. My name is Adele Martel and this is Adam Brant. Are you Mrs Annie Johnson?' she asked, a red tinge forming in each cheek.

'Yes.'

'We, er, my friend and I go to Dale School, part of the Jameson Academy.'

Adam felt scared now and wondered whether the lady had noticed the redness showing on Adele's face.

'And we, Adam and I, well, we want to do a school project over the summer about Rebecca Johnson. We want her to be remembered, that is to say, not forgotten, and we would be really appreciative if you would be kind enough, that is if you don't mind, telling us a little about her,' she continued in a babble of words projected far too fast. Adele stopped, waited and drew breath.

Adam desperately tried to gauge any expressions or emotions given off by this charming lady. He now felt quite awful about turning up – two young adults, nothing but strangers – at this person's door. She had suffered enough, and he wondered whether this was what it would feel like to be a reporter, turning up where you're not wanted and questioning people with no concern of conflict. It was exactly what his stepfather had accused him of, but he desperately wanted to know more: to find out anything that might help in the search for his sister.

The lady's face broke into a smile, perhaps a distant memory from way back when she herself had struggled to be brave in order to do something that was clearly difficult.

'You'd better come in then. Would you like some tea?'

They followed her into the house, across a narrow hallway and into a square lounge. The door had porcelain handles and fingerplate ironmongery. The room was minimalistic with plain cream walls. Along the left was a settee of beige, cream and gold that looked old-fashioned but was so pristine it could have just landed from a 1950s delivery truck. Against the wall and behind the door sat a dark wood drop leaf table, one half down and abutting the wall. The other leaf was up and complete with two matching chairs tucked neatly either side. In the opposite corner was a modern television that looked oddly out of place within this time capsule.

'Please have a seat. I'll put the kettle on,' she said, and as Adam watched the lady walk away, he felt a pang of guilt. He noticed her slightly bowed legs as she disappeared into the house. He exhaled and removed his baseball cap.

'Put that back on,' said Adele, forcibly grabbing it and helping him replace it.

'I can't sit inside with a cap on. It'll look odd.'

'If she sees you without it, we'll be thrown out, Adam. You really do look scary with half your hair singed at the front.'

He decided not to argue and they sat nestled in the soft yet firm sofa. His ears pricked up on a murmur of goings on from somewhere within the depths of the house.

Mrs Johnson returned sooner than he thought possible for a kettle to boil, pulling behind her a gold trolley. The top level housed a steaming pot of tea covered with a green jacket and a bone china jug of milk with three cups and saucers. The lower level held two plates with what looked like homemade shortbread biscuits. Adam poured the tea and they helped themselves to a biscuit, on Mrs Johnson's insistence. He realised that they hadn't eaten since that morning at High Peak School. They tasted delicious. Adam now considered how best to continue. Adele had done well so far, but he wasn't sure how to get the conversation going again. His momentary pause was broken by Mrs Johnson.

'I'm not really sure where to begin. I believe Rebecca was

much like yourselves. Is there anything specific you were thinking about?'

'Firstly, we must say we are really sorry for your loss. If this is too upsetting, Adam and I would perfectly understand and would absolutely not mind if you would prefer not to discuss Rebecca,' said Adele.

Adam struggled. He knew why she'd said this, but he for one was not for walking away. Not now.

'Thank you, I don't mind. What made you think about doing this for Rebecca?' asked Mrs Johnson.

'My friends and I have just spent a week at High Peak School and, well, we – that is our class got to talking about Rebecca, especially after the events of... of...' Adele broke off.

Adam realised how stupid he had been: how stupid both of them had been. Of course, Fraser Johnson – he would be another member of this lady's family. They had been so focused on Rebecca. Adam felt a huge wave of fresh guilt and embarrassment. Adele looked at him.

'I think you're referring to the accident at the school and my great nephew, Fraser.'

'I'm so sorry. I think we'd better leave. We clearly didn't think this through,' said Adam as he started to get up. Adele grabbed his arm and rose at the same time.

'Adele, is that right?' Mrs Johnson asked, not moving but wanting confirmation of her name. 'I'd like you to stay. It's been a dreadful time for us. My brother-in-law Bernard had two sons, Ian and Alan, and Ian married Gillian. They are currently in hospital with Fraser. We should all remain positive.'

'Mrs Johnson,' said Adam, removing his hat. 'I was in hospital earlier today and I've seen Fraser. He's doing really well.'

He saw Adele's eyes widen. She gripped his arm more tightly

and brought her other hand over to hold his.

'That's wonderful news... thank you. Have you had an accident?'

'It's a long story, but yes, I was caught in a fire explosion.'

'Oh, my word, young man! You should be at home.'

'Mrs Johnson, we believe the people who hurt Fraser and caused Adam's accident are... holding his sister and our friend Jonathan hostage,' said Adele.

Adam saw fear flash across the old lady's face.

'That's the real reason we're here.' Then he added, 'I must find my sister.'

'But what's that got to do with Rebecca?'

'We think she knew something, something about what was going on at High Peak, something that Dr Kovac was doing at his surgery.'

'Lilly has said how wonderful Dr Kovac is. He's cured so many elderly people in the village. There was a pause. You think that Rebecca didn't have an accident?'

'I'm so sorry, but yes, we are convinced after all that has happened that something else caused her to be in that storeroom, but we really have no proof,' said Adam.

'After all these years, I've never really been convinced about what I was told. Yet I chose to accept it. Never kicked up enough fuss, I suppose.'

Adam saw her elderly eyes glaze and stare beyond where he and Adele were sitting.

'If you could tell us anything about Rebecca it may help us. It may not solve the puzzle about her, but it might save my twin sister, Chloe.'

Mrs Johnson's eyes refocused on Adam.

'Of course, I've just heard on the news – Chloe and Jonathan.

That's terrible. What is it you wish to know?'

'Please, can you tell us anything about Rebecca?'

'Well, my nephew Alan sadly died many years ago, not long after marrying Katie. They had Rebecca, but Katie struggled after we lost Alan through a terrible accident at work. She didn't cope well and found solace in alcohol. At that point, Rebecca came to live with me. She loved the park and went to the library almost every day. Fraser often joined us back then and they would play in the garden. He was quite a bit younger than she, but Rebecca didn't mind. They were good times. Have some more tea. I find it always helps,' said Mrs Johnson.

Adam refreshed their cups and sipped the warm liquid. The heat soothed his sore throat and he thought she was right. It did make him feel better.

'Rebecca loved my stories of the olden days, of how Lilly and I would play tricks in the village at High Peak. Lilly is now the postmistress. She didn't ever move from that area. Quite strange how things turned out that Rebecca ended up in the same place.'

Adele looked a little sheepish.

'It was Mrs Forshaw who gave us your address,' she said, her eyes looking apprehensive.

'Ah, well, I'll phone her and thank her for some company. I don't get much of that these days,' she said, smiling at them.

Adam wondered if the old woman had actually remembered that he had told her his sister was missing. She was rambling on, not helping him find Chloe.

'Mrs Johnson, we would love to understand about Rebecca from Rebecca's point of view. Do you have any of the letters that she sent? Mrs Forshaw said she wrote regularly. I hope you don't mind me asking,' said Adele.

Adam felt elated. Adele was clearly brilliant, and he looked over at Mrs Johnson, who looked back at them both, a certain amount of guilt showing in the wrinkled lines of her face.

'I do believe I've been... well,' she got up slowly from the dining chair. Her stiffness appeared to ease as she moved further towards them and the door. 'Come upstairs with me, both of you. You can help me get the shoe box down in which I keep all Rebecca's letters.'

Adam and Adele followed the old lady out of the room and up the stairs. Each step took considerable effort and time as every move was carefully negotiated. In the back of his mind, Adam thought that she wouldn't be independent for much longer unless she had a chair lift installed.

Once on the landing, she moved more swiftly, entering a room on the left. All the doors at this level resembled the ground floor, with mustard-coloured opening leaves and white frames. The door Mrs Johnson had entered had a small ceramic plaque with 'Rebecca's Room' written on it with pink flowers dotted in the bottom right-hand corner. They followed and were immediately taken with the view of the park through the window. The old lady stood in the corner looking at the wall with the bed against it. Posters of Take That and the Stereophonics remained and to the left were shelves housing schoolbooks, some of the spines of which gave rise to recognition.

'Rebecca loved this room. I rarely come up here now. Up there on the shelf to the right of the books is a white shoebox. Can you reach it, dear?'

Adam, being taller, stretched up and pulled down the white box. To the right-hand side of the bed stood a low cream table housing a silver alarm clock with a white face, black numbers and hands. At the side of the clock sat a wooden frame with a photo of Rebecca standing next to Fraser. She was looking at Fraser with an expression of understanding, as though he had done something wrong which she knew about, and that he had at some point thought he may have got away with. Mrs Johnson had also focused on the photo.

'They were both so young, more like brother and sister really.'

For the first time, Adam saw the sadness in her eyes – life's screen cracking just a little. They made their way back downstairs, the younger ones ahead with the box held tightly in Adam's hands. Mrs Johnson pointed at the table invitingly.

'Please sit at the table. It will be easier,' she said.

'Are you sure about this, Mrs Johnson?' asked Adam.

'Yes, absolutely. You two carry on. Would you like a sandwich? It's well past dinner,' she replied.

'We really don't want to be any trouble, Mrs Johnson,' said Adele.

'It's no trouble. As I said, it's nice to have some company and I'm better known as Auntie Annie. Do you both like salmon?'

They looked taken aback at her generosity and thought she must be feeling very lonely with no children of her own and Rebecca now gone. Adam glanced at Adele.

'Yes, we do. That would be great. Thanks.'

'Wonderful. I'll go and rustle up something. Please, carry on,' said Auntie Annie, smiling at the teenagers clearly enjoying their visit. Adam watched Annie leave then turned to Adele.

'She's amazing. She takes everything in her stride, but I fear she's vulnerable. We could be anybody.'

'Yes, I know what you mean,' he replied, but his mind was elsewhere.

He glanced down at his watch and saw it was 8.30 p.m. He turned directly to Adele and mouthed 'two and a half hours left'. She ignored him. He refocused on the shoebox with the realisation that they might be holding the key to all the unexplained events that had occurred at High Peak. He pulled off the lid. He could hear cupboards opening and closing, and the sound of crockery tinkling on plates emanating from the kitchen. The box was jammed with letters. They were neatly placed, forming a row, and Adam could well imagine them being arranged neatly in chronological order. The lady who lived here wouldn't have done it any other way. His fingers trembled as they pulled out the first letter.

The edge of the envelope had been finely cut and on first glance it was barely noticeable that it had ever been opened. He removed the letter, unfolding it and smoothing it out flat on the table. He felt a sense of privilege: a strange honour to be allowed to read someone else's private script. His first impression was of its neatness. This letter had been written not long after Rebecca had arrived at High Peak School in her first year. It showed order and a structure Adam believed he himself wouldn't have possessed at the same age.

10th Sept 2007

Dear Auntie Annie

Hi, hope you are well. My first week at the school has been really nice. I was scared at first leaving home, but the teachers are kind and everyone else is just the same as me. We've been split into four classes. I'm told things get quite competitive between the classes, but I don't think I am really bothered about that.

I like it that there are not so many children here, not like my last school. There is loads of great stuff here. I've seen badminton courts, trampolines, even a climbing wall and canoes. Apparently there will be other schools and some people that go to work will come here to do activities, but that's not allowed yet until we all get settled into the place.

There is a dinner lady called Mrs Pig. I struggled not to laugh when I heard her name, but she actually knows Aunt Lilly at the post office.

Missing you. Lots of love,

Rebecca

There was something pure about it, with the intimacy of innocence. Adam started to reflect on what exactly they might gain from this review of general life at the school. After all, they kind of knew from their own experiences. Adele pointed to the opposite side of the box. Tightly packed against the end cardboard wall was a much thicker envelope. If it were ordered as he thought it should be, then this would be the last one that Rebecca had sent. Adam pulled out the letter. It was not just thicker but longer too than any of the others in the box. He turned it over in his hand and it was clear that, unlike the others, this had definitely remained sealed. Adam's stomach clenched involuntarily... a mixture of excitement with an overwhelming sense of dread. Adele focused intently on the package that Adam kept rotating.

'This must be it: the last one, the one that Martin sent. It's never been opened. The date on the postmark is 30 July 2010. That's after Rebecca died.'

Mrs Johnson returned, moving into the room closely followed by the trolley holding sandwiches, sticks of neatly cut celery, more biscuits and a fresh pot of tea all laid out on the same design of the bone china crockery service.

'Er... Aunt Annie,' said Adam, feeling quite odd using the title with someone he'd just met. 'This one looks like it's not been opened.'

She suddenly looked forlornly at the floor and sank lower into the folds of the settee.

She said, 'I'd completely forgotten or maybe I just blanked out that horrid affair. Somehow I could never bring myself to open it.'

'Well, it's not right for me to do it. We'll have a bite to eat then leave you in peace,' Adam replied.

'Adam, I would actually like you to open it for me.'

Inside Adam's head a voice was saying, 'I don't think I can, but I desperately want to'. He instinctively looked to Adele for support. She nodded. He simply couldn't rip it open. Tearing it jaggedly would almost be a crime.

'Do you have a letter opener, please?' he asked.

The old lady didn't move. Adele picked up a knife from the trolley and passed it to Adam, who inserted the blade under a tiny gap at the edge. He continued delicately along the natural crease. To keep it neat was more difficult as its contents were so compacted. Adam carefully removed the contents, his hands shaking as he tried to remain composed, if only for this lovely lady who had requested his help.

Within the folds was a set of pages stapled together in the top left corner. They had clearly been torn from a diary. There was also a separate sheet of normal A5 notepaper that Adam realised was an accompanying letter. He picked up the letter that was written in the same beautiful handwriting as the first he'd looked at and in the same formal manner. He thought again how meticulous this girl was and how very much like her aunt she had been.

10th July 2010

Dear Auntie Annie,

I'm writing to ask your advice and hope you do not think badly of me, or that I am being extremely silly. Your thoughts are very much cherished by me. I believe I may have witnessed something that has troubled me these last few months. One night after arriving back at the school late from a netball match, I was hungry so went to the kitchens.

The place was completely deserted apart from me, then I noticed Dr Kovac from the health centre. He did not see me, but I watched him. He was doing something to the food that had been prepared for our supper. Later, I saw Martin, my very good friend who I often write about. He was eating some of the same food that Dr Kovac was touching earlier. Then Martin fell ill. I was so worried and it all felt really wrong, but I could just be mistaken. Martin is fine now although he was off school for over a week.

I wanted to know if I had really been wrong. So I've been watching the kitchens at night in the shadows for months and the doctor returned many times, and each time one of the pupils has been taken ill within a day or so, sometimes they're off for a week like dear Martin, but sometimes only a couple of days. I have even seen Mr Lambert our PE teacher catch the doctor in the kitchen and he was really angry with him, but he left him there and went away and nothing has come of it, which made me more nervous. I don't want to talk to the teachers here in case they tell Mr Lambert, and he is angry with me for making up stories.

I have enclosed my diary that goes through the events and my school stats project that I decided to do so I could legitimately ask if students were absent due to illness. It clearly shows our school having the worst record for absent pupils compared with others in the Jameson Academy and also in comparison to other local authority-run schools.

I feel so much better just writing to you about this; it's been on my conscience for so long now I didn't realise just how worried I have been. I am probably being silly and I don't want you to worry. I am fine, just tired and a little achy; perhaps too much exercise. Please write back soon and tell me what you think.

Love you lots
Rebecca

Adam's eyes filled with tears. His suspicions were right. Something sinister was occurring, but he wasn't sure it would help Inspector Rumcorn. His eyes met the old lady and he saw she too was crying.

'Is it a suicide note, dear?' she asked.

'No,' replied Adam, which made the woman look curiously at him.

'Well, I guess that's something,' the old lady said.

How could he explain? At some point she would know, but the pressure on his young shoulders felt too much to bear. He didn't know how to begin.

'Rebecca is... er,' he paused, 'it's a school project.' He paused again. 'She's sort of asking for advice about it,' was all that came out.

'What kind of advice?'

Adam couldn't speak anymore. He handed the letter to her and she took it slowly, beginning to read its contents.

'Graham, I can't thank you enough,' said Adele, leaning around Adam in the front seat of the minibus to look directly at Graham Bates. 'I can't believe I left my stuff at High Peak.'

Adam just sat there trying to smile and make out everything was normal. Yet the day had been so far removed from normal he couldn't possibly start to run through it with Graham. It was dark now and the clock on the dashboard showed 10.30 p.m. A voice inside Adam's head said 'half an hour left'. There was no point in sharing this with Adele and he reflected on just how much he hated statistics. He knew one thing. He had to get back to High Peak. Somehow he knew Chloe was still there.

FOURTEEN

VLADIMIR'S PENITENT JOURNEY

SATURDAY 18 JULY 2015 – 08:00

Chloe felt mentally and physically drained. She watched the doctor pulling out bandages and what looked like tweezers from the cupboard as she sat on the edge of the bed. It was soft, clean and warm. She reflected on leaving the old schoolhouse. She hadn't been keen to go with Dr Kovac. She wasn't sure why she'd decided to trust him in the end. Jonathan had got up with some support and had just walked off, as though this were normal. Certainly the thought of leaving that awful place was compelling and when he cut them free of their bonds it all seemed too good to be true, but something still felt wrong. Where were the police? Even now, now they were back here at the school, or practically anyway, it was still only them. She thought Jonathan might be suffering from shock. He'd barely uttered a word, just followed like some sort of sheep after Dr Kovac. Did Jonathan not remember that this man was not who he said he was? He was an imposter.

'Why are you doing this?' she asked.

'Would you rather I'd left you in the old schoolhouse?' replied Dr Kovac, pulling open Jonathan's shirt and revealing the extent of the cuts caused by glass from the floor of the schoolhouse.

'That's just stupid. I'd rather you'd called the police and we got to go home.'

'You both need medical treatment. First aid is important.'

He sprayed something from a bottle that had no writing on it and pulled the tiny pieces of glass from Jonathan's side with tweezers. Chloe watched, somewhat bemused that Jonathan barely flinched.

'I don't need you to touch me,' she said. Then she thought about this school and the sick bay with its odour of bleach. She had no idea what came over her, but she asked:

'What happened to Rebecca?'

The doctor stopped what he was doing and turned to look at her. Slowly, he inclined his head and breathed out. His shoulders sank and he faced the floor before he spoke again.

'She became infected, infected with *Yersinia pestis* X1. There was nothing I could do.'

'The plague? Was she one of your trials?' Chloe asked, and then wondered why she hadn't been more cautious. A flicker of uncertainty shimmered somewhere within her.

'Absolutely not! I would never, never...'

'But you do carry out trials, don't you? On the students.'

'Minor ailments... I always have the cure. I just needed to get the balance right. It has saved hundreds of lives,' said Dr Kovac, his eyes now appealing directly to Chloe.

'That doesn't make it right. The students didn't agree to be guinea pigs.'

She felt sickened and wanted to be away from this man, far away. He made her skin crawl. It reminded her of when she had first set eyes on the doctor that day on their walk near the gorge.

'What were you doing at Padley Gorge? I saw you with a plastic bag.'

'I was collecting samples from a dead carcass.'

'That sheep. That really is disgusting. It smelled vile. Hungry were you?'

The doctor snorted with concealed laughter, but continued extracting glass from Jonathan's wound.

'I'd seen two patients with the same bacterial infection. They had both walked along that path by the gorge. They both had insect bites on their legs. I collected samples hoping to find the same bacteria. If the sheep was the source, then where the bacterium grows so too will a virus that will consume it. It's called Phage therapy. I can work the virus to create a cure for my patients.'

'Why not just give them antibiotics?'

'One of the patients suffers from stomach digestion issues and antibiotics would kill all the good bacteria. The patient would potentially suffer even more.'

Chloe shuffled uncomfortably. She felt saddened that this clever person didn't know where the line of acceptable behaviour lay. She hated him but perplexingly at the same time she admired the man.

'That disease... the plague. How did Rebecca get that, if you didn't infect her?'

'I've no idea. I did have cultures in my laboratory. I admit that. I was working on finding a cure; it has been my life's ambition, but that bacterium is safely locked away.'

'Clearly not that safely!' Then she thought about the fire. 'So you decided to save your own arse by covering up Rebecca's death in a fire.'

'You have no idea how this particular strain of the plague works. If I had not taken such action, hundreds if not thousands of people would have died.'

'Oh, spare me the bullshit. Maybe if you had called the right numbers. Then just maybe the right people and organisations would have solved the problem. Oh, hold on. You'd probably be behind bars where you belong.'

She got up and walked into the en suite. Splashing her face with water felt quite exhilarating. She realised just how thirsty she was and held her head under the tap, drinking like she hadn't seen water in weeks. She filled a cup and took it back to Jonathan. He accepted it silently.

'Are you okay?'

He just nodded as the doctor carried on, working his way down picking at the glass.

'So, where does Mr Ingham come into this?' she asked.

'He was from Russia. He and his family moved next door to me in Georgia. He was a good friend and helped me and Boyan escape from that country during the uprising, just at the outbreak of the civil war.'

'He must be a real pal. He decided to help you again, did he? To get rid of Jonathan and me because we'd discovered your secret. So you could carry on your cosy little lives.'

'You have no idea what it was like in those days.'

Chloe inhaled all the air she could muster before exploding.

'Really, you want to try being drugged, locked in a derelict building, tied up, gagged, and having to jump up and down on your best friend's back in the dark while he's choking to death on his own vomit. I can assure you it's not a barrel of fun, doctor.'

'I'm sorry. I'm so sorry about that. I can assure you I wish I'd never met Daviti, but please don't shout.'

Chloe watched him as he nervously looked towards the window and the door.

'What's the matter? Does he know we're here?'

'Hopefully not and I'd like to keep it that way. Hold this.'

Chloe put her hand on the bandage just where the doctor had indicated.

'Why are you helping us?' she asked.

'I fear Daviti has a different agenda. I believe he was planning to use YPX1 to carry out ethnic cleansing and keep the remedy for a chosen few. But I've stopped that. You see I have had a breakthrough. I...' He stopped and looked directly into Chloe's eyes. 'Stacey got me samples from Rebecca's body.'

'That really is gross. Just like you did from the dead sheep.'

'Yes, I found and isolated the virus that consumes this bacteria. I've already sent the bacteriophages that provide the cure to all the main laboratories in Europe. It will save countless lives. My quest is over. I'm a doctor and a scientist, not a killer.'

'Good to know,' she replied wryly.

'Now, are either of you allergic to paracetamol?' They shook their heads. 'Right, take a couple of these each while I phone the police. They can collect you from here.'

Chloe looked closely at the white tablets she'd been given and watched Dr Kovac pick up the telephone receiver that hung on the wall. She watched him press nine three times and ask for the police. This gave her some comfort, so she swallowed the tablets.

Chloe felt numb and sore. She ached. She laid herself down on one of the twin beds in the warm, clean environment and drifted off to sleep.

On the reception counter in the practice surgery below a light was flashing on the telephone. It indicated that the phone in treatment room two was in use, but it didn't have a direct line. The doctor calmly replaced the receiver.

SATURDAY 18 JULY 2015 – 22:30

Darkness waned gradually as Chloe came around for the second time in a strange environment with the realisation that the tablets she took were not paracetamol at all but a sedative that had induced a deep slumber. Outside the windows it was dark. They'd skipped a day. Her eyes met Jonathan's and he immediately asked if she was okay. This pleased her so much; he looked much better and it felt as if he'd returned from somewhere.

In the distance she could hear a voice coming from downstairs. She lifted the telephone receiver and listened. There was no tone – nothing. Chloe grabbed Jonathan's hand and guided him from the room. As they crept downstairs, she thought she would surprise the doctor this time and hit him with anything she could find. She stopped just outside the door, deciding to watch first and assess what he was doing before confronting him. Moving slowly she peered around the gap in the door and saw him seated at his desk. He was holding a vanilla envelope. Just as she was about to enter, he moved and picked up the telephone.

'I'm Dr Bence Kovac of High Peak surgery. I have with me upstairs the two students from Jameson Academy – the two reported as missing.' He paused and then continued, 'Yes, that's what I said. Now, please, can you send someone to take them home?'

Chloe watched him absentmindedly place the receiver on the desk and not back on the handset. Then he leaned back, taking something from his top drawer. She could hear a tiny voice in the distance, coming from the phone. She remained silent, immobile, rooted to the spot. She watched as he wrapped a strap around his bare arm just above the elbow and was transfixed as he held up a hypodermic. His eyes checked the tube and the fluid within. He inserted the sharp steel into his raised vein before she found the strength to move out from behind the door, followed by Jonathan still tightly holding her hand.

Chloe saw the doctor's eyes widen; he dropped the hypodermic to the floor as he got up, flailing his arms wildly.

'Go back upstairs! Don't watch this! The police are coming. I promise you I... I just don't want to spend the rest of my life behind bars. This is a better way... it's what I deserve.'

Then he abruptly stopped talking and his mass slowly dropped to the floor. He crumpled, helplessly losing strength. Chloe fell to her knees. Jonathan attempted to hold her as she struggled to get to the doctor. She watched the doctor's body take on a new involuntary state as a massive muscular reaction erupted and he started shaking violently. He shook continually, banging his legs into the desk and chair. Chloe started to scream. She felt Jonathan pull her back, his arms locked around her waist and then he tumbled forwards as something or someone shoved both of them further into the room.

'Well, here you all are. How nice,' said Daviti entering, closely followed by his brother. Daviti's movements quickened when he saw the scene before him. He snatched the envelope, ripping it open and reading its contents. He tore the pages and threw them across the room before striding over and gripping the doctor's collar. He lifted him off the floor by several inches. The doctor's entire body was convulsing now and foam was oozing from his mouth.

'You have betrayed your country, Vladimir, and disgraced your family.'

He looked around the room and forced the doctor's head around so he could see Chloe and Jonathan. Lowering himself, he whispered into Vladimir's ear.

'I know you can still see and hear everything, Vladimir. I can't allow these two to survive. You have wasted years of my life, it saddens me that the only vengeance I have now is to make sure you know Boyan, your son and Stacey are already dead. Know that... before you die.'

Jonathan made a move to escape, but Levan pulled a gun, pointing it at Jonathan's heart.

'How could you, Mr Ingham?' shouted Chloe.

Daviti turned around to his accomplice but replied to Chloe, 'I'm not who you think I am. My name is not nor has it ever been Ingham.'

He looked directly at his brother.

'We need to move fast now, Levan.'

Levan walked around the room and pointed his gun at the doctor's head.

'Leave him. He's dead anyway. We need to take these two for a walk.'

Chloe took her chance. She thought she had little to lose. They were going to kill her and Jonathan anyway. She shoved the man hard in the back at the precise moment he'd taken his eyes off them. It forced him to topple over Daviti. She glanced at the doctor's eyes as the two men fell over his body and thought she saw a small light of recognition, of hope. She grabbed Jonathan's hand, pulling him through the door, and they ran along the corridor.

They'd left the metal door to the consultation room corridor open. Chloe ran through the opening and then spun on the spot, yanking Jonathan around and using her free hand to throw the door leaf shut. They listened to the mechanism purr electronically. A tiny light on the pad went red then it purred again and went green.

'Oh no!' Jonathan wailed.

Chloe slammed a finger onto the keypad. Again the mechanism churned, sending the tiny light red; but this time it stayed red. Two shots were fired from somewhere on the other side, ringing out loudly like a gong being struck. The first lodged in the metal. The second hit the same spot and punctured through, splitting the metal and leaving a jagged hole at its centre. The time lag allowed for the narrowest of escapes for the teenagers as the second bullet, complete with tiny fragments of metal, zipped across Chloe's arm, cutting the flesh but missing the bone. She screamed as the searing pain registered in her brain.

The front entrance doors were locked, but only from the outside. The right-hand external door held the fire alarm – a condition the fire officer had insisted on following that awful night five years ago. Chloe hit the tube hard with her fist and it shattered, spraying the smallest of thin glass pieces and giving full access to the release pad. She pushed hard and the door flew open. They spilled out into the health centre car park. She held tightly to Jonathan. There was no way she was going to let him go. They had been through far too much to be separated now.

They ran as fast as they'd ever done in their lives and had just disappeared around the corner when they heard their pursuers. A bullet pinged off the corner wall of the building behind them, hastening their pace as they fled along the rear of the building. The gap between the school and the new sports facility was welcomed and they took it, removing them from direct line of sight, and in Chloe's mind, affording shelter from the bullets. The dirty boot entrance looked dark and foreboding. No use trying to break into the school. They continued straight out and to the front.

The main vehicular access meandered into darkness with the exception of the odd light perched on top of the bollards along the road's length. The lights seemed to do little to break the bleak depths of black nothingness. Chloe decided the best hope they had would be amongst the trees, to hide in the wood and possibly make their way back through to the main road. Then maybe a passing car would give them safe passage away from this place. She pulled Jonathan through the front car park and into the woods. At the sound of their pursuer's footsteps on gravel they froze, then jumped sideways, taking refuge behind two giant trunks and letting go of each other's hand in the process. She felt the cold night air on her clammy palm.

The light from a powerful torch spread its beam through the trees, casting shadows in all directions. It had gone surprisingly quiet with the exception of a slow breeze across the high canopy of old oaks. Chloe's heart was pounding and her arm was stinging. Her pulse was rapid and shallow. Shock was taking hold and she wondered whether the noise of her thudding pulse would give away their position. She remained rigid and almost on tiptoe, arms tight by her side – an illusion of thinness. She heard distant voices mumbling a language she couldn't understand.

A shot whizzed through the foliage, a more muffled thump than earlier, hitting a tree to Chloe's left.

A sound escaped Chloe. Their location was compromised. The dark stranger they now knew as Levan stood with his silenced gun less than four metres from her. Chloe became a solid statue of flesh, liquid and bone, fused to the spot.

Whack! From the corner of her eye she caught a glimpse of something flash downwards, thin at one end and wide at the other. It hit Levan smack bang on the back of his head. Daviti appeared, flashing his torch about searching feverishly for the assailant. The circle of light stopped moving and Chloe could clearly see her brother holding a club.

'Adam, you surprise me. What are you doing here? I had no idea you were so resourceful,' Daviti said smugly, as he moved slowly towards Adam.

Chloe's sharp intake of breath resonated with fear.

'You have to be stopped, Mr Ingham. It's over.'

'Oh, Adam. You look like you've had a hard day? We are very far from over; we are just getting started.'

Daviti moved stealthily and swiftly and with surprising fluidity for such an old man. He pulled a blade from inside his jacket and thrust forward with a trained stroke. Adam flinched to one side, but it was too late. The steel disappeared into him, twisting Adam's body around.

Whack! Something hit Daviti straight in the face. Its force sent him backwards. He staggered in the direction of Chloe, totally disoriented. Before he had the chance to take another step, Chloe kicked out hard, her toe gaining power from her whole body twisting. She released all the energy she had left. As she connected with his groin area, a crunching sound resonated through the night air and he fell to the ground.

The knife fell from his hand. Chloe looked up at the silhouetted figure of Adele holding a garden shovel. She had it poised at the back of Daviti's neck, making sure he wasn't going to move. Chloe moved as quickly as she could over to Adam. He was upright, but on his knees with his hand over the wound in his side. A red stain seeped slowly across the cloth of his shirt. She embraced him with her good arm, holding him tight. He wrapped his free arm around her and then placed his chin on her shoulder. She felt him settle as she took some of his weight.

Adam whispered into her ear, 'I'm so sorry, Chloe. I shouldn't have got us involved.'

'Don't be silly. You didn't do this, they did. You helped us. You didn't give up. We can go home.'

As Chloe said the last four words, she lost some of her strength and a little of the weight between them shifted.

'It's okay now, Chloe. John's gone and he'll never come back,' said Adam. 'I can't believe you didn't ever tell me.'

'He always gave me the creeps. He kissed me a few times and not like a father. I felt his eyes watching me. It felt wrong. There I've said it. I wish I'd told Mum, but I just wanted her to be happy.'

At that moment flashing lights erupted, complete with a cacophony of sirens disturbing the night.

Warm summer air drifted across the open-air leisure complex as screams of merriment could be heard on the other side of a deep blue pool.

'Now I'm in heaven,' said Jonathan, as he lay sunbathing on white wooden beds in the French region of the Rhone Alps just north of Bourg-on-Bresse.

'Well, we all deserve a break,' replied Adele. Then she continued, 'Chloe, I've wanted to ask you something about the old schoolhouse.'

Chloe lowered her book and looked around quizzically at her.

'What about it?'

'When you were tied up there, you said you thought there was a fire going in a corner of the room.'

'Yes, what of it?'

'Well, there couldn't have been. The old fire Adam saw was broken. He said it looked like it hadn't worked in years. And, anyway, why would Mr Ingham or his brother have provided you with a fire? It doesn't make sense.'

'I thought it was on.'

'Chloe, did you smell bleach at the same time?' pressed Adele.

Chloe thought back, initially with difficulty, but the memory was deeply engraved, the image of the conservatory at home and her mother's obsession with cleaning the floor with bleach.

'Actually, now you mention it, I think I did. How did you know?'

'There you go, then,' she said. 'It was Rebecca.'

'I beg your pardon,' said Chloe.

'Lisa told us that if anything strange happens at High Peak, it's always preceded by an odour of bleach. I think that when Rebecca died she was covered in bleach, you know, in the cleaner's storeroom,' said Adele.

'The doctor used it on her to kill any YPX1 bacteria when he and Miss Harper put her there,' said Adam.

Chloe watched Adam subconsciously rub his wound. The conversation, she thought, was causing him to reflect on that night.

'I think you're all being stupid,' said Chloe, but she was not totally convinced by her own statement.

'Chloe, tell me. Did the fire do anything? Did it make the room seem a little brighter or warmer?' asked Adele.

Chloe reflected.

'It did do one thing,' she mused, pausing for words. 'It gave me hope.'

Rumcorn took out a copy of the doctor's final note that he had personally stuck back together and felt moved by it, and not in a good way.

I take this final chance to pen a strong belief that has disturbed me all these years and I see no signs of change for the future.

Phage therapy in the West has not been taken on as anything like it should have. We as a race have known how to kill bad bacteria for well over one hundred years, but we remain ignorant of the practice in the West.

This is my view because of the difficulty an individual or organisation has to patent something that actually already exists in nature.

Therefore thousands of pounds, dollars or any currency could be spent investing in creating phage mixes and a competitor could take some or all of any profits.

So no one invests. Not even a philanthropic act, because even these like to see a 5% return.

I must therefore conclude capitalism clearly does not work. No one gains... no one creates. People die!

AFTERWORD

This story is fictional, however...

Felix D'Herelle and Fredrick Twort were two of the most brilliant underrated scientists of the 20th century. **True.**

Bacteriophages, viruses that eat bacteria, may save our civilisation as antibiotics become less effective. **True.**

The Russian army effectively used phage mixes on their skin in the trenches during the Second World War. **True.**

Sunday 9 April 1989, the massacre that ensued from the Russian army declaring martial law on Georgia, resulted in the deaths of around twenty people including women and young adults. **True.**

Tens of thousands of phage mixers that the eastern countries used to fight bacterial infections were destroyed over the four year period of the civil war in Georgia. **True.**

ABOUT THE AUTHOR

I am a Construction Project Manager with a head full of fluff, over a number of years I had made notes of a story about a group of young adults battling against a local doctor who displayed some poor behaviours.

I want to pay a very special tribute of thanks to my first wife, she was without doubt one of the bravest and greatest persons I've ever met, sadly she lost her battle with cancer in 2013.

Two years later, I was made redundant from the best job in the world to me. I decided to take time out from work and lost myself in a different world, whilst also caring and supporting my daughters.

I could not have created this work without the support of so many people whom I wish to give thanks. My editor, Julie Stafford (Word Perfect), who worked tirelessly with me for over six months; Typesetting, Dave Wright (Typo•glyphix); Cover design and photography, Christoper Howard (Cactus Images); Dani Murden, for agreeing to model the front cover. The support and encouragement from 'White Peak Writers'.

My gorgeous daughters: Alex, who has always been there for me, even at such a tender age, when a time was difficult for us both; and Hannah, who, as all of us, struggled through difficult times.

Thanks to my wife, Mhairi, who would have believed I'd be fortunate to meet another wonderful lady.

All other friends, too many to mention, who have put up with me over the past few years, thank you!

I sincerely hope you enjoy the read as much as I have in creating it.

Simon